PENGUIN BOOKS

ONE LAST LOOK

Susanna Moore is the author of four previous works of fiction including, most recently, the highly acclaimed novel *In the Cut*. She is from Hawaii and now lives in New York City.

One Last Look

~~~

Susanna Moore

PENGUIN BOOKS

PENGUIN BOOKS

Published by the Penguin Group
Penguin Books Ltd, 80 Strand, London WC2R ORL, England
Penguin Group (USA) Inc., 375 Hudson Street, New York, New York 10014, USA
Penguin Group (Canada), 10 Alcorn Avenue, Toronto, Ontario, Canada M4V 3B2
(a division of Pearson Penguin Canada Inc.)
Penguin Ireland, 25 St Stephen's Green, Dublin 2, Ireland
(a division of Penguin Books Ltd)
Penguin Group (Australia), 250 Camberwell Road, Camberwell,
Victoria 3124, Australia (a division of Pearson Australia Group Pty Ltd)
Penguin Books India Pvt Ltd, 11 Community Centre,
Panchsheel Park, New Delhi – 110 017, India
Penguin Group (NZ), cnr Airborne and Rosedale Roads, Albany,
Auckland 1310, New Zealand (a division of Pearson New Zealand Ltd)
Penguin Books (South Africa) (Pty) Ltd, 24 Sturdee Avenue, Rosebank 2196, South Africa

Penguin Books Ltd, Registered Offices: 80 Strand, London WC2R ORL, England

www.penguin.com

First published in the United States of America by Alfred A. Knopf 2003
First published in Great Britain by Viking 2004
Published in Penguin Books 2005

1

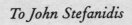
To John Stefanidis

One Last Look

On board the Jupiter, *2 February 1836*

There was another storm this morning, leaving a foot of water in my cabin, and now a rat scrabbles amongst my sodden books. There is a stench of rotting hides. My own excrement floats back and forth. The journal I began when we sailed last December is ruined. I have started anew—this is my first entry.

On board the Jupiter, *3 February 1836*

As sick as death, I've eaten only oranges, and the teaspoonful of arrowroot I take each morning (I just devoured the last five oranges in the world crouched against the bolted door of my cabin, terrified that someone would take them from me). We have not seen land, nor another vessel—not even a sea monster—in seventy-two days. There is no coffee, no biscuits, no marmalade, no ale.

Henry is not sick—he eats whatever food remains and dines

again with the sailors. They've grown fond of him, I hear. Harriet is not sick—to my astonishment, she's never been better. Cousin Lafayette, of course, is a good sailor. Henry convinced the crew to tie Lafayette to the mast for his twenty-fifth birthday and douse him with seawater. He spends much of his time with the ladies, particularly the lovely Miss Haywood—he aims to improve her whist. Frolic, like Harriet, is having a lovely time. The dog has a little window of his own, tacked with netting, where he sits and utters odd moans of pleasure at the foam.

Rather we were transported to Botany Bay in a ship full of Irish poachers than this! At least we'd have had the pleasure of a little felony.

On board the Jupiter, *4 February 1836*

I cannot conceive what it is like for the passengers below, packed tightly with the captain's private stores of cheese and hats to sell— the hatches are closed to prevent flooding. The wailing of the eighty-four hounds belonging to a Welsh army captain is ceaseless. A company of soldiers—who ate all the poultry before we'd left the Thames—drills up and down in new hobnailed boots, more thunderous even than the loose casks rolling across the deck. (We are most grateful that the crew is barefoot.) Harriet's maid Jones is so unhinged that Dr. Drummond has tied her to a chair.

Two sails were carried away in the storm and a drunken German piano tuner travelling to Ceylon lost overboard. Henry says it is a great pity, as piano tuners are hard to find in the East. There was a gathering on deck at sunset to ease his way to his Reward, but I could not bring myself to attend.

On board the Jupiter, 6 February 1836

My sheets are stiff with blood; my hair heavy with salt. There are no clean clothes. My nightdress is so soiled, I stuff it through the porthole and watch it disappear in the dirty yellow sky.

On board the Jupiter, 7 February 1836

I sleep when my exhaustion is so great that even I cannot resist—the click of the cockroaches cannot keep me awake, nor the sailors singing "May God Sink the Sea," nor the groan of the bulkheads as they strain to split in two. The ocean streams heedlessly past, so near that it seems to surge through my body. The movement of the ship both lulls and torments me—a glide forward and then a trembling pause until the ship relinquishes with a shudder and swoons into the trough of the next swell. It puts me in mind of the pleasures of love.

St. Cléry hides in his cabin with green-sickness, and Henry's manservant, Crick, is covered in boils.

On board the Jupiter, *8 February 1836*

No matter how loud I scream, no one can hear me.

On board the Jupiter, *12 February 1836*

I am feeling better now. It is so hot now we've passed the Equator,
I wear only a muslin camisole under my dressing gown. (By the
time that we reached Rio de Janeiro, I'd given up wearing stockings or dressing my hair.) My maid Brandt is disappointed that I
refuse to unpack my finery, in fear that soon we will be obliged to
dress like Ali Baba (she has never forgotten the evening that my
mother, who'd been once to Syria, came down the staircase wearing Damascene pantaloons and a jeweled dagger at her waist), but
she is too busy quarreling with the new half-caste maid, Rosina, to
make a fuss.

Harriet, good girl that she is, happily keeps up her regime,
wearing her corset without complaint, plaiting and plaiting again
her hair into two splendid coils, splashing in the buckets of salt
water the young officers conspire to bring her—Capt. Chesnell is
said to have challenged Lt. Galsworthy for twice going out of
turn. She busies herself writing longish letters when she is not
memorizing *Lalla Rookh*. I worry that my sister will have a difficult
time of it when we arrive. Harriet is used to comfort and quiet and
a certain kind of society. (That she is a trifling bit simple is an
advantage, for once. I sit in my cabin and think of ways to frighten
her. It is not as easy as one would think—she is not embarrassed
by fairies. I set off to find her with something akin to glee, but her

6

guileless gaze, turned on me in bewilderment as I prowl round her, robs me of purpose. She is so biddable, so eager to please, that I creep back to my cabin in shame.)

Life on board ship, while not being Paradise to all, as Brandt insists on reminding me, is nothing compared to what awaits us.

On board the Jupiter, 18 February 1836

Yesterday, an unearthly howl, one I've not heard before, racketed through the ship like a troupe of demons. (At first, I thought that I was howling.) I bestirred myself to the kennel where Lafayette keeps his dogs, but they were dumb with fear, cringing against each other. Eighteen puppies have been born in three months. I never liked a greyhound—too a-tremble—but these were pitiable in their distress. Even Capt. Llewellyn's hounds were speechless for once.

Tonight when I heard the horrible scream again, I slid from my berth, making my way as best I could across the fen that was once my mother's carpet (we were obliged to provide our own furnishings), and threw open the door. There was no one there. I could not bear to return to my berth—it reeks of too many other filthy souls—and found myself wondering if Henry were still awake. I went down the dark passage, my hands skimming the walls to keep from falling. Lafayette chipped one of his teeth in a fall last month.

The door to Henry's cabin was open. I stepped inside. He was sitting in an old armchair from Ravenhill, bent over a map. I made myself a place on a narrow bench built into the wall. There was a basket of mending on the bench, waiting for Crick to recover his senses, if not his skill with a darning egg. (I used to slip into Henry's room when he was away at school to look at his things. I used to take his stockings to bed.)

"You have worn your stockings to shreds, my dear," I said, looking into the basket. The bench was seeping and the damp wood was cool beneath my dressing gown.

"Yes." He made an attempt to move his chair closer to me, forgetting that it was nailed to the floor. I snipped a thread from my bodice with a pair of tiny gold scissors from the sewing basket.

"Shall we resume Mr. Berwick's *Life?*" I asked. I glanced at him, wondering if his curious giddiness of the last few weeks had finally passed. He still resembles a convict—the bits of hair clipped from his poor head for souvenir locks have yet to grow back, rendering his pale eyes too large for his face.

He put the map aside with reluctance. I lighted another lamp, and found the Berwick, its pages brittle, and opened it to my place: " 'I had long made up my mind, not to marry while my father and mother lived, in order that my undivided attention might be bestowed upon them. My mother, had indeed, sometime before recommended a young woman in the neighborhood to me as a wife—she did not know the young lady intimately—but she knew that she was modest in her deportment, beautiful and handsome in her person and had a good fortune. In compliance with this recommendation, I soon got acquainted and became intimate with her, but was careful not to proceed further, and soon discovered that 'tho her character was innocence itself she was mentally one of the weakest of her sex—' "

He interrupted me. "Do you remember the time Aunt Sally caught her skirt climbing a stile and tumbled head-over-heels,

8

landing on her feet with her dress over her head?" He began to laugh, scratching his short gray beard. Crick has been too sick to shave him.

"You always forget that I wasn't there," I said. "Harriet was there."

"And the next week Glamorgan had made a dozen tartan pantaloons for her to wear under her hoops. In Father's books they never wore underlinen. Much nicer."

"For all the times that you have told me this story, I wish I had been there." *With thee conversing, I forget all time.*

He didn't catch my tease. I wouldn't say that Henry has wit, although he is superb with puns. "I could swear that you were," he said.

"No. I've certainly come to regret it."

"Yes."

"Have you concern of these things?"

He was puzzled for the briefest moment. "These things?"

"Women's fashions."

"I leave that to my sisters." He was looking at my feet. As it is always my delight to oblige him, I lifted my dressing gown so he could see my ankles. I was wearing a pair of red morocco slippers; I was not wearing stockings. (When we were young, he liked me tied to my spine-board and trussed like a goose.) "Shall I read on?"

He grunted. I pulled the lamp closer. " 'The smirking lasses had long thrown out their jibes against me as being a woman hater, but in this they are greatly mistaken. I had indeed been very guarded in my conduct towards them, as I held it extremely wrong and cruel to sport with the feelings of any one of them in making them believe that I was in love with any of them, without really being so; in this (which was one of my resolves) sincerity and truth are my guides.' " I looked up and saw that he had gone back to his map. I laid aside the Berwick, of which I am not over-fond, and, rescuing Saint-Simon from the exile of my pocket, eagerly returned with him to Paris.

On board the Jupiter, *20 February 1836*

I am a disheveled jellyfish.

On board the Jupiter, *23 February 1836*

Last night I woke in the dark rolling, my soiled nightdress wrapped like a shroud around me, and I began to cry. I'd fallen asleep in a chair, rocked like a baby in a cradle. The carpet, still damp with the last of the flood, was cold beneath my feet. I could not see my hand before my face.

There was a smell of rum, and mildew. I'd been dreaming of Mademoiselle again. My father liked to visit the schoolroom of a winter evening. I often saw him there, although the first time it really was by chance. He was dancing with Mademoiselle, and she caught sight of me as she gazed triumphantly over his shoulder. I scurried out of sight like a rat. Her woolen dress smelled of sweat and tallow when she came to put me to bed, not unlike the way I smell now. I was unkind to her. I told her that my grandfather once dismissed a maidservant who'd had the ill luck to come across him on the stairs. Mademoiselle left me alone in the night nursery then, forgetting to take the candle with her, and I put my finger in the flame until my nail turned black. She did not stay long at Ravenhill after that. I told Henry. He accused me of the Sin of Envy and said that I must tell no one else what I'd seen. I lied to him, swearing that I had watched them only once. Sometimes I have difficulty remembering if my secrets are dreams or lies or if they are real (I at first wrote *had* difficulty). As a good Jansenist, I persist in believing that if I can imagine it, it must be so.

I lighted a candle and climbed into my berth. I wanted to look at my finger. There has been no sign of a burn for twenty years. There is not even a scar, these things healing much better than one would think. I lay back on the pillow and tried to calm myself: in the morning, I will go to Henry. If he isn't writing official letters with Lafayette (who amuses himself as Henry's private secretary), he will ask me to read aloud, his eyes strained by the smoke of the oil lamps, and I will read *Corinne* or perhaps Herrick until my eyes, too, begin to sting and I am forced to put aside the book. We will play chess and he'll let me win, and if his knee is not bothering him he will hum quietly to himself. I will be quite sure that I recognize the second movement of the Mendelssohn we first heard together in Hanover Street. We will sit for hours in the hot dark cabin, not speaking much, not reading, with the smell of the sea all around us and other smells, too, of tar and whale oil and the black blood of animals.

I closed my eyes and went to sleep despite myself. To spite myself. Sometimes I wake arguing.

Some of the English have taken to singing on deck of an evening. The gentlemen grow weary of shooting seabirds; they cannot retrieve the wounded birds and leave them to drown in the wake of the ship.

Henry lectures the sailors about drink again—he takes an interest in their welfare. Lafayette neglects the book he is writing on the Punjab to leaf through Miss Haywood's Souvenir Album for the fifth time. Harriet watches Frolic chase a rabbit which the soldiers obligingly turn out of its hutch so that the dog may have his run. He is no longer taken for his daily swim by the captain's boy, dragged back to the ship in the child's teeth—there are sharks in these waters and the young soldiers hang over the sides of the ship, muskets raised, looking for something to kill.

I read again my letters from Melbourne. He grows more appealing here in the middle of the ocean. I used to be frightened of him—all that cursing and the rumours of vice (he never once raised his hand to me). He sent me his own *Milton* the day that we sailed, with a note tucked inside that I'm embarrassed to say I didn't discover until today. *My Mother always used to say that I was very selfish, both Boy and Man. Very few events could be more painful to me than your going, and therefore I am not unwilling to avoid wishing you good-bye.* I am still angry with him—it was his recommendation of Henry that brought this misfortune upon us (does he replace me with the Hon. Mrs. Norton? Surely I am low on his list of loves)—and yet it is thanks to him that I at last understand that my place is with Henry. Melbourne helped me to know that I already have my mate in life. Besides, Henry is used to my faults. How could I be with another when he knows me so well?

It still seems impossible that we have had to leave our house and dear sister Mary and our friends. The last weeks in England were so distressing, I hardly knew what I did. It was not until Hampton Court that I at last admitted we were leaving England. I had thought our shaming expulsion from Ravenhill was the greatest grief I would ever feel for a place, but it was nothing compared to this. (I knew that Papa had begun his decline when he began to fill the house with dubious pictures and crates of porcelain, all bought with the scant remains of the money Maman had bequeathed him, necessitating within a twelvemonth the hasty sale of Ravenhill, and the inferior paintings and porcelain, and Harriet's and my removal to Henry in Hill Street. Were it not for Henry, we would be without a home. From that day, he and I swore to share our lives. We would provide a home for Harriet. Papa went to Paris and promptly died.)

The King had requested that Harriet and I bid him farewell, writing in his own hand to ask us to tea, adding that he had More than Respect for our Loyalty and Service. Harriet so admired his handwriting that I gave her the letter for her scrapbook (the same album with the thirty letters of condolence she received when her spaniel died). Now he must add Composure to his list of our good traits. He insisted that we see his pictures (after giving us cold sausage rolls, sherry and gherkins; Harriet, as usual, had no appetite, but unfortunately the drive had made me hungry) and we obediently trailed after him down the gallery. He was in very good spirits, despite his weakness of mind. "You know," he said, pausing before a picture, "the French Revolution was a lovely thing for us." We must have looked surprised, for he said, "You could pick up pictures for a song. Many of them purchased by your own father when he was ambassador at Paris, although you will no doubt have noticed that there are no religious paintings in my house. If I had my way, they'd all be destroyed." He was growing agitated, his pineapple head bobbing. Before a small picture of Jupiter seducing Io, painted by one Henry Bone after Correggio, the King said, "You see, my dear girls, why we favour cloudy skies in England? If only I could turn myself into a cloud, I would cover any number of naked ladies."

Would that I had my parasol. His gasps of glee rattled the feathers in Harriet's bonnet (he stood as close to my sister as her lovely nose would allow) and I found myself wondering whether he was the same with all his visitors or only with ladies. He reminded me of Lafayette when he was at school. I could not look at Harriet—not for shame, but in fear she would succumb to laughter. (Melbourne says that His Majesty does not possess the feelings of a gentleman. "He knows what they are, but he hasn't them.")

He stopped abruptly before one of his Brueghels, standing on his toes to drag a dirty finger across the painting. He found a dark figure of a woman squatting on her haunches and pressed the canvas with his yellow thumbnail, making her disappear. "Did you know, Lady Harriet," he said, turning to my sister, "that soon you will have to piss without a pot, like this lady here?" Before she could make him a clever answer—it was at that moment I accepted my fate: I apprehended that we were leaving England—we were carried along to the next picture, happily a portrait of his grandmother. I could see that Cleopatra applying her asp awaited us and I dreaded it, as much for Cleopatra's sense of things as our own, but with the fortunate arrival of Lady de l'Isle with twelve of His Majesty's wheezing lapdogs, the King lost interest in us and we were able to slip away unnoticed.

Harriet coughed (she even coughs with a lisp) the whole of the way home and I feared she'd taken a chill, but she insisted, wrapping herself in her cloak, that it was only a little dust from the King. She has always been inordinately sensitive. Harriet, less certain, less willful than I, is content to keep her thoughts concealed. She can, when she desires, assume an elusive airiness that puts her quite out of reach—only I know how galling a dismissal her compliance can be.

I waylaid Lafayette, who wore chamois breeches and a short tight jacket, in the ship's passage tonight in the hope of a game of cards, but he swept past me, looking haggard, and said, "Not this moment, cousin. I'm in love just now and rather unreliable."

On board the Jupiter, 1 March 1836

Even the moon is hot tonight. The air has thickened. Strange lights play about the ship. Flying fish throw themselves across the bow; the deck is littered with them. It won't be long now. I can even taste it—it chokes me. I am pressed against the Eastern Gate. I feel like cutting someone's throat. I am shocked at the violence I discover in myself. *From Heaven, across the world, to Hell.*

Bay of Bengal, 2 March 1836

The ladies were singing a much-practiced chorale for the captain and the gentlemen were on deck, casting for albatross. The sailors like to have the birds; they slice off the feet and use the bodies for tobacco pouches. I did not know what Harriet was doing— perhaps sketching the puppies.

I felt my way down the deserted passage (I am a pincushion of splinters) and knocked on the door to Henry's cabin. He could not hear me above the roar of the sea, so I pushed open the door and stepped inside. He was sitting at one end of his berth, near the open porthole, studying his grammar. He, too, was in his dressing gown, the scarlet paisley, and moved his bare feet to make room for me. I sat at the opposite end, my legs stretched alongside his legs, as we have sat many times. The soles of his feet were black. He wrapped his fingers round my ankle and read aloud a poem that he was translating from the Persian, shouting so that I could hear him. Something about "to blame the lotus in your hair." At that very moment, a violent lurch of the ship caused a bottle of claret left carelessly on a shelf above to slide towards me. I leaned to catch it, staining my dressing gown with wine as the bottle fell to the floor. The ship plowed once more into the sea and I was thrown against Henry, our legs caught in a soundless dance as we rolled back and forth with each lunge of the ship. I closed my eyes and began to laugh. I thought how strange it is that surprise lasts for so little a time and that he has grown thin and that the movement of the ship was like a woman who cannot sleep and turns to one side, then the other, in search of solace and that we were down to our last sheep. What will Henry eat? I couldn't breathe then and my body grew stiff. I could no longer laugh for my shuddering. Henry slid from under me, tying the sash of his gown, and pulled my dressing gown to my knees.

I went down the passage to my cabin. There was the sound of hurried, pounding footsteps and then a banging along the passage. Two sailors hurtled past, followed by Harriet, only slightly less urgent, her face flushed, her bonnet swinging around her neck. She'd come to tell me they had sighted land.

Calcutta, 3 March 1836

We sailed with the tide, the current running fast, birds diving in our wake. The river was brown, thick with silt. The sound of the sea grew fainter and fainter in my ears, escaping with each breath. My heart was beating fast. My feet were cold.

Harriet and I stood in a small open boat, at last done up in our finery (I could see my maid Brandt in another boat with the servants, nodding proudly at me), our feathered heads cocked like birds as we listened to the din of bells and drums coming from the temples along the shore. Lafayette, most handsome in the uniform of the 16th Lancers, whispered to us as he bounded past that it sounded like a veritable legion of devils let loose. Harriet laughed with pleasure. (Lafayette is her favourite; I'm not sure that she likes Henry at all.)

When I looked to see if my darling Frolic was happy enough in his swinging basket, I saw to my horror a brown stain all around the hem of my gown. The same with Harriet's Pekin silk, the sight of which, I'm ashamed to admit, assured me that it was not something I had done to myself. All the same, it was very distressing; the stain was climbing to my knees. I lifted my skirt and saw to my relief that it was only dirty water. I had not felt it at first because of the stiffness of my crinoline. My new blue boots were soaked through.

I touched Harriet's arm and pointed to her gown with the tip of my parasol. She stared at her skirt in dismay, her eyes near to popping. "It is bilgewater. My boots are ruined," I said. She held her arms in the air, fluttering them like wings, and looked in alarm to Lafayette, but he was standing at the bow and could not see her. She gathered her skirt and held it above the flooded boards and I did the same. (Father, like Chesterton, believed that a prepossessing exterior was a Perpetual Letter of Recommendation and I was gratified that he was not there to see us.)

There was a bend in the stream and all at once I could see the masts of ships, hundreds of them, and Fort William in the distance. Henry promises that the whole of the European community can fit inside Fort William for months at a time should it be necessary to seek refuge, although I believe its builders overlooked the necessity of a source of fresh water. I was so overcome at the sight of the ships that I could not speak.

Naked men leaned on long poles before a row of white palaces and men squatted in the shallows, pouring river water over their heads. Bullocks with gilt horns stood chest deep in the water and women washed their hair, their breasts bare. "No English-woman has hair like that," Harriet said. Her lisp makes her speech sound old-fashioned: "No Englishwoman hath hair like that." Of course she hathn't. Our great-aunt Winsome was known to lisp, so it is not an affectation. It is a family curse, as Maman always said.

There were schooners from America and Chinese ships painted red and country boats, their goods spilling carelessly into the water. Arab sailors sat in the rigging of what Lafayette said was a slave ship. One of the men swung round to shake his black hindquarters at us and the other sailors laughed. Tiny boats holding beggar men swarmed round us. The men knelt on straw mats dotted with coins and cowrie shells, screaming and gesturing.

Lafayette flung them a handful of coins, most of which fell into the river. The severed head of a goat, caught in the current, swirled uncertainly once or twice and was sucked into the depths.

I felt a sharp pain in the centre of my chest, a longing for Ravenhill and England so strong that I had to grasp the rail. Without thinking, I looked around for a place to hide, but there was no hiding place. I was filled with shame at my cowardice. I said to myself, as I have said hundreds of times, that I am here because I cannot be without him. I silently recited my Milton. *So dear I love him, that with him all deaths I could endure, without him no life.*

Knowing my thoughts as always, he looked back and beckoned me closer. His sunburned neck shone with melted pomade and I moved towards the bow to wipe his neck with my glove. Just as I reached him, the sailors threw their lines and the boat scraped noisily against a piling, knocking us off our feet. Before we knew it, Harriet and I, our skirts heavy with water, were lifted into the air by a gang of chattering bearers and placed upright on the quay. I looked round for our English servants, but they were lost in the crowd. I could not see Henry or Lafayette.

I took my first step on land in four months (to Harriet's delight, my boots squeaked). My head was spinning—black faces pitched all around us. I clasped my sister's hand (within moments, a small circle pressing curiously around us had grown into a mob of hundreds). I caught sight of Henry, Lafayette trailing skeptically behind, as he strode impatiently up and down the steps of the quay. I was relieved to see that they, too, were unsteady on their feet.

There was a melancholy absence of official dignity. There was a great deal of yelling and waving of arms, but it seemed theatrical and arbitrary—no gun salutes, no keys to the city, no orphans with bouquets. Hundreds of quarrelsome green parakeets lifted themselves from the branches of a dead tree, perhaps as a gesture of welcome; a corpse bobbed in the wake of a passing boat, the legs and arms singed black, perhaps as a gesture of warning; and a tight little group of disdainful Chinamen dressed in blue refused to look at us at all, signifying nothing.

The smell of decay was so acrid that my eyes began to burn. As I searched for my handkerchief, I noticed that my powder had begun to smell, too. "Do you smell my powder?" I whispered to Harriet. She was watching the women in the river and, to my dismay, waved to one of them.

She leaned towards me, the veil of her bonnet brushing my cheek as she took a discreet sniff. She shook her head. "I smell only the river. And the charcoal fires. It makes me hungry." She smiled as she turned away and, for an instant, I minded her lack of concern. But then Harriet seldom thinks about anything.

I surreptitiously sniffed my sleeve. "Perhaps I am imagining it, but it seems very strong. It revolts me—a mixture of sweat and dirty linen and wet dog and—are you certain? It is very disturbing. Does your powder not smell? Is this what it will be? Can you not smell it, Harriet? Tell me!"

"I promise you, I cannot smell you," she said, her voice a trifle loud.

As I found my handkerchief, a rush of shouting men seized us. There was movement everywhere—children black with flies and dogs and cows. A hundred black hands crammed us into a dank carriage and a hundred black hands smacked the rumps of the aged cab horses and we lurched away, driving along the shore as the river disappeared behind the white palaces.

The sky turned quickly to black. The road was unpaved, the only light an occasional lantern on a swaying stalk of bamboo. There was a smell of rotting fruit and rotting mud. A lady who appeared to be European—suddenly it was hard to tell—drew alongside in a new barouche and leaned forward to peer boldly at us, her eyes glinting in the carriage lamps. Beneath her satin bonnet, artificial vegetables flourished in a garden of false ringlets. I know from Henry that although the Mughals once made Bengal a place of exile, it soon became the richest province in their empire, a place to revel in debauch. Although it is no longer so corrupt, thanks to East India Company, I hope for Cousin Lafayette's sake that it hasn't become too Christian; like all of us, he is here to make his fortune. With a knowing smile, the woman pulled in her handsome head and the barouche drew ahead of us as we passed beneath a towering gateway guarded by the Unicorn and the Lion, coming to a stop before a large and imposing house that is the very image of Kedleston Hall, except for the black men in white dresses on the stairs. A rickety carriage followed us through the gates. The carriage doors flew open and Henry jumped out, his long frame bent in two, as Lafayette hurried to extract us from the swarm of native men surrounding us. For a moment, my sister's fairy face was illuminated in the smoking torches, and as the light played about her face, I thought how Queen Mab–ish she looked. For better or worse, Harriet is one of those people whose appearance matches their character. She seemed delighted by our reception.

We were led up the staircase, past a guard of native soldiers with blunt lances (Henry said the lances must have been left behind by Alexander the Great), all saluting with the left hand, and into an enormous hall with a black and white checkerboard floor where fifty people sat in a forest of potted palms, eating what looked to be grouse while a regiment of pipers played a reel. The ladies, fork in one hand and fan in the other, were dressed in low satin gowns with enormous sleeves many months out of fashion, I couldn't but notice. At the head of the table, a woman of a deep orange tint with six golden arrows in the bands curling around her ears (she had that particular second-rate look of an ambassador's wife) blinked uncertainly when she saw us standing there, our mouths agape.

It was soon explained that we'd been given up for lost. The steamers had been looking for us for weeks. Sir Charles, whom Henry replaces as Governor-General, is a smallish person, the very image of his great-uncle minus the revolving eye. He is rumoured to have a native companion and is exiled to Delhi. Lafayette claims that they used not to mind that sort of thing here; a native mistress (Lafayette calls them bibis) was better than marrying a Portuguese widow, but it is different now. I cannot help but like Sir Charles—they say his hobby is peacocks.

Because of the lateness of the hour, we were spared the more formal ceremony of arrival. Sir Charles swore in Henry right there at the table, as Harriet looked longingly at an epergne of fruit and the ladies looked at us. As Harriet and I were bustled away like maidens at our first assembly, I looked over my shoulder and saw that they had resumed eating. What they wanted in manners, they made up in appetite.

Men with sputtering torches took us down a dark gallery piled with bundles of linen. The rare lamp smelled of rancid tallow. There were paintings on the walls—fine men in ermine robes, I suspect. Maj. Quinn, our escort, pointed to the heaps of linen and asked if we'd be so kind as not to tread on the people asleep on the floor. Harriet jumped just in time to avoid trampling an elderly woman. We were soon separated—Harriet, with a whimper of dismay, was lured past some busts of the Caesars and carried to a wing of her own. Henry, I was assured in answer to my question, would not be far from me. I wondered where he was—perhaps meeting with his new political secretary, Mr. MacGregor.

My rooms were as spare as a gibbet save for the intimate adornments of the person, presumably a woman, who was living in them. A boy lounging sleepily on a blue-striped mat gave a surprised shout when he saw me. A string tied to the boy's big toe ran across the room to a filthy flounce of white cloth suspended a few feet above a bed set in the centre of the room. The cloth looked like an enormous fluttering moth. It is a punkah fan, my maid Rosina hastily explained, meant to keep me cool (she is a half-caste and knows these things). My first thought was that I would request a string long enough to reach the passage, where I will be happy for the child to pull to his heart's content. I do not like the idea of someone, even a servant, in my room through the night; I never have. Maj. Quinn, who appears to have a tic, said that the punkah boy is relieved every two hours. Maj. Quinn clapped his hands and a hundred servants seeped from the darkness to spirit away the belongings of my predecessor, before I'd even had a chance to look at them. Three smiling men in white dresses and gold sashes arrived with trays of covered dishes (I assume that it was food), but I was too tired to eat and I asked Quinn to send them away.

I wanted to stay awake lest Henry come, but the bed, although possessed of little more than a bolster and cotton quilt, was most enticing. The gauze bed-curtains were trimmed with swags of patched green netting. The legs of the bed stood in small dishes filled with water, a circle of peppercorns strewn around each dish. Brandt kindly beat the mattress for lice. Our trunks must be sitting on the quay; she was not able to replace the bedding with linen of my own.

I sent the twitching Maj. Quinn off to Harriet, and Brandt undressed me and took away my ruined gown and boots. There were raised welts up and down my sides, perhaps from the new busks in my stays (Brandt has sewn in silver ones which will not rust in the damp), and Rosina rubbed my waist to ease the swelling. My breasts were tender, having had only the comfort of muslin these last months, but I did not let her touch me there. Brandt placed Melbourne's *Milton* and my Prayer Book next to the bed and convinced Frolic that he should climb into his basket—he is to have his own servant whom we will meet in the morning. I insisted that Brandt and Rosina go to bed.

On looking closer, I discern that the peppercorns around the bed legs are beetles. I must ask for more candles. Now there is music outside my window, perhaps a snake charmer. Even that will not keep me awake. Nor the chatter of the servants in the yard, nor the smell of jasmine. It is my thirty-fourth birthday.

Government House, 9 April 1836

I wake to screams each morning, dreaming that I am on the river at Ravenhill, the room full of the cries of drowning women, but it is only the sound of crows. (Or drowning women.) I open my eyes, and only then do I remember where I am. It is not unlike that feeling of deepest grief that miraculously abates while we sleep, only to return on waking—but not before we have been deluded for a moment or two that we are innocent of sorrow.

We sit utterly exposed in a treeless yard. There are twenty acres of browning grass at Government House and not a leaf in sight; every morning the gardeners wipe the dew from the lawn so that the grass will not burn away altogether. It is most unnerving to live so in the open. I am used to the long avenue at Ravenhill, a wall around the park, a forest of beeches that conceals the house from the road; I am used to a house that seems to grow naturally from the earth. This house has been dropped here. And although we live so exposed, we are utterly isolated from the life that reels around us. We are here as conquerors and we are not inclined to let them forget it. I feel like a jack-in-the-box.

There is no main staircase in the house, only four small staircases leading to four wings at a considerable distance from one another— in truth, we live in four separate houses. One wing holds the Governor-General's private offices, the political secretary's rooms, waiting rooms, reception rooms, the quarters of the aides-de-camp and the offices of Henry's private secretaries, as well as those of the undersecretaries and clerks. I live on the second floor, above Henry. My sitting room is the size of the picture gallery at Grosvenor House, with three windows overlooking the town. Three more windows from floor to ceiling allow me to look onto the maidan (not intended for a common, as some believe, but to ensure a clear line of fire from the fort) and St. John's Church, with its little ramp for palankeens. To the west, I see the Doric columns of the Town Hall. I can just make out the memorial to Sir David Ochterlony for subjugating Nepal. Lafayette says Sir David would have been better honoured for the thirteen wives who followed him around the town, each on her own elephant (Lafayette was here three years ago with the 16th Lancers). Henry thinks that Calcutta is like St. Petersburg, but he's wrong.

I was surprised to see that many of the white palaces are already in shambles, their gardens overgrown by jungle. The buildings are not made of marble, as I'd thought at first, but a kind of stucco made from burnt seashells that is plastered over brick. The stucco soon chips away in this terrible climate, revealing the sham behind the facade or, as Henry says, the facade behind the sham. The natives live in huts built of mud with roofs of straw: Henry already suggests the prohibition of straw to lessen the occurrence of fire, and Mr. MacGregor already says the cost to replace the roofs would be too great.

Two punkahs run the length of my sitting room. Censers in every corner dispel plumes of incense. Large cupboards called almirahs hold everything from my Sèvres chocolate cups to my Windsor soap. At the doors are ribboned reed blinds, very pretty, wetted through the day to render the rooms a trifle less fiery than a kiln. As the windows are kept tightly shut from morning to night, a deafening contraption called a thermantidote blows iced air through the rooms. No effort is spared at Government House to assure our coolness; thirty-two men have no other concern than to keep us from dying of the heat. Night and day, they water the paths, pull the punkahs, dampen the blinds, moisten the mats.

As there are no bells in the house, we summon our servants by crying, Qui hy! which means, Is anyone there? There are hundreds of them there—rows of brightly coloured slippers crowd the verandah like schools of glittering fish. Harriet and I have seventeen walking-men between us, all dressed in scarlet and gold. Ten blackamoors from Bihar stand guard at my door. Seven pen wallahs come every morning to iron our clothes. Fourteen runners in gold turbans and sashes carry my letters (would that I had a correspondent). An Irish soldier lodged in my sitting room presents arms at the least glimpse of me. (He will be banished to the secretaries' rooms downstairs.) On my verandah, five owlish tailors sit cross-legged, sewing two dozen new nightdresses. Needles threaded in different colours are jabbed into their turbans; they simply reach up and pluck a needle as they need it. My new ayah, a gazelle of a girl named Radha, sits on the floor of my dressing room in a crimson saree, polishing my stockings with cowrie shells. My two child embroiderers—they do not *sew* children, they *are* children—sit by my side tatting lace. (The officious Maj. Quinn insists that I pay these last creatures myself.) A Chinaman with a waxen pigtail reaching to the ground paces scornfully amongst the natives, waving a big Japanese fan and kicking his braid behind him as gracefully as a duchess switching her train. He makes our slippers—I wear out a pair in six days. Men bring me water five times a day in a silver basin with a wide rim and filigree cover to prevent spilling—one man holds the basin, one pours water over my hands from a silver ewer, another holds the soap dish, one gives me a towel and one holds back my sleeves so that I will not be wetted. I've never been so clean.

A tall bearded gentleman named Zahid who speaks faultless English is to be my own particular servant, or jemadar; I am a bit frightened of him. When I asked him to remove a dead bird from my sitting room, his servant fetched the mali. As the mali is forbidden to touch dead birds, a man called a masalchee was summoned, but he could not touch it, either. After a day's discussion, a bearer was sent to the bazaar to find someone called a dome, who would remove it. Harriet's jemadar is a slender fellow in a sky-blue turban named Bhiraj. Henry, appropriately, has far more servants. (The world of men and women is divided in half, as we know, but now I am part of yet another division, which lessens me even further.)

I do have that greatest of luxuries, my own water-closet. An army of special servants comprising their own caste keeps it clean. It is most peculiar to entrust my private concerns to men who are nearly naked. I was at first disconcerted to see that a piece of white muslin is laid at the bottom of the water-closet each time that I use it, tending to make me think twice before soiling it. A bath stall contains a copper bucket, twenty goatskin bags and a low painted bench in the shape of a swan so that I may play at Leda. (I've asked Maj. Quinn to find me a proper hip-bath.) A mossy hole in the wall drains away the water, which makes a sound like thunder as it runs onto the glass roof of the conservatory. Brandt says that she will know who is clean and who is not just by the sound of sluiced water—as if we do not know already.

If I can find no particular work for my servants, I will make them sit to their portraits. It will take years to sketch all of them. I've made four drawings of the newtish boy who does nothing but pull my fan. When I look at my sketchbooks, it is curious to see that the natives I have already painted are possessed of far more spirit than my European subjects. Perhaps it is because their quaint faces are new to me.

Government House, 15 April 1836

We have fallen easily into our days.

We ride each morning before the sun rises. (In the stableyard this morning, Harriet said, "Have you ever thought how great an influence the horse has had on women?") The bridle paths of raised mud are just high enough to prevent our falling into the fetid swamp that surrounds us. There are little swinging bridges clearly designed to terrify the Cape horses, who are already petrified of cows. Brackish fields of rice stretch to a tremulous horizon. Pariah dogs lie panting in the dusty ruts, and buffaloes moan in the empty mud holes. In these last months before the Rains, there is a burning wind, charmed with death. The sun will turn even fiercer in the days to come—already I see that the shadows grow blacker.

By the time we return to Government House (I sometimes wonder if generations of privilege have conspired to inure me to this place; I see all the naked creatures squatting at the doors of their huts and feel nothing but disgust), the light reflected from the buildings is blinding. We stagger into the house; mercifully, it is as dark as the grave. Rosina and my ayah, Radha, who wears a ruby in her nose, await me with long tapers. They look as if they've come to bury me, but they wish only to remove my habit. Although I have brought trunks of gowns, I do not have enough. I've taken to wearing the same muslin morning dress (with corset) three days in a row with less ill effect than I'd imagined. Father was wont to say that a displeasing appearance was more than a pity, it was evidence of emotional disharmony. (I can hear Harriet pacing in the courtyard below, practicing her vocabulary—Qui hy? Qui hy?—as a hundred servants rush to her side.)

We have a little taste of coffee and biscuits when we return from our gallop, after which we rest until ten o'clock, when we are called to breakfast in the big marble hall with a brigade of Henry's aides-de-camp, Lafayette, Dr. Drummond, Mr. MacGregor (who speaks Hindi, Arabic, and Persian, the most ravishing language on earth) and Mrs. MacGregor, First Secretary Mr. Calvert (Henry tells me that he has translated a chaste *Mille et Une Nuits*) and anyone else who happens to have business with His Lordship. Silent native men with long beards stand close behind each chair lest one of us drop a napkin, their inky presence adding to the great heat. We are dressed in white, like clouds, and they are dressed in white; with their black eyes and floating faces, they hover over us like Orthodox saints. Native boys twirl branches of palm, the fronds bound together and cut into a shape that resembles a flag. It *is* a flag—the colours of the Empire thoughtfully have been painted on each, although all hodgepodge. As Governor-General, Henry is allowed a man who fans him with peacock feathers as well as the palm branch, but Harriet and I aren't permitted to be fanned with feathers in Henry's presence lest any undue respect paid us endanger his prestige. (Noticeably cooler than we were, Henry said this morning that it was clearly yet another feather in his cap, and Harriet, slipping into her new life like a powdered hand into a glove, said that she, at any rate, preferred a charbag to any fan. I had no idea what she was talking about.)

Harriet and I cling anxiously to the virtuous intentions of the newly arrived—after breakfast Harriet will play the piano; I will read, or write letters, or sketch—but somehow I find myself on my bed. (This morning I could just make out the strains of the Sonata in E—Harriet now plays a piece in its entirety; she used only to play the adagio.) Just as I am growing drowsy, half-mad St. Cléry, the Treasure of the Household, glides through the door in his red pumps à la Louis XIV with his book of receipts, eager to discuss menus (eager to gossip). "Mais, mon Dieu!" he says, his eyes like harvest moons in his black face. "Quel pays!" He has a loathing pour les pauvres sauvages.

Then luncheon at two o'clock (St. Cléry today gave us potage St. Germain, celery and radishes, salad and Tunbridge wafers, a forequarter of lamb, woodcock with prune sauce, some very good orange jelly and a Cambridge caramel cream with a perfectly fine Madeira that Henry bought in Funchal). The food is somewhat cold—it is carried two hundred yards across the desiccated lawn in iron boxes, St. Cléry in primrose gloves trotting alongside the terrified bearers. When we have finished, Qayum, the oldest footman in Government House, wheels around a large silver contraption holding a basin and ewer of water and a box of soap powder so that we may wash our hands. I have not mastered this ablution, and most days I leave the table wet to the skin (all the more reason to wear a corset).

After luncheon, Harriet excuses herself to take a plate of cheese to her room. Despite his often comforting lack of imagination, Henry has rather strong views on ladies and food—he suffers terribly should he see a lady eating cheese. He believes the practice should be limited to the boudoir. I'm more than happy to comply with any of his proscriptions, but Harriet finds it inconvenient. It is why she sometimes has an odour of cheese about her; she keeps some in her pockets for an opportune moment.

At five o'clock we at last drive out, heavily swathed in tulle and lace—even the carriage horses wear silk nets round their necks to protect them from insects, as does our coachman Webb, with the addition of a green opera hat draped in gauze—past the white palaces with their narrow flat roofs and too-slender columns, accompanied by outriders and a gang of footmen who run gaily alongside the open carriage. A spangled umbrella is held over our heads by a child whom Lafayette insisted be clothed (lest he prove a distraction?). It is unusual to see native women in the street, but there are tribesmen from the hills with fearsome countenances and tall native guards unusually fine-looking despite their tight-fitting uniforms—I find they look much better in native costume. It is even rarer to see a white woman in the street. In the cool weather, a few have been known to walk on the Esplanade, but Mr. Calvert tells us that it is not considered refined. (Mr. Calvert is called "Best Not" by his aides.) It is peculiar not to see poor white people in the street. Instead we are besieged by conjurers, snake men, puppeteers, fire breathers and mendicants who lunge halfheartedly at the carriage, leaping on spindly legs to avoid Webb's flicking whip. Every evening we see two elephants, each carrying sick Europeans to hospital.

In order to take advantage of the weather before the Rains come, we air ourselves on the river in a boat with a peacock prow whose oarsmen row us patiently from one bank to the other. Sometimes we ask them to take us across to the Botanical Garden so that Harriet may visit the World's Largest Banyan Tree. If we do not stop on the river or drive round and round the Course (there is no landscape here), we stop at the Europe-shop. The owner, an old Parsee in a peaked chintz hat, greets us with unction, the multitude of keys tied around his waist jingling harmoniously as he leads us down an aisle of filthy glass cases containing Windsor soap (I needn't have troubled to bring a trunkful of my own), pickles, yellowing eau de cologne and marmalade said to be made in Scotland but which Lafayette says comes from Surat. The shop is full of Europeans who seem to relish living en prince.

Most evenings, an Indian gentleman in a silver coach appears on the Course accompanied by a native servant who plays the French horn—not badly, to my surprise—while the gentleman nods to the ladies. He seems to have taken a particular fancy to our Harriet and she has begun to return his salutations. I notice, too, although I may be hindered by envy, that she is given to a more ardent style of bonnet since the Silver Gentleman first favoured her—last night, a pink Italian straw with tufts of white roses at her temples. Although no one enjoys an indiscretion more than I do, I pointed out that as we didn't yet understand the rules of this place, she may be accepting an invitation to join his harem. She sees my point, but it does not keep her from returning his smiles.

An even grander man who rides in a coach-and-six insists that his coachman, a retired Scots sergeant-major (everyone in

India is Scots), sit at a lower level than himself, with the unfortunate result that the carriage is pulled from a ditch several times a week. Hackney carriages career around the maidan, plump black natives hanging over the sides. Until the Rains arrive in June, a native band in English uniform will play each evening at the racecourse, their dusky faces illuminated by candles on the music stands. The lovely half-caste women tap their coachmen with the tips of their parasols in the hope of listening to the last of the music while their brownish children are led round the bandstand by their servants until it is too dark to see the path. Sometimes the white cows that live under our very noses pause to listen to the waltzes.

We return accompanied by torchbearers who replenish their flambeaux with oil they spill from little bamboo quills as they bound along, Harriet and I desperate the whole way that they will set themselves afire. We are lifted from the carriage and taken up the stairs, past the busts of kings stolen from a captured French ship, and down our separate passages to our separate rooms to be delivered into the hands of our jemadars, Zahid and Bhiraj.

The shutters are opened at last and Zahid brings me my cordial on the verandah amidst the shrieking of birds—hundreds of them live in the scrolls of the columns.

Government House, 18 April 1836

On Monday night there are fifty people to dine, the sort of people who have a child every year. I am much indebted to the musicians of the regimental band—it is impossible to make conversation over their racket. When Harriet or I so much as sneezes, they strike up "God Save the King." Thursday morning we have an At Home when we may expect more than two hundred people to call.

Many cards, called chitties, are left for us each day, written on violet- and rose-coloured paper alarmingly tied in the shape of Wellington's hat or the Great Pyramid. Papa would approve—he believed that the folding and sealing of a letter said a great deal about a person's true nature. Maj. Quinn tells us that fancy letter-work is the style here, and Harriet threatens to take it up. Perhaps it will give her something to do. So many cards have been left on us, we had to have more of our own printed overnight in order to return them en règle. As many more gentlemen are in residence, the ladies' dance cards are filled weeks, if not months, before a ball. Harriet has four quadrilles spoken for and the ball is not until July. I, for one, do not intend to dance. I am barely able to walk. I still have difficulty keeping my balance after the months at sea. Harriet tottered mistakenly into Henry's office, swaying as if she'd been drinking gin. Perhaps she had been. She announced at breakfast today that Indians look like rows of moths.

Government House, 20 April 1836

I was most disappointed to learn from Mr. Calvert that I will not be allowed to attend Henry's durbars for the native nobility (such as it is). I do envy Henry the company of men. I'm not used to spending so much time with women. I'm not very good at it—there is no conversation, no wit, no politicking. Unfortunately, it brings out the female in me. To make amends, Henry gave me James Forbes's *Oriental Memoirs* and a fat book of the Emperor Babur's life and one of Indian devotional poetry with a pretty title, *A Necklace of Fine Verses*. He wishes me to read the poems written for the Rains to prepare me for what is to come, expressing a hope that I not feel compelled to recite any of the poems over whist; a certain Capt. Hawkins, who had the foolhardiness to quote Persian verses at a regimental dinner, has been sternly censured by his fellow officers. I've glanced at the book and it seems unlikely that I'll be reciting anytime soon (my eyes fell first on the curious line, *The feet of the washerwoman are the highest truth*). We are to be treated to an amateur theatrical later this week entitled *Miss in Her Teens and the Padlock*. It is just the sort of thing that Lafayette admires.

This afternoon I watched from behind my shutters as a raja arrived atop a vast wooden tray, a few ragged drummers skipping behind. He was of an immense size—nineteen stone, at least—and had to be carried up the stairs by a dozen men. He would make a most comfortable banquette in a lodging house. I noticed that Henry had an aversion to taking His Highness's hand. The raja's attendants stepped forward with the usual salaams, each offering to Henry a handkerchief. It is meant to be full of gold pieces— you touch it with the tips of your fingers and the owner sensibly puts it back in his pocket. After Henry turned to precede the raja up the stairs, a native servant rushed forward with a brass bowl, water slopping over the sides in his haste, so that the Banquette could rinse his enormous hands. A much older aversion, I imagine.

Government House, 21 April 1836

Zahid said that the men on the riverbank with the long poles are there to keep bodies from washing up before the palaces. That stretch of the river is called Garden Reach.

A burning wind blows night and day. The stagnant vapours of the nearby mud flats hang over the house like a curse. The scorching winds confine us to the house. I've not been riding in six days and my body grows stiff and heavy.

Government House, 24 April 1836

A Mrs. Beecham, clearly not troubled by the sulfurous air, paid us a call today. We were warned by Mrs. MacGregor that she is notorious in Calcutta for collecting money for the poor and castoff clothes and underlinen of all kinds, which she piles high in a dog cart and distributes daily through the town. She has an establishment in Chowringhee where she cheerfully takes in half-castes. The girls' beauty does them harm; white women fear it excessively and refuse to see them (unlike their husbands). Mrs. Beecham herself is clearly of dark blood, perhaps Portuguese. Her black mittens were stretched to bursting across her plump hands and there were real flowers the colour of persimmons sewn under the brim of her rusty bonnet. Alert as a bird, she noticed Harriet staring at her coiffure.

"It is customary, my dear lady," said Mrs. Beecham, leering kindly at Harriet, "for ladies of quality like ourselves to have our hair dressed twice a day. I can recommend a Swiss gentleman much in demand for his skill with false hair, but you must swear to me that you will not give him to anyone else." She nearly shouted with the excitement of intimacy. I noticed that she held a thin chain; a hook at one end of the chain was attached to the hem of her gown.

Harriet was too fascinated to speak, but I quickly said, "We promise. Of course we do."

My jemadar Zahid nodded to the servants (who looked like little brown bears in nightshirts) and they began to pass trays of barley water and bacon sandwiches and seed cake. "It appears that there will be little else for us to do here," I said, watching the servants, some of whom had declared that they would not pass bacon sandwiches. "We are to do nothing for ourselves, it seems." There was a sudden odour of cess in the room—Saint-Simon writes that due to the mauvais airs caused by inefficient plumbing, it was not advisable to stop more than three months at any of the King's palaces That relieved me somewhat, although it occurred to me that Harriet might have secreted cheese about her person.

"You will soon discover that your Indian servant has every vice except rudeness and drunkenness. Their lack of insolence comes from their black nature as well as their utter indifference to us," said Mrs. Beecham. "I can't account for their sobriety." She handed her cup and saucer to one of the servants, who took it in his two paws and blew on the tea to cool it. I saw Harriet steal a look at Zahid, but his face was without expression. "You would do well to advise Capt. Lafayette to see that your bottles of wine are marked each evening." Mrs. Beecham pronounced Lafayette's name as if he were a vineyard, but I did not correct her. (My father's brother, in his perfervid admiration in equal measure of the French and of the rebels in the American War, slyly contrived to accommodate his idols by giving his son a name that flattered both.) Not troubling to lower her voice, she said, "The last mistress of Government House was dangerously sick for months after someone, I shan't even begin to suggest who, substituted river water for her sherry. It is the same colour, you see."

"Perhaps it is a religious stricture," I said.

"I beg your pardon?"

"Their sobriety."

"I know nothing about it," she said, "and I don't wish to. Truly, the less one knows of them the better, and that is the best countenance I can give you. They are the queerest assemblage of hobgoblins, these creatures, their souls past sorting out."

We said nothing. Harriet's cheeks were red, perhaps from the heat.

"I must warn you," Mrs. Beecham said, as she waited patiently for her tea to be cooled, "of a certain Mrs. Langley who is resident in this town. Oh, the ambition and the cunning!"

"We rather like cunning, I'm afraid. Don't we, Harriet?" Harriet, still in a stupefaction of wonder, had forgotten how to speak.

"Ne parlez pas trop tôt," said Mrs. Beecham, at last taking her tea from the servant. "Mrs. Langley, a widow-lady, is so proud of her white skin that she never appears without a Negress—her very own slave—simply to accentuate her beauty. The white against the black, you see. We are all shocked by it. But she fools no one. Luckily, you will learn to tell the difference between the civil service ladies and the military ladies in no time."

"Pray, how will we tell?" asked Harriet, speaking for the first time. She snatched Frolic from the mat and held him tightly in her lap.

"Your civil service ladies are quiet; nicely mannered, if a bit miss-ish. Not at all pretty, I'm afraid, but pleasant-looking. They may also, dare I say, be a little tiny bit dull. The military ladies, however, are noisy, coquettish, showy chatterboxes who twist their curls and flutter their eyelashes. Yes, they do."

I could see that Mrs. Beecham meant no harm. One might even say that she was sentimental. The smell in the room had grown unbearable, although I seemed to be the only one to notice. I resisted putting my fingers to my nose. Harriet scratched a bite under her cuff and Frolic seized the moment to jump from her lap to chase a crow that had wandered into the room. Mrs. Beecham opened her mouth to eat a second piece of cake and I saw that her teeth were black with decay.

"We will be delighted to pass on to you our démodé clothes, Mrs. Beecham—although our gowns will always be out of fashion here," I said, rising. I was near desperation for her to leave. Virtue is not its own reward—it may be anybody else's, but it is not its own. Mrs. Beecham's easy enthusiasm and earnestness, her attempts at polite chatter, not qualities I have ever admired, had exhausted me. "His Lordship has given us an army of tailors to copy our gowns, but, being a man, he doesn't understand that it's not copies we want, but the altogether new. Perhaps I'll take to wearing Turkish trousers."

Mrs. Beecham rose with all the tact in the world and made us a graceful curtsy, slipping the last of the cake into her piece bag. I wondered for the briefest moment if I'd offended her. "The first telltale sign, of course," she said, "is when a lady discards her stays and takes to laying about in a soiled morning gown. The dew of arrival is quickly exchanged for—how shall I say?—a certain sordidness."

"You must call again soon," I heard Harriet say, as I looked down at my dress.

"I have a great deal still to do today. Above all, I take pride in my matchmaking," Mrs. Beecham said to Harriet, with a sly smile. "It is only fair to warn you. Miss Da Silva is marrying Lt. O'Sullivan next month, and they met a mere two weeks ago. We have very short betrothals here; I must say it's much the best thing. People will die so suddenly! Mr. Burnet was perfectly amiable at luncheon yesterday but took a fit as he left the table and was as dead as a smelt by teatime." With a gay wave of farewell, she was escorted from the room by Zahid.

I went straight to my room.

As Brandt undressed me, an elephant fly the size of a hen's egg strutted from behind an incense burner. Having tried to kill one yesterday with my crop, I knew better than to try. I turned a bowl over it, hoping to capture it for Harriet. She has expressed an interest in collecting specimens for a cabinet of curiosities, but as a gentlewoman is not encouraged to venture into the wilds of the lawn herself, her eager servants have brought her only tumbrils of common black roaches. The bold creature made a noisy circuit of my rooms, the bowl clattering on its back, and I feared I would not sleep for the racket. I asked Radha to set it free.

Government House, 27 April 1836

We went yesterday to an afternoon party at the house of a Mr. Dwarkanath Chaudhury. I did not want to go in such felling heat—the wind and the air are aflame—but Henry insisted that Harriet and I accompany him. He does not ask many favours of us and I thought it well to oblige him. (I remind myself that I am here because I cannot be without him.)

It seems that a Miss Von Buren, a schoolteacher, threw herself down a well after the 20th's regimental dance, the very same Miss Von Buren who a week ago flung a roast chicken at a nabob's head after drinking too much cherry brandy, and Mr. MacGregor thought it prudent to show ourselves at Mr. Chaudhury's party. I wore a gown of gros de Naples the colour of bruised peaches with bunches of organdy lily-of-the-valley sewn by my Dacca children, white satin slippers with crisscross ribbons and a bonnet dashed with egret plumes. I carried the fan with my monogram in yellow diamonds that Henry gave me when we left England.

The house is situated five miles from town in its own park. We made the journey in persuasive pomp, Maj. Quinn and Mr. and Mrs. MacGregor in their own carriages and Dr. Drummond (Henry suspects that he drinks) with Harriet and Lafayette in the phaeton. Because of the black clouds, Henry and I went in the closed coach with our coachman Webb, the native soldiers running alongside, waving their arms and shouting Chalo! angrily at everyone they saw, particularly those standing patiently by the side of the road. It is all show, of course, like everything here. No one, not even a native, has the slightest intention of falling in the way of the Governor-General's coach. I was wet to the skin with perspiration by the time that we arrived, my undersleeves black. I arranged my shawl so as to hide the stains, adding to the great heat.

Mr. Chaudhury has built himself a villa said to be in the Continental style, although Henry didn't find it quite Continental enough. Mr. Chaudhury, who speaks very good English, had gone to no end of trouble, all with his European guests in mind—it is poignant when a man sets out to delight without truly understanding his company. The party was given particularly for us to meet him and, knowing this, Harriet (lovely in a dress of violet silk batiste, not stained with sweat, embroidered with lime-green parakeets) turned mute. She said later that she'd been Mesmerized by a row of waxwork soldiers melting on the verandah. Mr. Chaudhury's own face is pale—not as black as I'd expected—and he powders his head so that it will not show where he has lost his hair. He announced this to me and then I could look at nothing else.

White Persian cats sprawled limply on the lawn, the tips of their tongues dripping from their mouths. Screens of white silk had been erected near a trellis of withered sweet peas for the native ladies who keep purdah. Native musicians sat on the floor of the verandah, playing Neapolitan love songs. Several of Mrs. Beecham's comely wards were engaged in an archery contest on the lawn. A young prince (girlish, scented, delicate), dressed in gold tissue and brocade and said to be the favourite of the Dowager Begum of Ghanarao, strolled back and forth, the toes of his curled slippers just visible in the parched grass, surreptitiously glancing at the girls as they struggled to tighten their bows. The beautiful Mrs. Langley was there, affecting to be much naughtier than there is the slightest call for, accompanied, it is true, by a bejangled Negress who stalked proudly behind her. Quite understandably, Mrs. Langley has a look of exhaustion about her—as everyone who meets her falls in love with her, the extraordinary ingenuity that is required to maintain her impartiality must take its toll.

On the terrace, under a gold canopy, Dr. Drummond had been cornered by a Mohammedan who looked like a saint: lean, bearded, austere. "It is Dr. Khan—they are comparing receipts," whispered Mrs. MacGregor, suddenly behind me. She *will* keep an eye on me! Really, she is not an endearing woman. Resplendent in a merde d'oie crêpe gown trimmed with strands of gold, and a fichu of gold lace pinned with carnelians (I admit that her sleeves are better cut than I'd like), she held an open vinaigrette in her hand, the sponge ready to apply to her nose should she need it. Henry has suggested that I take up this Dr. Khan as he is certain to be more knowledgeable about Bengal and its ill effects than our own Dr. Drummond, but before I had a chance to engage him in mutually confusing conversation, luncheon was announced by a fanfare of horns, startling even the Hindu bankers whispering under the trees.

The rooms of the house were decorated a little too much for my liking: four Raphaels poorly rendered; four clocks chiming the hour at intervals of ten minutes (not the same ten minutes); two dozen hall chairs bearing the Sutherland coat-of-arms. White sheeting had been laid from one corner of the enormous drawing room to the other to protect a newish Aubusson (everything was European but the host) and the sheeting was already black with dead insects—the punkahs bestirred the wings and they rose and fell with each waft of burning air.

In the dining room, a long table was covered with what looked to be Holland damask. It was so laden that I could not be sure, crammed with bowls and trays and tureens of food, some of it amusingly mismatched—fish croquettes in an asparagus dish; cherry soup in a gravy boat. There was a great deal of champagne. (I longed to be in my bed with a supper of beans—broad beans and ham.) Harriet, her appetite insatiable, whispered happily that there were sugared almonds in the lobster tart. The food was an improvement, Lafayette said, over the Raja of Scindia's banquet for gentlemen last week where everything—game and jellies and casseroles—was made of sugar. Mr. MacGregor had warned us that there might be a pelting of bread à la Bengal, an exuberance that sometimes erupts here, but we had no such luck. A man named

Hennessey claims to be able to put out a candle at twenty yards with a piece of toast and I'd hoped to see him do it. The women cooled themselves with enormous feather fans, and bits of ostrich fluff and loose canary feathers rolled back and forth across the table, gently coming to rest in the jellies. My hands were so swollen with heat that I could not remove my gloves.

After tea, an elephant carried us to a lovely marble pavilion carved with birds and flowers (not very Continental) where we sipped pomegranate ices. The wife of a judge played a Welsh air on the harpsichord and a young lady recited a poem ("'Tis Dawn the Temple Gongs Proclaim") and Capt. McKay was prevailed upon to sing a song about Prince Charlie, which, I noticed, brought tears to the eyes of many of the ladies and two or three of the gentlemen.

We left after the Entertainment. I was relieved to go—the fingers of my gloves were glued together with the syrup of three irresistible dumplings I'd managed to devour when no one was looking. The men were encouraged to stay for an evening nautch party, but Henry insisted on accompanying me and Harriet back to Government House. I urged him to stay—it would have been just the show of manly English vigour that Mr. MacGregor desired— but he would not be persuaded. Wild horses could not have dragged Lafayette away.

As we made our good-byes, Mr. Chaudhury gave to each of us a necklace of pearls—thanks to a warning look from Mr. MacGregor I saw that we were meant to take them. Mr. Chaudhury could not fit them over our bonnets, and Harriet, seeing that I did not offer my hand (the honeyed gloves), accepted mine for me. As Henry climbed into the carriage, his new necklace around his neck, the pearls caught on the helmet of a bodyguard and, badly strung, broke apart. We watched, frozen in embarrassment, as the pearls, one by one, rolled hesitantly down the carriage steps. There was nothing for it but to pretend it hadn't happened. As we turned out of the drive, I looked back and saw one of Mr. Chaudhury's secretaries plucking the pearls from the gravel and dropping them into his white glove.

Government House, 28 April 1836

I was in bed when Lafayette crept into my room this morning, still wearing his black dress-uniform with the added touch of a rather tired bracelet of marigolds around one wrist.

"There were dancing girls," he said, falling across a divan. "The most ravishing creatures, I must say. I could see only their hands and feet and a part of their soft little middles, but it was enough to make anyone want more. There was one, most enchanting, called the Lotus." He reeked of attar of roses. This frog he would a-wooing go. "Such arms!" he said with a sigh. "I doubt I've ever seen a better-bred wrist."

"What is the strange hum that I hear?" I raised my netting. A gang of disgruntled bees seemed to have gathered on the verandah.

He lifted his head to listen, trying to summon interest, but he could not do it and let his head fall back on the pillow. "I'm sorry that Cousin Henry didn't stay for the nautch. He'd have liked it immensely. Even Crick was there. He was so appreciative he had to be restrained at one point from joining the ladies' dance. Mr. MacGregor managed to persuade him that it's not quite done here."

Brandt handed me a lace cap. "Crick was there?" I asked in surprise.

"Judd, of course, contrived to take offense at the whole thing. He complained to Chaudhury that nautch dancing was not Christian." He laughed and began to cough. "Too much hubble-bubble," he said with a gasp, thumping his chest.

"Did Mr. Judd leave?"

"Oh, no." Lafayette smiled—he has had his tooth repaired by an army surgeon, who patched it with a chip of elephant tusk. "But poor Jackson was rushed from the room like a madman. He had to be held down lest he tear his skin away. He's covered with sores again."

I gestured to my jemadar to give Lafayette tea. "Henry says there will be talk," I said.

He lifted his head to squint at me. My cousin has a habit of tapping one end of his moustache with a forefinger—it gives the impression that his moustache is thinking hard about something.

"It seems that half the town violently disapproves of our calling on Mr. Chaudhury," I said. "We're meant to set an example. The other half of the town, of course, was there."

"Mr. Chaudhury is jolly nice."

"Natives putting on airs."

He groaned.

The jemadar placed a tea tray on a table next to Lafayette. "I'm feeling a bit grisly this morning," Lafayette said, waving him away. "After the dancing, I sneaked off to the stables for some cockfighting with the grooms."

I begin to see that while this space of half the convex world, as Henry calls it, is a different universe for women, for men, Calcutta might just as well be London. The ayah put tamarind jam on a piece of toast for me. I've developed a passion for tamarind. The bees were grown louder. It was a curiously pleasing sound. "Can you not hear that, Lafayette?" I asked.

"It's Harriet," he said, yawning.

"Harriet?"

"She has the natives play her a morning raga. My darling cousin seems to be making a life for herself." He closed his eyes.

"Would you like some breakfast?" I asked, changing the subject as I held out my hand for more toast. But there was no answer. He'd fallen asleep.

Government House, 2 May 1836

I see Henry only for a few hours in the early morning when we ride the black Cape horses. When I complained that I see so little of him, he asked me to join him in his Hindi lessons, but I told him that I will make do with talkee-talkee for now. Getting to know them and learning their language would bring responsibilities with it: this servant will want three months' wages to celebrate his daughter's wedding; that one will need tincture for the fingers he claims were chewed by rats as he slept. It is best not to be able to speak. Besides, they make no effort to learn our language. They cannot even say my name. Rosina tells me that Lafayette is called LaughingYet by his servants—a name I'm sure he'd admire if he but knew. I must tell him. I wonder what I am called.

I spend quite a bit of time each day tending to the domestic dramas of our little court. Of course, there is fighting amongst the servants and the occasional missing plate and Crick's increasing boldness and scheming aides-de-camp and their nattering wives. The native servants, on the other hand, are most accomplished at a provoking kind of stillness. They possess a sly trick of making me feel awkward of limb and uncommonly loud. (They themselves are, I cannot deny, the most graceful creatures on earth.) Privacy is impossible. There are no locks on the doors—indeed, there are seldom doors! They do not wear shoes, gliding soundlessly over the floor, and I have often turned to find one standing inches from me. They will wait for hours, their eyes, with their faintly mocking glint of humour, never straying from me, their hands held together as if in prayer, awaiting my orders. I suspect it will be the death of me. Zahid says that servants like to work at Government House, as it is one of the few places where they are not beaten. A true gentleman, he says, would never defile himself by touching a servant.

Harriet amuses herself with her commonplace book. She records Oriental proverbs, Persian verse, the way to make ice and how to tie a saree, and lists of trees with both their Latin and vernacular names—this from the girl who was convinced that birds kept fireflies in their nests as lamps. I myself have been buying Mughal miniatures, and seventeenth-century black-and-gold calligraphy from the Dara Sukoh album. I made a quite good drawing last week of a fakir with fingernails so long they'd grown into the flesh of his palms. Harriet made a sketch of him as well. It was the sort of thing that once would have turned her stomach, but she surprised me by taking one of his pierced hands in her own to draw it more closely—something I could not have done. At least she does not limit this bewildering place to the picturesque. No longer satisfied with the wheelbarrows of household cockroaches that the servants collect for her, she has, with the help of her jemadar Bhiraj, turned a small gatekeeper's lodge into a laboratory. She analyses everything; revelation is no longer an accident. The sentries bring her the rat snakes they find near the kitchen and she wastes no time having them cut open (the snakes) to see what they've had for luncheon—not St. Cléry's meringues, but in one of them a little frog which, after a few moments on the tile floor, began to stir. In fifteen minutes, it was recovered enough to hop out the door. Last week, Bhiraj dragged in a crocodile that Harriet had shot on the ghat—it was more than four feet long and its stomach contained, according to their notes: 32 water beetles, 15 giant water bugs, a lady's garnet ring, 14 paddy grains, 1 large frog and 16 small stones. Bhiraj holds the belief that the crocodile swallows a stone a year, thus making it quite easy to determine its age. Bhiraj hasn't the grave dignity of Zahid; he does not order the world for my sister's protection, but, despite his tendency to clumsiness, he is honest and not without humour. His wife is ayah to Maj. Quinn's wife.

Government House, 5 May 1836

It appears that Lafayette has angered Mr. Calvert. At Mr. Chaudhury's nautch, Lafayette, much taken with the beautiful dancing girl called the Lotus, gave to her the bunch of pearl flowers that Mr. Chaudhury had presented to each of the gentlemen. Calvert stamps his feet in girlish injury, vexed at the great loss to the company's Treasury.

At last I have a diversion! It is called Barrackpore, a house sixteen miles from town laid out by clever Lord Wellesley twenty years ago to resemble an English country house. There are ferns in the lanes and white arum lilies and the inevitable ruined temple (and a gloomy banyan grove). And indeed, despite its shabbiness, it is most pleasant, which is perhaps why I feel so much better. I am able to spend several days a week here. It is a respite from the ladies with their greasy mittens and their gossip—oh, for a little chat! (When Caroline Lamb asked Melbourne's brother if perchance he knew the Eleventh Commandment, he said, "Thou shalt not bother.")

The house, rather like the dwelling of an unmarried officer, encourages us to organize along the lines of a gentleman's club. The great height of the rooms adds to their already considerable charm. There are thirteen jalousies (but no doors) in an immense drawing room, six of them opening onto a deep verandah that surrounds the house on four sides, twenty feet deep and very lofty, with Tuscan columns draped in trailing beaumontia and clematis. The floors are laid with coarse date-leaf matting said to deter white ants, then with cotton mats woven in stripes of indigo and white—the ants *are* diabolical; they fall into my soup, into my bodice, into my hair. Hammock chairs and zebra-skin rugs are scattered studiously about the place, away from the walls, to discourage reptiles. There are no pictures, no curtains. The high ceilings make for airiness, the black beams exposed so that the ravages of insects will not go too long unnoticed. Blinds called tatties, made from the roots of fragrant grass, hang at each window to spare us the dust and the heat, and the interior doorways-with-no-doors have blinds of bamboo or muslin.

Chunam, the lime made from seashells, covers the walls and columns, whitewashed and then waxed to such a high sheen that at first I mistook it for marble. It is particularly beautiful in candle-light. The size of the rooms requires an endless ingenuity of light. As we throw open the shutters at night, as well as use the punkahs, the hundreds of candles must be protected with glass shades; the effect is fairylike, the air sparkling with the reflection of blue glass teardrops and festoons of cut-glass icicles. The swinging lamps of painted glass illuminate then darken the walls with each waft of air and sometimes I feel as if I am underwater. Shadows leap and sway along the white walls, hovering like haunts. I never knew the arrangement of black and white, of dark and light, could be so attractive—it is all that I see now.

The park is long and undulating in an English way, the long lawn sloping to the river, full of unknown trees trimmed to look as much like English trees as possible, some of them very fine, and an English flower garden that needs tending, and a not very English aviary, and a dilapidated zoo, most definitely not English. (Harriet has already adopted a lemur she calls Rolla and a gazelle whose mother was stoned to death by the river.) A tribe of Chinese pheas-ants resides in a peeling Moorish arcade built around a tank of stagnant black water. Two mournful cheetahs, more princely crea-tures, fittingly live in an odoriferous neoclassical temple. There is another temple, the Temple of Fame, built in honour of those killed in the Conquest of Java, but it does not hold cheetahs.

We loll on the verandah after dinner in our camp chairs—to get out of the natives, Henry says; to eat the air, the natives say—and play chess or écarté. Harriet reads Tennyson aloud (. . . *they came upon a land in which it seemed always afternoon*) until the ham-mering of the tin-pot bird drives us to our rooms, hands over our ears. Lafayette and the other secretaries sleep in thatched bungalows in the park, so I have the comfort of knowing that Harriet and I are alone in the house with Henry, even if I rarely see him. He comes in great pomp on Friday, displayed uncomfortably on his black and gold yacht, accompanied by hundreds of boats and a military band playing the "Puritani." He is nothing to the nabob who trails from his boat fine gold chains with vermeil fish wriggling on silver hooks. Sometimes the bodies of children are caught in the chains.

Henry claims not to feel the shocking heat, and indeed he sleeps very well here. I discovered a ruby-coloured blister fly in his side whiskers last night. It was only with difficulty that I removed it, sending Zahid running for my sewing box; had I crushed it against his dear face, a large and painful blister would have instantly raised itself. He was so pleased with my fancywork, he agreed to ride the elephant this morning to some ruins a short distance away that Mr. MacGregor had assured me were worth viewing: a tomb and a white marble bathing pavilion smothered in pink creeper, hidden amongst the tangle of the park.

He frowned with boredom the whole way (Mrs. MacGregor considers all Hindu temples to be imitations of the Royal Pavilion), pulling out his watch at every turn, as if time mattered in this place, and I swore aloud that I would not ask him again. He only smiled, knowing that I did not mean it. His restless glance seemed not to take in the great wands of Assam orchids hanging from the trees, even as he impatiently waved them aside. His quickly changing mind does not always admit ease. I must remind myself when I grow impatient that it was Henry who insisted that Harriet and I be admitted to the schoolroom when Herr Schmidt first came to Ravenhill—going so far as to vow that he would not benefit one single conjugation from the presence of Herr Schmidt were Harriet and I not allowed to share his lessons. What a sublime delivery it was! To be free of Mademoiselle, who placed slates next to Harriet's and my bed each night so that we might list the Sins of the Day, and to fall under the sway of stern, droll Schmidt. Harriet swears that Mademoiselle began each day with the reminder, "Souvenez-vous, Mlle. 'Arriet, que vous êtes la personne la moins importante ici," but I have no memory of it. (Harriet could run like the wind.) It has always puzzled me why my mother, who openly disdained Mademoiselle, was so heedless as to put us in her questionable care. I first knew how much my mother hated Mademoiselle when she said, "She is the kind of person who wraps presents." Perhaps it was that Maman did not believe in too much accomplishment. She held that a child quick at lessons made for a disappointing adult. One must be ordinary to be a successful person; to excel bespoke a certain vulgarity.

I pointed out to Henry the place in my new garden where the malis are building a mud-and-wattle altar. They'd asked my leave, of course, promising not to harm the English flowers which they find both comical and a source of pride. (Watching them this week, I had the idea of making a large public park where people may meet and walk in the cool of the evening. I saw some land not far from White Town, near the river—there are some fishermen in reed hovels on it now—and I asked Henry if I could have it and he gave it to me.)

We sat in the howdah, our legs pressed against each other, my hand in his lap. There was a breeze from the river and I did not feel the oppression of the air as I sometimes do. The flock of pelicans kept by the dying King of Oudh rose all at once from a tank and flapped clumsily past, barely clearing the trees. Henry and I made a quick survey round the temple; good statesman that he is, the Reluctant Imperialist feared offending the servants if we did not dismount. Really, such an odd idea. Not that they cannot be offended; rather, they can't have had the slightest concern of us.

We climbed the little ladder tied to the side of the elephant and turned for home, the mahout bobbing beneath us, his white turban absorbing all the light in the world. *Elephants endorsed with towers. Dusk faces with white silked turbans wreathed.*

"I hope there is Périgord pie for luncheon," said Henry.

Barrackpore, 17 May 1836

Squeals of feminine laughter float across the garden from Lafayette's cottage—it is one of those long evenings wet with the moon. He must have invited some of the merchants and officers and their wives to dine. We have no choice in this place but to consort with types we've never met before—for the professional soldiers and civilian administrators, Calcutta is a pot of honey.

Lafayette himself has a scheme to grow tea in the Assam hills. As he is not accustomed to the philistinism of the middle class (only that of the nobility and gentry), I do admire him. A man who in London is dutiful, hard-working, even somewhat constrained on two hundred a year, here adopts all the privileges and even vices of aristocracy—he keeps a mistress, gives big supper parties, orders expensive carriages, sends his soiled shirts to Lisbon, buys packs of hounds, falls into debt. (In seventeenth-century Auvergne, the nobles were first aware that revolt was in the air when peasants began to buy gloves.) It would not occur to even the least prepossessing of the Europeans to attend a supper party without his own hookah burdar to prepare his pipe as well as three servants to wait on him at table—and that is in addition to his palankeen bearers, his mace bearer, his messengers and his runners. It is no wonder that they think themselves gentlemen. (My father agreed with Pascal that if you managed to be well-born, you saved yourself thirty years.)

I have a new bird, a myna, which pretends to be a kind of starling. Everything I now know, I know from the Emperor Babur. *We used to think that parrots and myna birds said whatever they were taught, not that they could think on their own. A member of my close retinue told me something strange. He had covered the cage of a parrot . . . and the bird said, Uncover me. I'm stifling.* It puts me in mind of Sterne's caged bird who would only say, *I can't get out!* My myna has already learned to call Qui hy! and when the servants rush to my room, thinking I've summoned them, I am certain that the bird smiles.

The gazelle that Harriet found by the river has proved to be European. With a show of contempt, she refuses to let any of the servants lead her. She kicks at them halfheartedly, knowing instinctively that half a kick is as good as one. They call her Guzzle behind Harriet's back. Harriet pretends not to know in order to give them pleasure.

Government House, 29 May 1836

I had not known that the strain of falsity, of being polite, of being conspicuous could be so deadening. It is most extraordinary that the balls given during the worst heat are always the best attended. Because this place is obsessed by precedence, I am seated each night between the same two perspiring men—Dr. Robertson-Swinton and Sir Jocelyn—and all three of us ran out of conversation months ago. Dr. Robertson-Swinton, the former Lord Rector of the University of Edinburgh, discusses with me eschatology, linguistics and Jewish Intellectualism. In the beginning, he expected to be both contradicted and bored; needless to say, he isn't bored. If I can enliven a conversation with a little untruth, it makes the talk less tiresome. It also helps to keep hidden my real thoughts.

Despite the suffocating heat, we gave to Harriet a small dinner in honour of her thirtieth birthday—I invited Sir Jocelyn, Dr. Robertson-Swinton, the Calverts and the MacGregors. There was music after dinner (there was a minor stir when the trombonist found a snake in his instrument), and Henry led Harriet in an allemande. I gave to her a drawing I made last year of Ravenhill, and Mudie's *Feathered Tribes of the British Isles*.

Government House, 30 May 1836

The danger of this place is that I am learning to deny myself nothing. At first, I minded giving trouble to my servants, but now I think nothing of it. It has all happened with such little effort on my part. Nothing in my life has ever happened so quickly. (Sometimes I have the idea to take off my clothes and sit in front of the house.) In truth, I've done all in my power to resist. Sometimes I even weary for a child to talk to! I must ceaselessly remind myself that Henry is here to do good work and that I am here to help him. We are not like other administrators, infuriated by India's untidiness. Our stewardship will be maintained by intelligence, not pride or contempt. Besides, I cannot bear to think of Henry alone in this terrible place.

This morning, Bishop Maxwell-Lewis came into the garden room where I was sitting. I barely managed to hide my still-uncut Balzac in the sofa cushions—there was no time to do up the hooks-and-eyes at my waist. My slippers were across the room. My black sash lay like a viper under my chair. Drenched with perspiration, my hair hung in sodden strands around my face. I was not wearing a corset.

Fortunately, His Lordship seemed distracted, fanning himself with his limp hat while he stared with an incurious squint at his dirty canvas shoes. He looked up when Zahid came in with more lamps. "Have I interrupted your reading?" the Bishop asked politely, gesturing towards the book jutting from the cushions. I pulled it into my lap, showing him the cover, *Le Lys de la Vallée*. "A study of garden bulbs," I said shamelessly.

"Ah," he said.

I thought for a moment that he'd believed me, until he said, "One of the many things I hold against Carlyle is his insistence that French literature is corrupting." Wiping his face with a large black handkerchief, he seemed not to notice two great beetles trotting across the floor like a pair of coach horses, even when Zahid shooed them from the room like tiresome children.

"I feel that I should ask right out," he said abruptly, putting the handkerchief inside his hat, "if you are a believer in the three C's."

I gave up trying to retrieve my sash with my toe. I would have paid cash money for the Bishop to disappear in a puff of smoke.

"Commerce, Christianity and Civilization," he said.

I weighed for a moment my answer, confused by his tone, confused by the place, confused by all of it—I am so unlike myself that I wanted to give him the answer he desired.

"That is why we are here," I said. "To be agents of change. Beneficial agents, of course."

To my surprise, he was disappointed. I wiped my forehead when he looked down at his sunburned hands.

"Ah. Agents of rapacity, more like."

"Surely this venture has always been about profit," I said.

"Were it only profit. My heart sinks and sinks. The shining light of Christianity is growing very bright here. Some of the ladies are much concerned with it. Saving the ignorant savage from his vicious ways. They believe that India must be rescued from the Indians." He paused. "I do not encourage conversion. The ladies enjoy praying for the poor pagans, but it is neither my concern nor my interest. I am only impressed that people have so effortlessly absorbed what is so alien into the deep stream of their own traditions."

I nodded in agreement.

"You will see that the colleges are attended by all kinds of Calcutta people—even men of high caste study English law and literature. That has told me everything."

I'd misunderstood him. He was speaking of Indians. "What is your concern, Bishop? I hear that Dean Frasier keeps racehorses."

He paused. "I am possessed by Chinese gardens." At my look of surprise, he said, "The East India agents bring me rare specimens in return for certain dispensations. Now that is commerce for you. Opium for lotus roots. Perhaps you will be so kind as to call on me when the weather cools."

"Nothing would please me more."

He was silent for a moment, considering his words. "I think I should caution you, Lady Eleanor, that you and your family will be the subject of countless anecdotes—not all of them kind."

"At least amusing, I hope."

He stared at me, taking my measure as he pulled his handkerchief from his hat to wipe his face once more. His cheeks were like two plums. "I take it that you have not been to any of the parties given by the Parsee vendors. There is far more gossip than custom."

I wondered if he had a perception of the ludicrous, after all—it was impossible to know. He does not seem to have a weakness for heroines. His eyes have the indistinctness of eyes that are too blue. His irises are transparent; my own eyes watered if I looked into his eyes for more than a moment. "The women arrive in a group of forty, glower at our hats, yawn once or twice in unison and then pick up their skirts and stagger home—most uninteresting fare," I said.

"Even if you said or did nothing, they'd invent it for you. There's nothing else to occupy them. It is very difficult to know people here. Women cannot walk in the town. They cannot visit the sick. There is nothing for them to look at. All they have is their emotions, which can be a hazardous thing here. Of course, the more English you are, the better your prospects. The worst thing you can do is to go native. That is much frowned upon, even if you are Indian."

"Perhaps they should put themselves under the protection of our local goddess," I said boldly.

He was too intelligent not to see that I was trying to provoke him. But as I, too, am intelligent, I knew he would come up with something far more interesting than distaste.

"She is a most compelling goddess," he said. "Perhaps the most compelling." He wiped his face. "To meditate on the Dark Goddess is to remove one's self from the knowable. Kali makes bearable those aspects of their highly refined world that remain inexplicable. We've nothing like her. Except Satan, of course."

You see that I was right. He didn't disappoint. Highly refined Bishop.

The room was stifling. The dead petals of the Gloire de Dijon rolled back and forth across the mat with each wave of the punkah. The bamboo blinds, meant to keep out the flies, let in visible streams of heat. The smell of mildew made me ill. I longed to open the shutters, but the heat would be too great. I went to the desk, my hands at my waist to hide my undress, collecting my slipper on the way. I could hear the tonjons rolling down the drive, their bells ringing, the runners grunting, Tovie-tovie-tovie, to ease their loads.

"All my life I've prided myself on not being afraid," I said. "One of the advantages of privilege. But when I understood that His Lordship meant to accept this appointment despite my appeals, I was very distressed. I went straight to the museum at India House—to learn what awaited me, to calm myself, or perhaps to frighten myself even further. I was so disheartened to leave England, you see. I had succeeded in drawing a magic circle around us; to venture outside was unthinkable. It was not that I hadn't been about in the world. I was born in Paris, after all. Everyone else considered India a good appointment. Lord Melbourne had generously pressed for His Lordship, even though there were men better-suited for it. I'd had the same confusing feeling after Waterloo when everyone was joyous and I felt a terrible sadness as well as pride."

He looked down into the garden.

"The museum at India House has a most valuable possession: Tippoo's Tiger. It is a wooden tiger with a European in his mouth. I'm sure that you, too, have seen this famous tiger. The whole of London has seen it. Visitors cannot resist turning the handle that causes the tiger to roar and the dying man to scream in agony. The sound is utterly unbearable. I fled the museum."

He turned his head. "Poor tiger. He holds all the terror of the East. Our dear lambs and hedgehogs, what are they compared to crocodiles and leopards? Of course, the more we are afraid, the easier it is to remain good Englishmen."

At that moment, Zahid came into the room with biscuits and sherry, and I wondered, for the first time, if he had been listening. The Bishop wanted nothing and we chatted earnestly of other things (the Rains, the Hot Weather, the Cool Weather), the way we do when we have tired ourselves, and he soon found an excuse to leave, threading his way across the room, Zahid leading the way.

I wandered listlessly down the passage. Within moments of reaching my bed, I was asleep, dreaming, and when I awoke hours later, my legs heavy, my mouth dry, it took me some time to remember where I was—and when I did remember, such despair came over me that I was convinced I would never get up again.

But then foolish Rosina came in with a fresh muslin gown and Radha brought me a glass of wine, her earrings of white jasmine buds hanging to her shoulders, and the boy who pulls my punkah woke from his own nap and began to pull so fiercely that for an instant I was caught in a draught. Harriet skipped in gaily in her scarlet riding habit with a note from Henry to say that once again I'd neglected to attend the meeting of the Asiatic Society. As his hostess, I am Honourary President. This month's topic of discussion was, thanks to Bentham, "The Greatest Happiness for the

Greatest Number (as Applied to Empire)." Is it any wonder I forgot? The members are so grave that my lack of gravity becomes unbearable.

I have so little strength, so little interest in anything, that even Harriet's good spirits are intensely jarring to me. I bite my tongue to keep from carping at her: Must you wear that jasmine in your corsage? Must you collect black spiders? Must you read *The Last Days of Pompeii*? It is the strain of the heat that robs me of my calm. (In the garden tonight, fireflies cluster like jewels, illuminating the world for a moment before plunging it into darkness again, pulsing with each slow breath of the earth.)

Rosina and I took turns fainting as she dressed me.

Barrackpore, 2 June 1836

I used to disapprove of the way that women treat their servants here—not that they are unkind, but too trusting. I see now that the social hierarchy is so clearly defined, there is no need of aloofness; a native servant hardly need be reminded of his place. Native servants are present at moments that do not customarily allow for witnesses; their opinions and advice sought and often taken. Mr. Mill, who has told us that they are unnatural, offensive and not infrequently disgusting, might be surprised to learn that my jemadar Zahid has become my stay and support. He brings me fresh watercress every morning, washes my painting box, takes care of my money. He makes sure that my bathwater is cool, and he watches (from a distance) as the chobdars clean my rooms. He is faultless, as subtle and as silent as night, except when he shouts for his god Hari's protection (I thought at first that he was calling my sister) against devils leaping into his mouth when he yawns. Yesterday, he suggested that I might like to taste the flower buds of the asoka tree. He claims they are a cure for grief. He also claims that the asoka will burst into flower if kicked by a maiden— perhaps Harriet would oblige me.

Government House, 12 June 1836

Three days ago while I stood at the window watching the heavy white sky, a sudden breeze rose in the east. The air smelled like metal. The sky turned to black as twisting clouds moved heavily across the horizon and sheets of silent silver lightning flattened the plain. The river turned to glass. There was a terrifying silence. For a moment the world ceased to exist. And then the house began to shake.

I opened the window. My room filled with insects. Men ran shouting across the courtyard, their arms in the air. There was the sound of glass breaking and trees splitting in two. The shutters were ripped from the windows and bounced across the lawn. Chairs flew from the verandah. Small boats caught on the river spun in wild circles. Carriages overturned on the road; there was the sound of horses and women screaming. The sepoys poured from the guardhouse, pulling off their clothes. Women rushed singing from the servants' huts as a rope swing was hastily thrown between two columns.

The rain foamed with pleasure as it soaked into the dry earth. I stood in a trance, wet through, suffused with such joy that I could not move. I slept that night for the first time in weeks.

Barrackpore, 19 June 1836

The park is deep in water (it is nothing compared to town, where the water in the streets rises to the waist). The river has over-reached its banks. The servants, convinced that the fish fall from the sky, rush about the lawn catching them with their hands. The gardeners spend the morning slaughtering reptiles—snakes of every size and colour bound fearlessly through the house. The outbuildings have turned black, streaked with streaming water. The pages of my books are green with mould, my sketch-books in blisters. My only pleasure is to watch as my handsome bodyguards—barefoot, six feet tall, covered with the gold amulets of the goddess—cool themselves with their tiny hatchet-shaped fans. There are rush stools along the colonnade so that they may sit cross-legged—their preferred position—above the snakes.

Zahid tried to lift my spirits with the news that a Capt. Hing-ham rides to the club every evening in a horse and carriage while Mrs. Hingham runs behind, but I felt only contempt. I have lost all my strength, even for the most trifling of things. I can barely lift a pen to write.

Barrackpore, 21 July 1836

Oh, the dazzling greenness! The greenness of Bengal! The air is heavy with the scent of queen-of-the-night. The river is a silver stream. Even Harriet's hair has changed colour. I thought at first that she'd resorted to henna, but it is only that it is always wet.

I went this evening to view a famous bel tree. The bel tree is so sacred to the natives they will not use its wood for fuel. Bearers ran alongside holding numerous umbrellas over my head, dueling with each other for precedence, with the result that I was soaked to the skin. Men with panniers of birds splashed after us in the hope that I would throw them a coin to free a bird in my honour. I emptied my coin purse and two dozen startled doves were prodded out of their cages, several of whom fell dead in the mud.

The tree was not impressive, but then it's not like a visit to Chartres. I found the tree both haughty and skimpy. Later, when Harriet tried to tell me that the tree is a god, I was glad that the outlandishness of this place, its excess and exaggeration, serve most complicitly to keep me from being too much affected.

Barrackpore, 24 July 1836

Henry sat with me tonight on the verandah, Henry drinking tumblers of iced claret. He told me that he has determined, with some prodding from Lord Palmerston in London, the necessity of making a Grand Progress to the Punjab as a way of consolidating our position in the north of India. It is of the utmost importance that we make the Maharaja Ranjit Singh our ally. Our mission to Amir Dost Mohammed in Kabul does not go well and the Russians encourage the Persians to make forays on the Afghan border. Although his people revere him, we aren't meant to like Dost Mohammed. Of course, Harriet and I will accompany Henry, but such a long trip will mean laying aside our busywork here to attend to the grander interests of Empire. (I heard Mr. MacGregor say to Henry, "My Lord, you must assume all your invested legitimate power to depose Dost Mohammed in Kabul and put someone who likes us on the throne—by force, if it is necessary. Or, rather, someone we like.")

"I loathe living in tents," Henry said to me. "There will be ten thousand people in our cavalcade, ten miles long, the best part of it our Bengal and Bombay troops, but all the same we will be a spectacle. All so that no one objects too much when we take Afghanistan." He plucked a pale green lizard from his trouser leg and dropped it over the balustrade. "You must help me to select gifts for the endless Magi who will present their noble selves. I've noticed that the farther East one goes, the more one gets out of a piece of bunting; all their bravery is upon their floors. Anything but horses! I last sent Ranjit Singh a matched pair of English cart horses who were fed a box of Turkish Delight and promptly died."

Henry is convinced that the native nobility living on boiled rice and fancy titles may be managed most effectively with the smallest effort and not much cost if we but appeal to their finer sentiments: a bit of silk, a diamond aigrette, a case of champagne. Rather like women. With this in mind, he's asked Lafayette to design a book of emblems so that the princes we meet on our journey may pick a coat-of-arms and crest for themselves—an elephant couchant here; an emblazoned lotus there. England will define what it is to be Indian. A good way to start, of course, is to make sure that Indians look like our idea of Indians. Turbans and sashes thought to be Mughal will do nicely. Even the English officers of our native sepoys will affect a touch of Indian costume; it is good for the morale of both. We will win their loyalty and gratitude without giving up a thing.

As Henry rose to bid me good-night, there was a frightful shout in the garden and a horde of naked men burst from the darkness and ran in alarm through the rain to the flower garden. It frightened me until I saw that their altar, laden with flowers in honour of the goddess, was disappearing before our eyes. The men tried frantically to save it, but it was impossible. Henry began to laugh at the sight of them flailing in the mud as they tried to hold the sodden platform together with their hands. To my irritation, I felt as if I were going to cry and I tried to hush him, if only because Zahid could hear him. I laugh less easily at this sort of thing than I once did.

Barrackpore, 30 July 1836

I drove here this evening in a silver mesh of rain with Lafayette in his new wicker pony trap—it is still too wet to ride. He cuts quite a figure and I understand why women like him. Mrs. Beecham has even had a hand at matchmaking, introducing him to a young lady with the ominous name of Miss Almeida, but he claims to be too occupied with his hounds to give a thought to romance. I wonder.

I prefer to leave town in the early evening. It is too hazardous to travel after dark; there are no watchmen and the roads are lighted only by the occasional sputtering lamp. Lafayette has landed more than once in a ditch. As we leave the European compound, which looks exactly like St. John's Wood with its little houses and little gardens, the air is filled with the calls of the boys hawking sweetmeats down the lanes, shouting so as to be heard in the women's quarters. *The melting voice through mazes running.* In tiny hutches at the side of the road, men sell rush candles and cheap cloth and amulets to keep away demons. The women in their yellow and purple sarees start in alarm when they see us, covering their faces with their hems as they run away. I cannot help but steal a look into their shelters. Sometimes I have seen a naked child standing on a dirt floor or a woman oiling her hair and for just a moment it seems lovely here and even blessed (although not what we would call comfortable). They seem not to mind their destitution.

It grows cooler in the falling blue light. The flowers that bloom at night tremble with impatience in the fast-descending darkness and it seems as if the clay cups of oil are lighted in the little wayside sheds just to guide our way. (I refuse, however, to drive past the village for the old and the sick. If a man is not mindful, his impatient relatives will catch him and ladle river water into his mouth until he expires—and if that fails to dispatch him, they will stuff his nose with mud.)

As the trap is narrow enough to move easily down the lanes, I asked Lafayette to stop in the bazaar. I'm no longer surprised when a half-naked man emerges from a ramshackle shop to run through the rain with a bundle of the most ravishing brocades and embroideries, some of them so fine they are meant to wear out in a single night. I can't help but want all of them. Maj. Quinn, of course, forces us to give to him all the gifts that we receive. The extraordinary things given us by the rajas and nabobs are snatched from our very hands and taken to the Toshakhana Treasury for the benefit of East India Company, to be given in turn to some sulky raja in need of placation. I say that it is Harriet and I who need to be placated, but Quinn does not agree. My heart breaking, I had to relinquish an emerald parure that the Raja Rana of Dholpore presented to Henry for me. Henry bought me a shawl to make up for it—a cream-coloured Kashmir stitched in a gold-thread paisley—and I shall wear it next week when Sir Harry comes to stay. Barrackpore is no longer so restful. It has grown more tiring here than in town—there, we are alone all day until the dreadful At Homes. Now that we are established and open for business, so to speak, Barrackpore is packed to its black rafters every weekend with official guests and visitors from abroad with questionable letters of introduction (an Irishwoman, Lady Fitzgibbon, announced that she was acquainted with my sister—"Her Highness the Countess" were her words—but when I pressed eagerly for news, she admitted that she only saw Mary at the opera).

Barrackpore, 4 August 1836

I cannot sleep tonight. I would ask Radha to sing to me (*Ramprasad says, Lift the mosquito net and look at yourself*), but she is asleep. I begin to prefer her company to that of Brandt or Rosina. She brings me almond soup made with buffalo milk—I daren't let St. Cléry know. I quarreled with Maj. Quinn about her. He discovered that she'd purchased her letter of reference in the bazaar and wanted to dismiss her. He claims that most of their attestations of character are inherited if they are not bought. I lied, saying that Lady Steadman had sent her to me herself. He knew that I was lying.

The subtle, exquisite Bengalis—I begin to think our servants very poor judges of character. They are too easily convinced of our superiority. Sometimes they put me in mind of children who have been brought up for a life of debauchery, seemingly innocent of guile but a trifle too eager to please.

Government House, 17 September 1836

Harriet and I have been greedy—I suspect it is something that happens when one first sees the splendour of these jewels and shawls and paintings and carvings, and all at such a reasonable price—with the result that we have already spent the money we carried with us. We want everything we see, sometimes snatching it out of the very hands of the merchants, squabbling as to who first saw it. It is one thing to be short in London, where one's bank manager is endlessly obliging; it is altogether different to find oneself in Asia without a penny. I'd thought that the three hundred a year that Harriet and I each receive from our mother's estate would go rather a long way here, certainly farther than at home, but then we were not buying emeralds in Hatton Garden. In addition, certain necessities are very dear here: drawing paper, for example.

I determined that there was nothing for it but to apply to Henry. I was under no anxiety that he would refuse us—it is simply a matter of introducing us to his banker here and establishing our own credit—but it is never a conversation a woman likes to have. (I can already see that in keeping with the gentleman's club atmosphere of Calcutta, women, while certainly not allowed inside the club, are encouraged to find a convenient place nearby where we may be worshiped at a safe distance as symbols of Purity, Empire and, not least of all, Whiteness.)

With this in mind, Harriet and I went before tea today to his private office, where I knew him to take a little rest after luncheon. The servants were resting, too, and there was no one about but Crick, who, to my astonishment, considered for a moment turning us away. We brushed past him.

Henry was lying on a chaise, an arm thrown across his face. He lifted his head and smiled drowsily (I know that smile), gesturing to Crick to light some candles. Despite the punkahs, the air was clouded with incense. The shutters would remain closed for another two hours. He was most exotic in a gauze nightshirt.

"Do forgive us, Henry," I said, "but it is the only time I knew we'd find you alone. We've come to ask a favour that is private in nature, and we did not relish the presence of your two hundred aides."

His eyes lighted with interest, even if he yawned.

"It is far less mysterious than you imagine," said Harriet, sitting in a silver chair. "We simply need money."

"As we haven't the convenience of a Mr. Hoare here in Calcutta, we must come to an arrangement with the Company banker," I said.

"I'll give you money," he said. He seemed a trifle disappointed that our difficulty of a private nature should turn out to be so conducive of remedy.

"I don't want your money," said Harriet, wiping the perspiration from her forehead with the back of her hand. "I just want to get at my own."

He stared at her for a moment before allowing that it would be easy enough to do and we settled that one of East India Company's agents would call on us as soon as it could be arranged. He offered halfheartedly to send for lemonade, but we could not tarry as Harriet had engaged a snake charmer. Henry found this most amusing.

"Surely you don't—" he said.

"Surely we do," Harriet said.

"—believe in that rot? It's all a trick. Like most things here. Sleight-of-hand. I'm rather surprised at the two of you."

"Sleight-of-snake," said Harriet.

I couldn't bear his condescension. This from the man who believes that Bacon's writing is mistakenly attributed to a W. Shakespeare. "As strange as it may seem, we are able to distinguish between what is real and what is fancy," I said.

"And the thing of it is," Harriet said, in her deceptively sweet (or is it sweetly deceptive?) voice, "it doesn't make the slightest difference. We don't care if the snake charmer is a charlatan."

I like it when Harriet shows her sansculotte side. I liked that we were a team, even if I were riding postilion. "Forgive us rushing off, Henry," I said, rising from my chair.

"I was rather hoping to see you both, as it happens," he said. "There is something I wish to show you." He lifted himself from the chaise and went to the window. He pulled open a shutter, beckoning us to look. The sudden light rendered his nightshirt transparent.

On the verandah was a little pile of red cloth and black feathers. He reached his bare leg to turn it with the tip of his slipper. It was a dead crow, its beak drilled through and strung with cowrie shells. It is the method the bored sepoys on guard duty use when they divert themselves killing birds. Harriet has tried to stop this practice, but with little success. Here was proof of her failure (as if there were any hope of preventing it). The crow—it takes two days for it to die this way—wore a tiny red soldier's tunic complete with brass buttons and a sergeant's stripe on the chest, its wings squeezed tightly inside. It looked like a puppet.

"Where did they find those buttons?" I asked. "I have been looking for small brass buttons."

"Must you be so arch?" Henry asked angrily, causing Harriet to stiffen and me to blush.

Harriet reached to pick up the crow.

"I wouldn't," Henry said, stopping her. "You don't know where it has been." An enormous crane called an adjutant landed heavily on the balustrade. Like the jackals and crows (and the starving), he keeps the town clean. Like Henry, he was very interested in the dead crow.

"No," Harriet said, looking puzzled. "That's quite true."

He swung the shutters closed in irritation, catching the hem of Harriet's dress. "I am worried about insubordination and you are worried about dress trimmings."

I suddenly had a rare and unsettling glimpse of the future. I do not mean that I anticipated a mutiny in the guardhouse, but that I grasped for an instant a future that awaited us. "I do not believe the torturing to death of a crow is a sign of insurrection," I said slowly, "nor a threat to our safety, even if the crow is wearing a uniform." As I said this, I admitted to myself the clever insolence of the crow and his uniform, but it did not frighten me.

"It is a threat to crows," Harriet said, opening the shutter to free her hem. "Surely you cannot object to one less of them."

As he looked at her, I could see him weighing whether it was worth his while to dispute her. He decided that it was not. "I'm relieved you aren't concerned then," he said coldly.

"Perhaps you should tell Mr. MacGregor," I said, feeling a little remorse.

"Yes," said Harriet. "Mr. MacGregor doesn't like crows *or* natives."

I looked at her. I can never tell with Harriet. "Thank you, Henry, for this matter of the bank," I said quickly, catching her eye.

"Surely the least I can do is look after you." He was still speaking of the crow, I knew.

Harriet and I smiled and nodded ourselves out of the room as if we were ten-year-olds brought down from the schoolroom for our first grown-up tea.

We raced down the stairs to the lawn. "We were appalling," Harriet said.

"I *am* looking for brass buttons. Where can they have found them?"

As we crossed the lawn, Mrs. Calvert, protected by three umbrellas, came into view. "Mrs. Calvert, what are you doing out?" Harriet asked, a trifle presumptuous. Mrs. Calvert has been known to swoon from the scent of queen-of-the-night flower.

"I might ask the same of you," she said, as primly as if we'd been caught on our way to the barracks.

"Do come see the snake charmer," I said.

Mrs. Calvert demurred. She was returning from a luncheon meeting at the Women's Auxiliary where she and the other ladies rip used paper into minuscule pieces to make proper mattresses for the sick. Shaded by her patient (but possibly mutinous) bearers, she bid us good day.

The snake charmer was in the stableyard, sitting on a cool stone mounting-block with his basket next to him. He'd been there an hour, awaiting us in his polite way, and was not cross that we'd kept him waiting. There was the appealing smell of horse mixed with incense and wet earth. We apologized for our lateness and sat in two cane chairs placed for us under the eaves.

Harriet's snake charmer did not disappoint. Among other wonders, he pushed a reed-thin bright green snake up his nose and pulled it out his mouth, to the astonished murmurs of the syces gathered around us.

Barrackpore, 7 October 1836

Feeling this morning that I could not look at one more card from the ladies of Calcutta (watercolours of Vesuvius in eruption and fitting lines from Byron in Gothic lettering), and wondering if I've been neglecting what His Lordship the Bishop might call my spiritual life (I tend to doubt it: my life, inner and outer, near to bursting with all kinds of spirits), I took out my prayer book—not only neglected, but the red morocco cover with the Oliphant coat-of-arms now possessed of a parrot-green patina of mould—and found myself at the page with Prayers for the Royal Family, where the names *George* and *Charlotte* had been crossed out with a pencil by my mother and the names *William* and *Adelaide* substituted in their place. I began to read for the hundredth time the Prayer for Travellers in Foreign Climes, but was interrupted before it could do me any good when Zahid came in with a note from Henry. It appears that now I have been remiss in reviewing the week's menus with St. Cléry. What is more, I forgot to engage the company of French players visiting from Pondicherry.

St. Cléry is behaving even more strangely than he usually does; perhaps he has fallen, as others have been known to do, under the spell of this place. He is a Creole, after all, and it may be in his blood. Aloof and offended, he sits in the kitchen house on a sofa covered with a white sheet, giving his orders, refusing to use other than silver pots and pans. He has taken altogether on his own to slipping rather unexpected dishes onto the table; we are given a cashew rice with curds and a spinachy dish with shrimp and chilies called puishaak and spiced pomfret curry and a sweet drink called a lassi. The surprising thing is how much I like it—having been brought up with the idea that too much interest in food bespeaks both vulgarity and greediness, I do admit that I grow hungrier and hungrier. I'm not sure, however, that it is the sort of food to serve the European contingent. I may be wrong; I'm losing my confidence about these things. *Slain-Stags teares: the unctuous dewlaps of a snail; the broke-heart of a nightingale.* They would not eat it.

Barrackpore, 15 October 1836

My father, adamant in his belief that fine ladies did not diminish their fineness one bit by indulging in the physical, would turn over in his French grave did he but know that I resort of late to a sedan chair carried by two of my bearers, Salim and Khalid. I am utterly, luxuriously dependent on them. They leave me only when I retire—and even then I am reluctant to let them go. They squat contentedly on the verandah until Radha gives them a sign, when they rush inside with my chair.

I have discovered a number of suttee tombs as they carry me about the place. It is considered a great honour to have a suttee widow as an ancestor. Upon immolation, her sins are forgiven and, most important, in her future life she is freed from being female. (I could not tell if the mounds were poignant, or melancholy, or simply mounds. I have no opinion—or, rather, I am fraught with opinion but have no conviction. I no longer know what I think.) There are another ten suttee tombs in a copse of tamarind near the river. Happily, my bearers are not Hindu or we'd have to pray at each of them.

Barrackpore, 20 October 1836

There was another festival tonight and I used it as an excuse to set free my servants so that I, too, could watch the mysterious procession of gods and goddesses along the river. I extinguished the candles and stood in the dark. (The music alone would terrorize a Christian into belief.) The idols, large clay dolls dressed in yellow silk, riding gaudily painted peacocks with spread tails, were borne on the shoulders of the worshipers. Zahid says that they cut off the nose and ears of the goddess and make her new ones. (To my surprise, I understand that. I would like someone to do that to me. Perhaps Zahid would do it. Or Radha; she will do anything I ask. I would like everything new.) And then they drown her.

I tore myself away with difficulty and climbed inside my net, but the clamour of horns and banged pudding pans would not let me sleep. I wondered if the racket was keeping Henry awake, too. I put on a dressing gown and went down the stairs with a candle. It felt most odd to be walking; I am so used to being carried that my legs are weak.

There was no answer when I knocked on his bedroom door, and I let myself inside. He wasn't there, although the lamps were lighted and Crick had turned down the bed and laid out his night-clothes. It gave me comfort to be in his rooms. For a moment, I even forgot where I was; I thought I'd stumbled into a gentleman's bedchamber in Wiltshire. I picked up his brushes, the silver ones I gave to him when he gained his ascendancy, and I smelled them. Henry likes my odour—he prefers it to all others—but since coming to this place, my body no longer smells as it once did.

There is a miniature of Lawrence's portrait of Papa on his desk and one of my sketches of our sister Mary. The miniature of Papa gave me a start and I couldn't think why. When I returned to my room this morning, I remembered that the original portrait hung in Papa's library—the room where Henry taught me to look at things. Of course, I had seen animals mate, but it had never occurred to me that human beings would do the same thing until Henry showed me Papa's books. I was never frightened by what I saw (all one had as a girl was looking, and looking was a way of knowing), perhaps because the pictures were deliberately gro-tesque and sometimes even humourous. A pretty woman in dia-phanous muslin lifting her skirts to the delight of a French hussar; a plump acrobat displaying her charms in an enviable somersault. Henry's favourite was a drawing of a woman with unmistakably English breasts bursting from her bodice, standing on a table laden with food and drink, surrounded by unmistakably English gentle-men, including George IV, as she urinated into a champagne glass held by the King—uncharacteristically, her English buttocks were not displayed.

The portrait of Papa was the last thing that we would see when we blew out the candle. I was convinced that he watched us; in truth, he was too far above us to countenance so undignified an exercise as spying on children. He was always kind, without too much feeling behind it. Henry never understood what I meant when I said that Father used to look right through us. I sometimes think I carry within myself Henry's sins as well as my own. He knows there is reason for shame, but with his splendid manners, he kindly allows me to feel it. I have never deceived myself that love bestows any rights. *To haunt thy days and chill thy dreaming nights.*

A picture book lay on Henry's dressing table. I took it to a chair near the cold fireplace (I must tell Crick not to arrange cascades of scalloped paper shavings in the grate; it looks as if a woman has fallen down the chimney) and opened it. The paintings showed men and women in the act of pleasure. "Even the Moth Is My Disciple." The private parts of the women were without hair, the opening a furled lotus bud, a pale pink almond. Clefted. The figures were in profile. I could see them, but they could not see me—nay, they had not the slightest interest in me. As I wondered if the keenness of desire causes us to think too well of love, Crick appeared in the doorway. I closed the book quickly and put it aside. Henry, pulling off his black sash and sword belt, was behind him.

He was happy to see me and sent Crick away for the night. Crick gave me a knowing look as he left, almost insolent, which made me think that perhaps he had seen the book in my lap. Henry plumped wearily into an armchair across from me and I leaned forward to pull off his boots. Crick had left brandy and ginger nuts on the desk and Henry poured out glasses and handed one to me.

"What a pleasure to see someone who does not live to thwart me," he said.

"What have they done to you now, dearest?"

"Do you think it can be a question of manner? I know that I lack a certain grace, but it doesn't seem to have harmed other men. Lord Russell, par example."

"It would be difficult for me to say, knowing you as I do."

He poured himself another glassful. He was exhausted, working as he does from six in the morning until late at night. "My responsibility, of course, is to carry out the needs of East India Company in fruitful conjunction with the requirements of Government." There were black demilunes under his eyes. "Company's commercial policy, that is, in accordance with Government's political aims." (Is there any difference? I wondered.) "Do you know, Eleanor, I have the power to declare war or make peace? Honour or dishonour myself? Anything that I desire." He paused. "We will make a fortune here, you know. You shall have your villa in Kensington Gore."

"We must make more schools," I said. "I'll help you."

He leaned back in his chair. "Yes. Yes, I know you will. You're a good girl."

He reminded me of Rochester wooing Jane Eyre: *You, poor and obscure, and small and plain as you are . . . accept me as a husband*. I gave a little smile to let him see that I didn't mind. "Hardly a girl." I wanted to ask about the picture book, but only when he was through with governance.

"The Calcutta Board of Control is secretive," he said. "Clever, ruthless. Which, of course, one must be with a native population. As for the native leaders, they are the worst of all." He paused, thinking. "Surely we're meant to agree with Macaulay—

we must develop a new class, Indian in skin, but English in thought. English in morals."

"But our books lie rotting in Bombay. Three hundred copies of *Pilgrim's Progress* translated into Bangla slowly devoured by white ants. Four hundred copies of *Aesop's Fables!*"

"Quickly devoured. And by black ants," he said.

"Have the books sent at our expense." *To sit in darkness here hatching vain empires.*

He thought for a moment. "You are a very good girl."

This time his compliment made me blush. I rose from my chair, changing the subject. "Lafayette and I arrived late this evening. There was such a sky. We were gallivanting for jewels. I made him give me a present of some black pearls."

"More than a few?"

"A basketful."

"Greedy thing." He closely examined his fingertips, then bit off a piece of thumbnail. His hair has grown back, but it is whiter than it used to be.

I opened the shutters despite the clamourous drums and horns. "Harriet has gone all jungly, have you noticed?" On the river, fishermen slid past in boats shaped like the new moon. The garden, scented to decay, held wisps of fog. In the highest branches of the trees, the moonflower hung in chaste clusters. Withered and drooping by day, it lifts its languid head with the coming of night. From the bacilli tree came the fragrance of a million star-shaped flowers. The ground under the tree would be littered with blossoms by sunrise, when Radha would gather them for the goddess. The fragrance falling from the trees hurt my head.

"Give your brother a kiss," I heard him say behind me.

Henry has asked me to draw up the guest list for the ball. It will not be difficult, as everyone is invited. The whole world comes to Government House; no one is turned away. That's the way it is here and I can't say it's a bad thing, although I have felt Henry flinch as the half-caste Lady Howe, a rotund creature with a red wattle, makes him a wobbling curtsy. The great gulf that exists between us and our native subjects and between us and the lower types does not prevent an alliance between persons who would at home be shocked, if not offended, to find themselves in the same room.

I wonder sometimes if it has nothing to do with India. The world seemed to shift about eight years ago. It is most odd to know that one is living in a period of change. My kind begins to grow ridiculous. (It will be good manners that keep us from seeing the truth.) I smile to think that my brother-in-law Buckingham removed the cannons from his yacht to his lawn for fear of an invasion—not by the French but the rick-burning mill hands in his town. But, after all, it is Buckingham who likes to say, "I adore privilege."

Barrackpore, 11 December 1836

I was in bliss, settled with a pot of sweet milky chai and a trashy yellowback book from one of the American schooners (the more trash the better), when Dean Frasier was announced.

Full of religious swank in his Episcopal gaiters, the Dean twirled his gold-knobbed cane in the doorway, waiting sniffishly. I fear I scowled at him resentfully as I put aside my book, wondering if perhaps the Dean had come himself to present my note-of-hand. As it is considered unseemly to carry cash money here (we all live en prince), we drop our chits in the collection plate each Sunday to be redeemed later in the day. His long face, almost attractive in its severity, caused me to wonder if he'd heard my complaint that Service is too long—dozens of ladies faint away each Sunday morning during devotion—perhaps with devotion, but all the same. Must I listen to benumbing sermons extolling the Virtues of Faith? I know the Virtues of Faith and find them less compelling than I once did.

Because this place is excessively moral, it lives for gossip, a good deal of it supplied by our servants. (Does not the world seem more melodramatic now?) I cannot begin to keep up with their tales. The ladies of Calcutta might be shocked to know that I find it more disheartening to see a husband and wife seated next to each other at a supper party than to hear of Mrs. Langley's latest seduction. A great deal of mischief is caused by the endless to-ing and fro-ing of chits; entrusted to native servants, they are frequently put into the wrong hands. Lafayette tells me that a certain Miss Saintsford, believing her note on its fragrant way to Dr. Mulrooney, was astonished to find the curious Dewan of Moolrah at her door. Even smiling Rosina tries to tempt me with her tales of romance and betrayal, but then she is half native. She is convinced, for example, that Harriet's jemadar Bhiraj has a brother confined to a madhouse in Lucknow who was dragged from a wolves' den! I am not unhappy to depend less and less on Rosina. It was not uncommon to ask for the pease-porridge taffeta and be brought the pink crêpe de Chine ("Missy Sahib like?"). I leave all that to Zahid now. His understanding of colour and texture is refinement itself. I depend on him to tell me when the blond on my cap is too blond or my stockings too dark to wear with muslin. In the evening, he sees that a gown, gloves, shawl, jewelry and slippers are laid out for me—all which he chooses himself. With her lady's maid contempt of foreigners, Brandt doesn't like it, sometimes pulling my hair a bit roughly when she affixes my ringlets, but she knows not to speak against him. She has tried to draw Rosina into her camp, but Rosina is too happy to be relieved of any responsibility to take sides against Zahid. Rosina is cheerfully convinced, however, that I am in danger of a poison spell. She claims that there are as many spells as there are hairs on the human body—which by her count is three and a half crores, or thirty-five million hairs. She's trying to teach Harriet's maid Jones how to tell a man's fortune with beans. (Henry cautions me against taking too great an interest in my servants' lives. A gentleman was pelted in the street yesterday for showing Bengali boys the proper use of a fork.)

"Were you aware, ma'am," the Dean asked, "that your servants are working on the Sabbath?" He affected the kind of smile displayed by someone who has convinced himself he is a gentleman.

I could feel my face flush, not with shame, but with anger at his high tone, especially as I virtuously had determined not to take one with him. "I'm not sure I understand," I said, at which moment there was the distinct sound of the malis breaking rocks. He smiled in pleasure. (Melbourne once said, "Things are coming to a pretty pass when religion is allowed to invade private life.")

"I will see that His Lordship is told of your concern, Dean," I said. "In fact, my brother has been preoccupied with religion lately."

The Dean looked interested. If he were one scintilla less false, he'd be intolerable.

"He is abolishing the Pilgrims' Tax. We intend to continue neutral as regards religion here." I paused. "I had no idea you were a Sabbatarian. Surely you understand that it is not the Sabbath to an Indian?"

He turned away. "Lovely sissoo tree," he said, looking into the garden. "The country was very bare when we took it, you know."

I said nothing.

"Quantities of trees were planted in the Punjab. I don't imagine you've been there. We rode with native soldiers, one carrying the teapot, another my sermons. The Sikh chieftains rode down from the hills to greet us. We hunted birds. They worried themselves no end over my dear wife, confused because she had no beard and yet rode a horse."

"I have yet to meet your wife," I said, in placation.

"She is buried among streaks of tigers," he said.

"I'm very sorry." I *was* sorry, but I didn't like to be put in my place by romance—not for a place or a person. Or even a sissoo tree, for that matter. I don't take to moralizing, even when it's geographical.

"Have you heard the news?" The Dean, perhaps sensing my irritation, strove to please me. "The Raja Bandu is building an enormous palace made entirely of marble. Not chunam, mind you, marble. They say he has received a hundred crates of pictures from Europe. Of course, the French buy them for him. Paintings of Napoleon. Paintings of our Christian martyrs. But that is not the worst of it."

"No?" I asked. "What could be worse?" The Dean's latest project is a subscription to raise money for the construction of steeples on Anglican churches in India.

"The figures in one of the paintings, a Last Supper, I'm told, possess the faces of the important men of Calcutta."

This from the gentleman who is said to hold the monopoly in

Bengal on beef, a man who takes the new Christianity seriously. "I should like to see that," I said, meaning it. "Although I must admit to feeling left out. Do you think it's too late to be included in one of the Raja's paintings? Should he care to commission another, the beautiful Mrs. Langley would make a fine Récamier."

He picked up his hat.

"Surely you will have tea?" I asked, ashamed for just a moment, but only because I feared that Zahid had heard the unkindness in my voice. I cannot bear him to think ill of me. (I've noticed lately that it grows easy for me to disapprove of my own kind.) The Dean happily saw that it might be unwise to take a stand. He put down his hat and accepted a cup of China tea.

"It's rumoured there is to be a Theatrical Event at your ball," he said, forcing a smile.

"Oh, yes," I said.

"Will you and your kind sister be taking parts?"

"I think it unlikely."

"And to what, may I ask, may we look forward?"

"*The Duchess of Malfi*," I said.

He put down his saucer and cup with a little rattle and we sat there in a silence sufficient to extinguish a candle, I perfectly happy, especially when my angel Frolic raced in, followed by his servant, Jimmund—Jimmund, as always, a little out of breath. He almost drowned two nights ago retrieving the dog from the river. Lafayette had to rescue both of them. He stopped short when he saw the Dean, and Frolic bounded into the garden. With a shy smile at me, his cheek bulging with pan, Jimmund tiptoed across the room and sped after him.

"The natives believe a dog is the reincarnation of an adulterer. Or is it a thief? It is their prophet Mohammed who deemed them pariahs. It is the only explanation I can make of their cruelty," said the Dean. A frown of false concern crossed his face. I did not answer and when he rose to leave, a whiff of Tartuffe-ish disapproval trailing in his wake, I did not stop him.

Government House, 15 December 1836

A bundle of fat letters, posted in Paris in August, arrived yesterday afternoon—many from my sister and friends and, of course, my dear Melbourne, and the added treat of the first chapters of *Sketches by Boz*. Mr. Dickens can make me laugh, but he cannot make a nobleman to save his soul. I have thought from time to time in my life as to what it means to be female, but never before did I consider what it signifies to be English; now I think of it endlessly. Mary sent me some very fine otter brushes and watercolours from that shop in the Palais-Royal—would that she'd thought of drawing paper—and several books, among them two volumes of *Lady Morgan's France*, which I've read, and a book by a Mr. William Playfair entitled *France as It Is, Not Lady Morgan's France*, which, I'm happy to say, I have not read, as well as the memoirs of Count Lavallette and two volumes, just published, of Fanny Trollope.

Oh, the pain of sitting here at the end of the world, a few days before Christmas, thinking of Paris! She doesn't mean to provoke, but how could it not agitate me? She went to the Comédie the first night, of course, and as many nights thereafter as she could manage, writing that there is nothing in the world as nice as French wit. She likens it to being invited into a salon of the merriest, wisest, wickedest creatures in the world who speak as if you were not really there (a more pleasurable arrangement, surely, than mine, with my silent servants who really *are* there). The audience, she writes, is altogether saintly in comparison to an English mob.

I am sick with envy. I have pined, even sickened at the loss of that world. To be a bas bleu in India contains its own highly arch unlikelihood (it is too hot for stockings), if not mordancy, although the idea of standing in a long line in the hope of Louis-Philippe gracing me with a banality, even if it is a French banality, which is never so banal as any other, seems so trifling, so meaningless an occupation that I wonder I ever did it. And yet Mary does it, even does it charmingly, and she is not a fool. It is this monstrous place that confounds me, confounds even my memories—I once thought that nothing in the world would ever be as sublime as going to Paris with Henry for my twentieth birthday to see Mlle. Noblet as the violet in *Flore et Zéphire*.

Mischievous Melbourne sent me a novel entitled *Ourika*, "a story of the forbidden love of a black girl for a French nobleman." I can picture him rubbing his hands in delight. His sister, Lady Cowper, sent me four months of *Fashion as It Flies*. "Lord Brougham," writes my friend Catherine, "kept us spellbound at breakfast talking about the habits of bees."

Government House, 23 December 1836

We drove to the races today through a thick white fog. The Oliphant Cup was to be presented by Harriet; Lafayette had spared no time and expense on an enormous gilt chalice made by the Mohammedan silversmiths. As expected, Sir Jocelyn's bay horse won by twenty yards. In the winner's circle, the horse dropped to the ground at Harriet's feet and died instantly. The cup was awarded to the dead horse. It did not help my headache.

Zahid just brought me a box of narcotine and laudanum.

Barrackpore, 25 December 1836

This is our first Christmas here. The servants hung garlands and generously wished us in Hindi a Happy Christmas (I think). A moment of despair passed over me, filling me with such shame. I have been doing so well. It is exhausting, this occupation of being full of hope one moment and revulsion the next; a robber one minute, a spendthrift the next. Although I am capable of deceit and selfishness, I am not a hypocrite. Both sides of me are real.

I gave to Henry for Christmas *Le Père Goriot* and Mary Shelley, to Lafayette a watercolour of Eton College Chapel, and to Harriet an apron of black Alençon lace and an ivory box of fans. As is our custom, we read *Twelfth Night* aloud Christmas Eve; Henry, of course, was the Duke. (Last Christmas at Panshanger, Melbourne would not read. He believes *As You Like It* the prettiest play ever written and refuses to countenance any other.)

Although she insists that she's never been so well, I am uneasy about Harriet. She is impulsive, paradoxical, avid. She said an extraordinary thing in the stableyard this morning, her heel in the palm of her syce's hand as she mounted: "Do you reckon, sister, that whiteness is really a means of not being black?" For the briefest moment, I thought I saw the syce's eyes flicker with interest, but then I remembered that he does not speak English. With a gay wave, she rode off to her zoo. She's had the head keeper dismissed for cruelty. The zebras had rusting iron bolts pierced through their nostrils in an attempt to break them. The keeper knows nothing about animals but is, in fact, a blacksmith.

She came to my room this afternoon. Falling into a chair at the side of my bed, she opened the black tin box in which I save the plum cake I carried from England (I keep it close to me—it would not last a minute out of its tin and not only because of insects) and began to eat it with her fingers.

"Mind the crumbs," I said.

She licked her thumbs. Her fingers were red, the skin around each nail cracked. A girl with skin like a magnolia.

"I would like to give you a Christmas gift, Ellie, of a little black flying squirrel," she said. "I think it will do you good." She rose from the chair, brushing the crumbs from her skirt.

As I leaned over the side of the bed to collect the precious crumbs, I realized that my company did not please her. "I don't want a squirrel, dearest. I can barely take care of myself." I did not tell her that I feel as if I am floating, lost in a dream. Yesterday Frolic jumped into my footbath trying to catch a little frog and I thought how much he was like us—we are living in a marsh catching golden frogs.

"I am thinking of making a journey," she said, going to the window. "Lafayette is off to the hills to hunt tiger." She turned back to the bed in excitement. "He has invited me along. We will have two tents each, one for sleeping and one to use as a sitting room." She paused. "Of course, you are invited, too, sister."

I knew at once that I would not go. "I couldn't leave Henry for that long a time."

She said nothing, but I could see that she was not disappointed. "Yes, you must keep an eye on him. I thought the other evening that the ravishing Mrs. Langley fancied him."

"You have no cause to worry. Need I remind you of the German princess? I'm ashamed to admit that I lost all bodily sensation from the waist down for a fortnight, but he did not wed."

"A wasted mortification, as mortifications tend to be. Did not the German princess elope with the Elector the day after Henry's proposal?"

"Causing Maman to lose feeling in her entire body and prompting Henry to remark that the princess did not forbear to Hesse-tate."

She prised open the louvers with her fingers to peer through them.

"They still correspond," I said.

"Who is that, dearest?"

"The Electress of Hanover and Henry."

"I cannot not go," she said, with a sudden gasp of joy. She pushed open the shutters. I could hear her feet on the seashell path, running; and the creak of the punkah as it moved ceaselessly over my head, now and then brushing the rotting lace of my cap; and the sound of Lafayette, humming the "War March of the Priests" from *Athalie* as he practiced his sabre strokes on the side of an unhappy bullock; and the kitchen crows shrieking in outrage as the sentries snicked them with cricket bats; and the clang of the gong, ringing through the house as the watchmen marked the time; and the voices of the Bhils as they drifted into the banyan grove to sit on their haunches and smoke; and the calls of the sweepers as they carried away the household waste, shouting their approach lest they cast a polluting shadow on a man of higher caste; and the native guards playing chess in the stableyard, every move endlessly, furiously debated; and the dhotis as they ruined my linen, slapping it with sharp cracks against the steps of the ghat where the bodies of the poor surge, the ones whose families cannot afford wood for a pyre—it is all too poetic. I loathe it.

Barrackpore, 8 January 1837

My little squirrel is extraordinary, very fond and merry, with three beautiful white streaks down his back. He runs up my gown to my shoulder when I bid him attend me. I keep him locked in the bathroom, but last night I awoke to find him stretched across my neck, whimpering plaintively and patting my face with his little black hands. He must have escaped through a window. I woke Radha, who sleeps in my room now, and she carried him back to the watercloset. Shortly before dawn, I was awakened again. I thought it was a rat at first; the squirrel had slipped inside my net and was sleeping pressed against my bare leg.

Barrackpore, 10 January 1837

The sky was so black I thought that the moon and the stars had fallen into the river and drowned, but I was mistaken: thousands of bats filled the sky. Lafayette swore that they were rooks, but birds are not my cousin's area of knowledge. Famous battles and horses, certainly women, but nothing with wings; he claims that the cannons at Bijapore, where he was garrisoned three years ago, are made in the shape of dragons with diamond earrings and ruby tongues. Most risible, he finds everything about the natives wildly droll, unable to keep from laughing immoderately at every excruciating speech and comical habit, and it is difficult not to laugh with him. He's grown adept at a jest called chicken pop in which a rooster is slipped inside someone's mosquito net. (Yesterday at breakfast he said, rather mysteriously, "You can't conceive the fun that's to be got from a grasshopper and a wineglass.") He sleeps with a mongoose—he'd rather be bitten by a mongoose than killed by a snake. He appears to have lost all interest in writing his book on the Punjab. I tell him that he must take up his work before there is too much to know, before the tumult of history is too overwhelming for just one mind, but he only smiles. Harriet tells me that he lost three hundred pounds last month at the rhinoceros fight.

Government House, 14 January 1837

I had quite a start this afternoon. I have been feverish and conserving my strength for the ball, but I wished to remark the arrangements of the ballroom before the arrival of our guests (in Calcutta, they are always on time). As the jeune première in the travelling French troupe I'd engaged had taken sick and our play cancelled, Harriet contrived in its place a show of fireworks, knowing that the native guests would particularly like it.

I called for my chair, but my men could not hear me over the strains of a mazurka—the military band was rehearsing on the lawn—and my other servants, busy ironing false hair and picking tiaras, had disappeared (Brandt had chosen that particular moment to sulk because Zahid refuses to introduce her to his wife).

Halfway down the staircase, my hand gripping the rail, I saw a swirl of white below me—skaters gliding on a frozen pond, their hands clasped behind their backs, chins high in poised aplomb as they flew gracefully across the ice. I rushed down the stairs only to stop in astonishment when I saw that they were not skaters at all, but servants with chamois leather tied to the bottom of their feet, giving a final shine to the white marble floor. They saw me and stopped abruptly; we stood there, stiff with alarm, as if the addition of my weight on the frozen ice would cause it to crack open and we would drown.

I slowly made my way up the stairs, calling for Zahid. It is Zahid who keeps me from falling through the ice. It is his faithfulness that compels me to duty. What is more, I cannot dress without him. He'd chosen for me the figured russet satin I'd ordered from Paris—it was quite à la mode with the new sleeve, trimmed with a slender band of chinchilla. Brandt helped me into it. As I twirled girlishly before the glass, I noticed that one of the sleeves had a tiny rent in it—it was almost too small to see. Zahid had laid out a headpiece of rubies and pale rose stockings with black lace on the instep (openwork stockings invite bites). *Bells of silver round the knees . . . Sandals of gold & pearl, & Egypt and Assyria before me.*

As I reached to tilt the looking-glass, there was a disturbing rip under the arm. I lifted my arm and the bodice disintegrated into fluttering strips around me. Brandt was left holding a sleeve in her hand. I could already hear music in the ballroom and the growing hum of voices. It was Zahid who calmed me. He chose instead an eau-de-Nil silk à la Sévigné (the spots of mould blending nicely with the colour), the sleeves draped with three flounces of just-beginning-to-rust tulle, faille slippers the colour of a violet snail, with topaz buckles, and an amber fan. In truth, it is wiser to appear in a gown of a few seasons past lest undue envy be excited. He wanted me to wear a black velvet ribbon around my neck, but for once I disagreed; I'm too old for that kind of coquetry. I chose instead the tobacco-coloured diamonds. As I no longer pretend to any graces, my underskirts did not need to be shortened for dancing. My neglected corset made it difficult to breathe—I had forgotten how to take those quick, shallow breaths that make it bearable. Harriet tripped into my dressing room with little Versailles steps to ask Zahid's advice on her gloves, white doeskin with a row of citrine buttons. Her jemadar Bhiraj does not shine in this area.

Brandt stepped aside to allow me to admire my coiffure in the looking-glass. My little flying squirrel lighted on my shoulder to make a few unexpected adjustments to my chignon, but my ringlets remained firm—perhaps too firm. I know that I can no longer rise to an effect. No more charms and wiles. All the same, I can be tempted by the luxury of regret. As I stared reproachfully at my reflection, my chobdar Ali came in, carrying a bouquet of roses that violet-brown colour of burning paper, a present from Henry. I held the flowers to my face. (As a child I'd been outraged to learn that flowers are the sexual organs of plants. I loudly refused to believe it and Herr Schmidt was obliged to ask me to stand in the passage until I could collect myself. He was so discomposed, even shocked by my ignorance, that he was silent and cold to me for days after.) With a last glance at Zahid for approval—he nodded his satisfaction—I opened my fan and followed him down the stairs to the ballroom.

A thousand people stood under the great chandeliers. The arches of magnolia, ordered by Harriet, over the doors and windows and the ropes of jasmine encircling each column filled the room with a heavy scent that just managed to obscure the smell of camphor drifting from the ladies' gowns. The light of a thousand candles was reflected from the silver medallions of the stewards and the officers' gold sabre hilts and the vast white canvas ceiling and the diamonds of the women—even the far edges of the room sparkled with fire.

I looked for Henry, but I could not find him. The Europeans sat on blue silk sofas along one row of columns and our Indian guests sat in a row across the room. The musicians were playing a gavotte and I saw that Lafayette was dancing with the lovely widow known as Mme. Sublime. He was exquisitely dressed, as always—perhaps too exquisitely. He seemed to be wearing two waistcoats, one of them a gold kincob that set off his fair hair and pink-and-white complexion. He affected what I can only describe as elf locks at his temples. He reminded me of a Regency dandy of my father's time. He'll grow tiresome with age, I suspect. I often wonder if his charm and good manners serve only to mask his emptiness. I must ask him one day. His lovely partner gazed avidly around the room, her lustrous eyes gleaming with triumph. She must have Irish blood in her—she had that particular enchantment of face and manner that only Irishwomen possess.

I had decided that I might be able to dance, after all, but only if Henry asked me (he knows that my legs are grown weak). He is a very fine dancer, despite his instinctive reserve. It is always a surprise to me how sombre, even forbidding, others find him when he is so easy with me. I wish they could see him as I do. He's not allowed the credit he deserves. He was my first partner and so he will always be. I've known gentlemen to claim that there are only two or three women in the world with whom they can bear to waltz, but Henry is different—he can waltz with only one.

I took my place as arranged on a large crimson and gold chair set on a dais, fringed with native boys in silver dresses waving yak-tail fans. As I was climbing into the preposterous chair that once belonged to Tipoo Sultan (he of the noisy wooden tiger), I heard a gentleman whisper urgently behind me, "Permit me, madam, to remove the blister-fly entering your bodice." I made a quick perusal—happily he was not speaking to me but to a youngish woman who burst into tears. Wreaths of evergreen with *EO* and *HO* woven in forget-me-nots were attached to the dais in extravagant swags. My position, a foot above the ballroom floor, made me appear like the presiding judge of frivolity.

I could see Mrs. Beecham in the crowd, accompanied by a flock of lovely black-haired girls. (I must remember to write to her—she sent us three dozen candlestick shades for Christmas painted with scenes from the Old Testament, all done by her wards.) And the Bishop in brocade breeches rusty with age, fastened with what looked like jade buckles. The servants, wearing new black lace-up shoes that made them uncustomarily awkward, moved amongst the guests with trays of champagne and strawberry cordial, trying not to look at the white women dancing in their low gowns, several of whom, unusually spirited given the press of the crowd, were leaping about like calves, dancing as if they hadn't another minute to live. A portly woman in black bombazine approached my chair with a cry of disappointment. "I'm bereft! Bereft that the play is cancelled!" she shouted at me. I nodded in agreement, not wanting to converse with her. We were never going to have the Webster; I was just impatient with Dean Frasier. Lafayette had asked for *Ma Tante Fifine*, anyway.

There were many attractive men in uniform, far greater in number than women. The ladies who didn't wear hats had stars and shafts of lightning (I also espied the planet Mars) arranged in their hair. The headpieces of some of the women had gone awry, revealing the evenly spaced marks left on their temples by a treatment of leeches. Several of the ladies—they must have been Mrs. Beecham's military wives—wore velvet Gypsy hats, and not all the gowns were newly clean.

I at last caught sight of Henry moving uneasily through the crowd, swarmed by his aides. He seemed a trifle underexcited. Mr. MacGregor, wearing large blue spectacles, marched behind him, steering Harriet with a gloved hand. Dr. Drummond escorted Mrs. MacGregor; she was wearing a most splendid tunic of Grecian blue silk with a skirt of silver lace. Although her diamonds were inferior, it was my first moment of envy in months. Mr. MacGregor looked a bit worn (he's been here since 1809, after all), but Harriet was lovely in starched white gauze with an underdress of marigold organdy embroidered with golden insects and a bandeau of sapphires in her hair. She was carrying the mother-of-pearl fan I gave her for Christmas—I could see her blush at the deep regard she was drawing: she was a slender-waisted Bee Priestess. The guests cleared a way for Henry, nodding in the hope that they might be mistaken for acquaintances. As he stopped to greet the Nawab of Kampore, I caught his eye. The young Nawab, foundering under ropes of pearls the size of white mice, was doing his best not to touch any of the Englishmen, hopping from one white-stockinged foot to the other as he evaded the hazards of the dance floor. He nervously made his way to his scarlet cushion, where he sat himself down in relief.

Henry detached himself from his convoy and approached my throne, smiling when he saw how uncomfortable I was with my placement. He made a quick bow at the waist, one hand held to his chest. He was dashing in his black evening clothes.

"I lay down my arms before you," he said. "As always."

"I thought you'd done that years ago. What else do you offer?"

"Will you dance?"

I listened to the music—they were playing "Le Remède Contre le Sommeil." It was my mother's favourite waltz.

I went into his arms, his hand at the small of my back, my body pressed against his as he drew me into the spinning circle of dancers. I believe that people turned to look at us. He brushed his mouth once against my cheek and the coolness of his skin told me that my body was burning. We have danced hundreds of times, I thought, and each time it is unlike any other—although this time he was wearing a scruple of musk.

He stepped on my toes, bringing me to my senses, and squeezed my fingers in apology. I fear that it was my fault; I am unused to being on my feet and it renders me awkward. I could see Mr. MacGregor dancing with the beautiful Mrs. Langley, although he held her at such a distance she had to trot alongside just to keep in step. As I was about to ask Henry if we mightn't sit down—my legs were weaker than I'd known—there was a scream at the far end of the room. The dancers shifted as if it were part of the waltz, swaying towards the corner where a small crowd was gathering. Something had happened—I hoped not a quarrel. Henry takes a hard line on duels. I saw Lafayette gesturing to me over the heads

of the dancers. One of the aides-de-camp made his way with difficulty across the floor and leaned into Henry's shoulder to whisper
to him. Something had happened to Harriet.

Lafayette carried her upstairs and laid her on her bed. Insects
swooped through the room to celebrate our arrival, putting out the
lamps. I sent him away and called for Harriet's maid Jones, who
was watching the dancing from the gallery. I undressed Harriet,
wrenching free her damp corset and peeling off her gloves. The
maids hastened to light candles. Her ayah Myra bent over the
bed, solemnly petting Harriet's bare arms. The lemur Rolla
watched dispassionately from the top of the pillow, the only one
not concerned.

There was a deathly smell—a tortoise shell was drying on
the verandah. On a table was a small bronze sculpture of a god
dancing on the world, one foot raised (freeing our souls from the
snare of illusion?), and next to Harriet's writing table was a large
sandstone Buddha with pleats of drapery so fine I had a sudden
violent impulse to disturb his dress. Against the bookcase was a
row of Persian tiles. Trunks of boots and dog-skin gauntlets and
butterfly nets and gaiters and sketchbooks and brass telescopes in
readiness for her hunting trip with Lafayette stood open against
the wall. She has turned her room into Calypso's grotto.

Jones arrived at last, her face flushed, and when she fussily
shooed away the ayahs I saw how envious she was of them. She
leaned around me to chafe Harriet's cheeks and I could smell that
she had been drinking. I sent her downstairs to fetch some ice from
the sherbet boxes.

Harriet opened her eyes. I sat on the edge of the bed and took
her hand in mine. "You fainted in the ballroom, dearest. Lafayette
carried you here."

A goddess wearing a necklace of skulls sat atop my sister's dressing table, a handful of red petals at her red feet.

"There is a song to that goddess," Harriet said, following my gaze. "I will sing it for you: '... If you take refuge at her red feet, what is there to fear?' "

"There is nothing to fear, dearest."

"They say she is very fond of those who approach her and will look out for them." (I am familiar with Harriet's religious transformations. Maman introduced into the schoolroom one summer a companion named Mlle. de Préydelle. I was later to learn that she was the natural daughter of my mother's sister, Clemmie, and had been hidden in a convent near Lyons since childhood. She introduced Harriet, who was the youngest, to the mystery of the Immaculate Conception. Maman made no objection until Harriet felt it her responsibility to convert her. Mlle. de Préydelle, who was our cousin, after all, was convinced to return to the Continent to attend the old Duchesse de Languedoc as souffre-douleur when Harriet adopted the habit of curtseying to the East while reciting the Apostles' Creed.)

"Do you not feel as if you were living at the entrance to a cave?" Harriet whispered to me.

Before I could contrive an answer, I heard myself say, "Yes."

Jones bustled in with the ice and edged past me to hold it to the nape of Harriet's neck. Harriet gasped.

"Has this happened before, Jones?" I asked.

"Oh, no, madam. There never was a sweeter person than Lady Harriet."

I suddenly couldn't bear the presence of Jones or any servant—or anyone, for that matter, other than Harriet—and I realized that despite my great isolation, I am never alone. I asked

Jones to leave and she tottered angrily out of the room, her feelings injured. I sat so that Harriet's head rested on my chest.

"I am not as content as I was, sister," she said.

"Nor I, dearest."

"I am not talking about England." There was a sudden swooshing sound from the lawn and the white light of the first Catherine wheel shone for an instant through the blinds. There was the smell of gunpowder. "I have been safe from myself for so long," she said. "Such profusion! And ours for the taking." She was growing agitated. "And I have never been so happy. That is the most confusing thing." She grasped my hand. "The silken veils—we conspire in our own blindness." She closed her eyes. "We would die of despair if we could but see."

I had not at first been able to make out the nature of her distress, but I saw then that it was grief. I stayed with her, listening to the last of the fireworks, her fireworks, and the hubbub of departure in the yard below: the shouts and cries of the palankeen bearers as they pestered the guests, refusing to let them pass 'til they were tossed a few more coins; and the equally vehement shouts of the English officers as they cursed their bearers, demanding that their chairs be brought at once; and even the raised voice now and then of a woman shouting Jehannum! Jehannum! at her servants, which I believe means, Go to hell.

At length she fell asleep and I went to my room. Radha was waiting to undress me. I must remember to tell Dr. Drummond one less egg for Harriet at tea and fewer leeches.

Harriet has gone to the hills with Lafayette. I've already had four letters from her. She has been presented with two peacocks, a pot of honey, and a pet deer by an attending raja. The deer travels in her howdah with her. He has his own spoon, teacup and saucer. She has had her dinner on a sandbank in the middle of a river (but was disappointed to find the table set with Meissen). She has ridden in a line of thirty screaming elephants in chase of a rhinoceros. She has refused to sit hidden in a mahua tree to shoot the deer tempted by the scent of the flowers. She has played whist under the yellow gaze of hyena dogs. She has seen scorpions the size of biscuit tins, boa constrictors twenty feet long and a jungle of white roses. And she has been seen by natives who never before looked upon a European woman.

She writes: *On the other side of the Hooghly, we found our palankeens. I felt as if I were climbing into my coffin. However, there was a comfortable bed made up in it. The evening was beautiful and it was not the least hot. Lafayette and I were carried side by side with the doors of our palankeens open, and though it was soon bright with moonlight, the bearers who ran by the side lighted great torches. Lafayette amused himself by catching fireflies in his hand and throwing them into my palankeen. We got on quickly, every now and then having to get into a boat to cross a river (truly the Hooghly is a very inferior article to the Ganges—that last sentence is what I call real Indian patriotism). My servants are quite unlike the fussy lady's maid and valet who dispute every inch of the carriage and expect tea, beer, and feather beds at every bad inn on the road. These people must have been magnificent before we came with our bad moneymaking ways. We have let all they accomplished go to ruin, and all our excuse is that we do not oppress the natives so much as they oppress each other.*

I had not known Harriet to have such strong opinions. She can feel but not understand—the opposite of myself. Clearly she has found it stimulating to reflection to be two weeks in the bush. She complains that Henry has turned despotic (I think she is mistaken, despite the occasional mild Voltairean blasphemy) and that I am aloof—she has had to leave town in order to tell me this. She wishes to give me the raja's deer as a present. She says that she had not, in truth, been feeling well in town but she now has twice the strength she had in Calcutta. *Like my beautiful white mare, I can sleep standing up if I wish. I've been practicing.* (Lafayette writes that she has made trouble by refusing to allow the bearers to doctor the water holes with opium; the tigers become addicted and she will not have it done. She has also tried to stop the villagers throwing themselves flat in the dust as she passes, but with less success.) She longs to go out alone, but the servants will not leave her side. *One servant carries my gun, another my sketchbook and pencils, a third an armchair, a fourth a footstool, a fifth an umbrella, and all of them prostrate round me. I went home in utter desperation and drew a cooking tent instead.* She is low at seeing no monkeys.

Barrackpore, 5 March 1837

I've had another bag of letters from Harriet. She and Lafayette were given a durbar where fireworks were lit on their behalf, causing the assembled elephants to run wild, killing three of the native bearers. Fortunately, the collector acted with haste and intelligence. Lafayette says that the Triumph, if not the very Efficiency of Empire, rests on the heads of these brave Englishmen—a good many of whom waste away with loneliness, not seeing another white face for years on end. He hopes that when the historians write our version of India, they will not neglect the sacrifice of these men. Harriet, for her part, cannot say the respect she has for elephants. Though they are not naturally witty, she suspects that they have more common sense than we do. Her elephant lifts its trunk to make sure that branches do not sweep her from his back. A great deal of trouble, certainly, is taken with his dinner; he is given cakes and wine. She's met a Lord Morlington, who once had his head in a tiger's mouth and has been an amateur tiger hunter ever since. He wears a long black beard which he divides in two when he dines, looping an end behind each ear. A numismatist and scholar just come from the Levant in search of old Hindu coins, Morlington has already given her an armful of books to read, including the *Mahabharata*. She wonders that there is no such thing as a proper Hindu history. *The ancients exceeded themselves in art and astronomy and architecture and medicine but left little written history; did you know there is none to be found until the Mughal invasion? Since the only accounts come from foreign travellers or conquerors, Lord Morlington strives to make his own contribution.*

She claims that while strolling about on an elephant—*I do not know why it is, but the instant I am on an elephant I do not feel the least afraid for myself or anybody else*—she and Morlington came upon a temple with a black stone idol in it. Around the idol was a railing of bloodstained iron spikes where human victims are sacrificed. She insisted on drawing the idol as well as the bloody railing before the arrival of the two tigers who come every day to sweep the courtyard clean with their tails. Is it any wonder she disdains coming back to our great hot shut-up prison of a palace?

Government House, 24 March 1837

My squirrel, now left to his own devices, no longer locked in the bathroom, which makes us both happier, could not be found for all the emeralds in India when I left Barrackpore last Monday to return to town. I was not very worried, as he often goes off on his own. The khansama sent word two days ago that the squirrel still had not been seen, causing me much concern and the servants much trouble. I resigned myself to the truth; he had been taken up by a hawk. I was very sad to lose the poor thing.

This afternoon a hircara brought me a note from Barrackpore: "Madam, I have the honour to inform you that the squirrel returned home at twelve o'clock today, ate a good dinner and immediately went to bed."

Barrackpore, 31 March 1837

Because there are myriad dangers surrounding their camp—snakes, jackals, tigers, even brigands—Harriet finds it an unexpected gift not to be, for once, the most troublesome creature around. *What a relief I felt when I realized that for Lafayette and the other gentlemen of the expedition, I was not a worry, at least while there are real man-eaters about. It wouldn't serve any of us very well if I were to maintain my girlish ways. Would you believe me if I said I killed a scorpion with a knitting needle in Mr. Thackeray's camp last night? Lord Morlington doesn't find me mysterious or weak spirited or incapable of logic (I'd like to hold on to just a little mystery, thank you). What do you make of it, dearest? I wish that you were here to feel it, too. On top of everything, I've dispensed altogether with my pantaloons, which allows me to refresh myself easily in the field. You know how difficult it is when we are in distress with no hope in sight. No more soiled frocks! So long as my skirt does not fly up, no one will be the wiser, although when I returned to camp last night, I found that my legs were streaked with blood. How did we exist before?*

My sister and I have never spoken of our body's blood before.

Government House, 2 April 1837

Yesterday Zahid brought me a chitty bearing Mrs. Langley's name, come to present her niece, just arrived, who had kindly carried from London a packet of letters for me and Harriet and four trunks of gowns and bonnets. So irrational have I become that for a moment I considered turning them away. It is this desperate heat. I asked Zahid to show the ladies to my sitting room.

Brandt fetched a black net cap for my head—it is too hot even for muslin—and handed it to Radha, who affixed it to my head. I took a little sip of my special concoction—it calms me—and went to meet my visitors.

Mrs. Langley, without her Nubian but with a niece, Miss Rose Sheridan, jumped up as I entered the room, pulling the girl to her feet. With all the queenliness I could summon, given that my false hair was already sliding down the back of my head in the heat (Radha has not yet perfected the dressing of hair), I invited them to sit down. As she settled herself, Mrs. Langley dropped to the floor a little white French dog that I had not noticed—to further emphasize the chalky pallor of her own skin? In truth, she is whiter than her dog, who, with the mange that is common here, displayed great patches of gnawed pink skin. She was wearing a most pretty cornflower-blue challis dress laced up the front with white silk cord, a hat lined in a darker Popinjay blue velvet and green kid gloves, and the young lady, despite the unbearable heat, was no less elegantly bedecked, although I can't recall seeing anyone quite so shrouded from the elements as was Rose Sheridan—unless it were Harriet and myself eighteen months ago. It would have taken an hour to unwrap her. A large rice-straw bonnet and a curtain of gauze covered her face. Swags of white silk protected the back of her neck. Under a swarm of shawls and mantles, I espied a pelerine of jersey atop her sagging shoulders. Two sweeps of lace were tied around her throat. Looking at her, I began to fear for her health. As it is an accepted fact here that a young lady come in search of a match has but forty days before her complexion is ruined, she had by my reckoning a little more than a month to justify her aunt's expenditure. She was reluctant to close her parasol until her aunt, for the third time, insisted.

"Thank you so much, Miss Sheridan," said I, "for bringing the letters and trunks. I am quite in your debt. But I have one more thing to ask, if you will oblige me: will you remove your veil and mantle?"

Before the dazed girl could speak, Mrs. Langley said, "She's a lucky creature. To think that your bonnets might have been lost in a shipwreck! But then she's always been a lucky little thing, haven't you, Rose?"

Rose wasn't so sure.

"Was it a difficult passage, Miss Sheridan?" I seemed to have forgotten that had I been possessed of a keg of powder, I'd have blown up the *Jupiter* and myself on it.

The girl's muffled chin appeared to nod. She was suffering from heat exhaustion. I gestured to Zahid to take her shawls and she reluctantly allowed him to unwind her just a little, staring at him with a look of deep mistrust. At last I could see her—her piquant little face was shiny with perspiration, her two cheeks like ripe lady apples. Tidy side loops of yellow hair were wound tightly into fat braids at each cheek, covering her ears to shut out anything unsuited to purity.

"I am so looking forward to the next tableaux vivants," said Mrs. Langley. "I've told my niece how your entire family excels at the game, especially Capt. Oliphant. I confess to having seen a number of Theatricals in my life, but truly I've yet to see anyone better at it than the Captain."

It was becoming clear that here was a woman who could judge artistry, a woman who'd spent a good part of her life in lively drawing rooms—but then her father, they say, had been equerry at Dublin Castle. She turned to Rose in an excess of enthusiasm. "You must prepare yourself for the most delightful evening of your life, my pet!" I was disquieted to see that she meant it. "I'm hoping," she said, turning to me, "that the Captain will take an actor's interest in Rose. She is a very good amateur performer— she was first at her finishing school in Rhetoric."

Rose looked surprised.

"I am sure that she was," I said.

It was Mrs. Langley's turn to look surprised.

"If she takes after her aunt, there is nothing she cannot do," I said.

Mrs. Langley smiled with pleasure and snatched up her little dog, who'd begun to bark furiously at the servants come to replenish the lemonade. In the little silence that followed, Mrs. Langley understood with a sudden gasp of embarrassment that it was time to say good-bye. We shook hands and she curtsied and the ugly little dog snarled and the niece said not a word. As Zahid took them to the door, Mrs. Langley paused to point out to Rose a miniature of Lafayette that I keep on a desk. It was clear that the Captain has been a subject for them. Mrs. Langley has very high hopes indeed of Miss Sheridan. But first she'll have to persuade her to speak—not too much; Lafayette doesn't require great knowledge in his companions, but he does like a little chat.

Barrackpore, 3 April 1837

Harriet returns tomorrow.

Government House, 6 April 1837

Feeling unusually restless in the suffocating heat (I can see the humidity), I climbed into my chair this afternoon with the little deer that Harriet brought me, and Salim and Khalid carried us across the courtyard to her rooms—she is at least a mile away.

She was sitting on the floor, cross-legged, with Gazelle's head in her lap and something in her mouth. At her side was a plate of cheese and sweetmeats, a copy of *The Calcutta Literary Gazette* and a bucket of mangoes in cold water. Wisps of pale smoke encircled her head—she was a smoldering volcano.

She gestured to me to sit down. She was smoking a hookah. Oddly enough, I was not surprised. It made a lovely odour—sweet grass and tobacco and cardamom. She pulled the tube from her mouth. Rolla sleepily lifted his head to gaze at my deer, decided that he was not interested, and lowered his head and went back to sleep. I saw that Harriet had dispensed with her bed and exchanged it for a native one—a charpoi—which she has had placed on the verandah. She saw my look of surprise. "To catch the eastern breeze," she said, pulling the pipe from her mouth. "If I had my choice, I would never sleep in a house again. You can read by starlight in India, sister."

I noticed that her hands were spotted with fleurs de cimetière.

"Would you like to try?" She gave a little cough.

I hesitated, unsure of her meaning. Her room was fragrant with the aloeswood incense she burns to keep away mosquitoes.

"Many ladies do it," she said. With the leather coils of the hookah wrapped around her, Gazelle at her side, she was a Minoan goddess. "It's considered a great compliment, sister, to be offered one's hookah."

I lifted my skirt and sat next to her on the floor. The deer circled me twice and curled himself around my feet. Harriet passed the mouthpiece to me. I put it to my lips and found that the taste was very pleasant.

"You missed Mrs. Beecham's visit this morning. To welcome me back to Calcutta," she said, placidly stroking the deer's spotted back.

"Not altogether by chance. I had a note from her. On the back of her very scented envelope she'd written, 'Qui me néglige me perd.' I thought it foolish to persuade her otherwise." I handed the pipe back to her and she took a long pull on it. The water bubbling in the silver bowl had a comforting sound, not unlike a kettle on the boil. Gazelle's round black horns looked like polished river stones.

"She had hoped to introduce me to a gentleman with the lovely name of Tinker Taylor," she said. "But I'd taken the precaution of asking Jones if she knew anything of Mr. Taylor." She turned mischievous eyes on me and it crossed my mind that her blandness was a deception. Had always been a deception.

I waited for her to continue. It was comfortable resting on the bolsters. She seemed both less female and less English (I think I am envious of it). As a girl, she had difficulty pursuing any chain of reasoning that was likely to end in an unhappy conclusion; now she is utterly imperturbable.

"And?"

"And it seems that Mr. Taylor already has a companion with whom he is particularly satisfied. A fourteen-year-old Maratha girl who is said to cull his eyebrows."

I blushed. Harriet didn't blush. From the verandah came the harsh, grating scream of the male blue jay. It must be courting season. "What can she be culling, do you imagine?" I asked.

"I've wondered the same thing. It hasn't to do with lice, do you reckon?" She smiled and stretched her legs. She wasn't wearing stockings. Her legs were pale, hairless. She leaned forward to clean Rolla's ears.

The chobdar brought a bowl of clove water to fill the hookah. I was light-headed from the tobacco and I used the interruption to get to my feet. Bhiraj, as cheerful as a bird, appeared with the lamps, followed by a bearer swinging a brazier of screwpine chips and another bearer with Harriet's pet lizard, on a silver tray, which is kept in the bathroom at night to eat mosquitoes. She has insisted that only wax candles be used in her quarters so as not to give offense to her servants by burning the fat of animals (Mohammedans think that tallow is pig fat; the Hindustanis think it cow fat. Of course, it is neither. It comes from sheep).

"I think you are well out of it," I said, teasing her. "Perhaps he has a brother."

Jones let out a loud snort of laughter. I don't believe I'd ever heard her laugh before. Truly, I thought to myself, the world has turned upside down.

"I'll need your help," I said, as I walked to the door. "Henry thinks there should be a play at our Thursday reception."

"It is all a play," I heard her murmur, as Khalid helped me into my chair.

Barrackpore, 12 June 1837

The sun has at last moved to the south; the clouds, laden with darkness, gather themselves like an army of elephants. There has been thunder and lightning for days. A hot wind rattles the desiccated trees, flinging branches and leaves across the parched lawn. I've been watching the sky—the thought that it might not come fills me with despair. I calm myself by imagining its path: it will gather force in the black oceans, ripping in two as it reaches India, flooding the south before it moves up the Western ghats to Bombay where it will rest against the hills for a moment, gathering clouds before it flies east across the parched Deccan plain. Spinning about, it glides across the water to Ceylon, reaching Burma only to turn back on itself luxuriously, streaming west, then north to Bengal, skimming over our own scorched brown fields until it is stopped at last by the white Himalayas.

This morning, Zahid raised the blinds and we waited for it together.

Barrackpore, 25 July 1837

The sky is black. The birds no longer sing. The peacocks have disappeared. It has been raining for a month. There were two days of clear weather when the world turned green and then the rain began again. The vines grow ten feet every night.

Something is happening to me, too. Something *has* happened to me. Fits. They wrap me in wet sheets.

A mad dog ran into Harriet's room last night—Bhiraj quickly closed the shutters and she shot it. Often I cannot remember what it is I'm not meant to forget.

Government House, 8 August 1837

Henry and Lafayette were attending one of Mr. Calvert's bachelor dinners at the Bengal Club—Dr. Mulrooney is marrying Miss

Saintsford to protect her honour, which is a far better solution than a duel with the lovesick Dewan of Moolrah, who thought for one confusing afternoon that the lady was his own. Lafayette told me this morning that Harriet's episode at the ball was occasioned by an effrontery made by a Capt. Woodson to Harriet's admirer, the Silver Gentleman of our evening rides on the Course, when the Gentleman was thought by Capt. Woodson to have asked Harriet to dance for him rather than with him. It seems that Harriet, although I find it unlikely, was about to comply when the Captain intervened. The Silver Gentleman was seen to leave the ball soon after, so it is possible that offense was given. Lafayette is outraged at Woodson's rudeness. Henry confined himself to remarking that she simply should have said, "Thank you, but I'd raja not." The aides boast that until an Indian gentleman allows them to meet his wives, he cannot dance with their wives. It also seems that Lafayette's waltz partner, Mme. Sublime, is not a widow, after all. She is possessed of a husband very much alive in Lahore, although this news seems not to deter my cousin.

Despite the suffocating heat, Harriet and Bhiraj, who grows indispensable to her, were working late in her laboratory. They soak the skins of birds in arsenical soap. Our Taxonomists wrap their heads in muslin and draw it across their faces so as not to poison themselves—they look like Berber camel drivers. I'd sent my gentle Radha to the Chinese market for a new rain hat for Squirrel. (I've asked my child embroiderers to make a little coat with silk ivy leaves and a silver breastplate for Frolic, to wear on our journey to the Punjab to meet Ranjit Singh, and three blue twill jackets for the squirrel.) Brandt was confined with boils again and Jones was turtledoving in the park. I happily settled down to read. *Although he was a bachelor, he had held some ladies in his arms, before this time;*

I believe indeed, that he had rather a habit of kissing barmaids, and I know that in one or two instances, he had been seen by credible witnesses, to hug a landlady in a very perceptible manner . . . but, who can look in a sweet pair of dark eyes, without feeling queer? "You will never leave me," murmured the young lady. "Never," said my uncle. And he meant it too.

I couldn't keep my mind on the story (it reminded me of Lafayette). I put away the pages so that the ants could not get at them and went quietly into the hall—I didn't want the servants to hear me. The marble tiles felt cool beneath my bare feet. As I started down the stairs, mindful not to fall in the dark, the squirrel darted past me. He bounded along the banister in his white nightshirt like a ghost. I coaxed him into my arms and carried him back to my room and locked him in a wicker hat box, out of breath with the effort, then once again crept down the stairs with my candle, nodding as I always do to the portrait of Wellington.

Henry had not returned from Mr. Calvert's party. The shutters in his sitting room were open to the river. The rain made a clattering sound on the glass roof of the orchid house. I lighted a candle on his desk, which was covered with government despatch boxes and maps; it is no wonder that I see him only in a crowd. There was a letter from the newly widowed Electress of Hanover (she who did not Hesse-tate), who appears to thrive as an epistolary admirer. It seems that her elderly husband is killed in a boating accident on Lake Constance. I threw the letter under the desk.

The book was on a shelf between Berwick and Dr. Johnson. I took it down, clearing a space for it on the desk, and opened it: *Un Guide au Sept Cent Vingt-et-Un Positions par Yasodhara.* I turned the pages slowly; heavy with moisture, they smelled of mould. There was the banana tree, just as I remembered; the banana tree with its pink bud hanging. The red-stained hands and the feet, the long black eyes. The lotus, opening. The king, the pearls, the pearl. I pressed my hand against my skirt. Through the muslin, my fingers found my parting.

There was a noise in the next room. Crick. I picked up the candle, leaving the book open on the desk, and slipped into the passage, where I had a view of Henry's dressing room. His black uniform was laid out for the morning's levee; his boots, a sword in a silver scabbard. His dressing gown was hanging over a corner of a screen where he'd thrown it. There was the umbrella stand made from an elephant's foot and the bamboo easel holding Mr. Danicll's drawing of the Red Fort. There was an odour of musk. Although there was no one in the room, I felt myself watched. It made my hair stand on end.

As I hurried up the dark stairs, I thought, I am going to walk tomorrow. Khalid and Salim will be dismayed, but I will reassure them that they must never leave me, even if I no longer use the chair.

Barrackpore, 18 August 1837

Henry is tempted to put off this Great Progress of ours to Raja Ranjit Singh in the Punjab. He fears among other things (Ranjit Singh) that the hard travelling will cause me and Harriet too much discomfort. It never occurs to him to leave us behind and it doesn't occur to us, either. Who would look after him?

To my surprise, his concern released a torrent of complaint from me. It was as if I'd at last been given permission to express all the accumulated aggrievement I'd been safeguarding, nourishing in secret pride and silence until the moment someone, in this instance Henry, begged my pardon: Why must we travel with scribes, equerries, victualers, cooks, officers with their wives and children and parrots and spaniels, tent pitchers, herdsmen, syces, grass-cutters, musicians, dancing-girls, water bearers, butchers, sweepers, tailors, valets, hairdressers, the Bombay Troop, the Queen's 12th Regiment, the Irish guards and two thousand native archers?

"There will be more treasure than you can imagine," he said. "You shall have your pick of the East."

I said nothing, both Indians and women being easily placated with treasure.

"You are less easily pleased these days," he said, when I did not speak, picking up the despatch box that Mr. MacGregor leaves for him every night. I waited as he went through the box and then his letters. He looked up from one of them. "There has been an outbreak of cholera in Ceylon so ghastly that in one madhouse all the survivors went sane."

Crick stood in the doorway, fiddling with the punkah string. He yanked it hard and on the other side of a screen a boy yelped in pain.

"Surely Crick can go to bed," I said.

"Yes." He turned to dismiss him and a smile of contempt crossed Crick's face, even as he bowed his head to bid me goodnight.

At last Crick went away—it seemed to take a lifetime. Across the verandah, on the floor, three of Henry's bodyguards lay sleeping. Figures moved on the lawn, their faces black in the darkness; the aides-de-camp returning to their quarters perhaps. The maidservants stealing home until we call for them in a few hours. Lafayette on his way to the nautch, Lafayette in love again.

"I cannot make this journey without you," he said, looking up from his letters. "Sometimes I feel as if we are sinking in quicksand."

"We are," I said.

"Do you think so?"

"I know so."

"Ah. So I'm not mistaken."

"At the Kali festival, her most fervent adherents pierce themselves with hooks attached to swinging ropes. To show their readiness to suffer on her behalf."

"That is what we face?"

I nodded. "I admire them. It terrifies me."

"How sentimental you've become."

"Sentimental. Full of soft thoughts. You may have to beat it out of me."

"Across my knee?"

"I can't think of a better place."

"Nor I."

"Being ordered to do a thing is so much better than being asked."

"I must get my crop then."

At which moment his sirdar, lying unnoticed behind a chair, leapt to his feet to fetch it for him.

Government House, 20 August 1837

There is cholera in the town—hundreds die every day.

I live in complete darkness. I am in a stupour of blindness.

Rats run across my bed. Insects cling to my face. I plead with Zahid to open the shutters, but Dr. Drummond forbids me air. I have not the slightest doubt that there is something out there, waiting. It is patient, expectant, concealed. Secret, black, reproachful. But I cannot see it. Zahid reluctantly raises the blinds and I am stunned by the sudden light. He moves my chair to the window— one of the traditional places, after all, of women. I hold tightly to the balcony rail, afraid that I will fall and roll helplessly across the lawn, where they will find me and do something to me. (It does not stir my emotions, but it does give me a thrill.)

I have an insatiable longing for Patna rice, the perfect pearl, the perfect bite, but I cannot eat.

Government House, 30 August 1837

The smell of sour curds awakened me. I couldn't imagine at first who she was—who is she?—but when Radha stepped out of the blackness to take the bowl, it was my sister who leaned forward to put it in her hands.

I am sick with fever, she tells me. I have no memory of the last few days. They took my little deer and the squirrel from me. There was the incessant screaming of birds. I'd no idea how much I loathed them. I would have poisoned them had I the strength. Melbourne always claimed that birdsong was over-praised.

Government House, 4 September 1837

The agony settles in my arms and legs; a kind of derangement. Harriet gives me narcotine pills. I only want my native servants, not Rosina, waving her arms and speaking in tongues, or Brandt, with her crushing notion of Empire—I shouldn't mind, I am much the same as Brandt, although unlike my maid I take an interest in the low as well as the high; it is the middle which is intolerable. My native servants appear different to me now—they are beautiful; their smooth arms. Perhaps it is the fever. I must be very wicked indeed to be given such confusion.

Government House, 14 September 1837

They tell me the Rains have ceased at last.

Harriet is very good to me—so deft to oblige, impossible to frighten now. I cannot read, indeed I haven't the slightest wish to, or for Harriet to read to me, although I find comfort in her presence. She works on her commonplace book and it is calming to open my eyes to see her measuring the wing of a moth. Zahid rests on a pallet alongside my bed, separated from me by a white muslin curtain so that we may maintain our propriety. Radha lays neem leaves across the bed.

These shivering fits are familiar to me. Maman once sent me to Beaulieu-sur-Mer with Mrs. Millington, all because I could hear Mr. Percival reciting passages from *Paradise Lost*. I didn't tell her I had visions of death, too. (I know the difference between real voices and conjured voices—that is the very thing that makes it such a torment. If I really believed that Mr. Percival could speak to me, what would there be to fear?) That is when I became so fond of my journal, lying on my sofa from week to week, interrupted only by the heavy tiptoe of Dr. Gaumont as he made his way across the room, bearing a platter of leeches. It was disconcerting for poor Mrs. Millington to be forced to listen to Mr. Percival declaiming on the terrace when she, too, knew that he was in Scotland with his widowed mother. To my surprise, it is not so easy to die of a broken heart.

"Tell me again about the tigers," I said to Harriet, as Zahid laid a wet cloth across my eyes. Never was there a more gentle hand.

"One night near sunset," I heard her say, "I walked to a water hole in the hope that the tigers would come to drink. I told no one that I was leaving camp and I did not take my gun. I wished to be alone—there were two hundred people in our party—although at first if Lafayette were out of sight for five minutes, I screamed that he was abandoning me in the middle of Asia. I sat there 'til dark. The tigers never came. They knew that I was waiting for them. On the way back to camp, there were hundreds of peacocks flying in the jungle—it was then that I at last accepted that I was not dreaming."

I took the cloth from my eyes to look at her.

"The next morning, we went out with the elephants to look for a tigress who had killed a hundred villagers. The jungle was full of cotton trees: no leaves, only enormous crimson flowers, and white boulders rising from a thicket of vines. I heard a shout and there she was—lounging atop a rock, calmly gazing down at me. It began to rain. I lifted my gun and looked for her in my sights, but she had already slipped away. The beaters soon came upon the body of a woman, her foot and leg eaten to the knee. The tigress had arranged the woman's saree to conceal her so that she could return to finish her feast. We'd interrupted her, you see. Bhiraj says that tigers prefer the foot and leg to any other part."

"Like Henry," I said. I do not think she heard me. She jumped up, opening the shutters with a gesture of such exuberance that I had to turn away. I know that I have lost her. "The natives believe," I heard her say, "that when a man has been killed by a tiger his spirit ever after holds the deepest hatred for his own kind."

My bolster was wet through with sweat, and although it felt cool against the back of my neck, Zahid took it away.

Government House, 22 September 1837

I am recovered at last.

Government House, 25 September 1837

On the way home this afternoon from a meeting of the Poetry Society, Harriet asked if she might take me to see something she had come upon, something she thought might be of interest to me. Of course I agreed, and she directed Webb to change his route.

We left Park Street and turned to the north, driving along the Esplanade. Men were flying pigeons to celebrate the end of Monsoon, the birds shifting direction and speed with the wave of a wand—they were dashes of ink across the sky. They returned to their tall bamboo poles, only to be prodded into the sky again by their sombre keepers. The sound of their wings was like the clapping of gloved hands.

"Lucknow pigeons are the most prized, they say. Are we going to an English-shop?" I asked, as I watched the birds. "I am in desperate need of black lace for our Great Progress north."

"It is a surprise," she said.

I noticed that we passed the mansion of the Maharaja of Mewar twice—thirty families live in it now, the Palladian portico hidden behind banners of yellow and pink sarees hung to dry from the upper windows. Our coachman Webb was unsure of his way, I realized, but like a native he would never admit it.

"We are in that part of the city where the potters live," she said, "and the men who make the clay idols for festivals. I chanced upon this place while searching out more pieces for my cabinet. You've seen the statues of Saraswati that they throw into the river—the white-armed goddess riding her swan." I had seen the goddess. As her black hair is pasted only to her forehead, the bald dome of her head looks like a big white egg spinning down the river. Harriet has assembled a collection of Hindu gods, including two bronzes from the Chola dynasty of a dancing god and a god who is half man, half woman.

At last the carriage came to a stop. Harriet alighted first. She gathered her skirts and led the way past a small whitewashed shrine in which there was a likeness of Hanuman made of dried mud. Behind the shrine was a small dirt courtyard with a pipal tree in the centre. Strands of red yarn were wound around the trunk of the tree and terracotta cups and dolls and tinselly things were tied to its branches.

"There it is," Harriet said.

I looked around but could see nothing. She pointed to a large rock, perhaps six feet high, around which the tree had grown. The roots of the pipal clasped the rock, embracing it. The rock was painted a bright saffron yellow.

I wanted to please her, but I was bewildered. I understood that she was eager and excited, but I could see nothing. I wondered if it were the objects hanging from the tree that aroused her interest.

"Forgive me, sister, but what is it that you wish me to see? I fear it eludes me."

She gestured to the yellow rock. "The goddess," she said. At that moment, two old women in white sarees came into the court-yard with brass water pots and a bowl of rice. One of them carried a broom of willow switches. They barely glanced at us.

"It is the goddess," Harriet said again.

I was loath to meet her gaze (Harriet's, not the goddess's), dreading that she would see my amusement. I was fighting the most childish impulse to giggle. Something about the place made me ill-at-ease. I could not contain myself a moment longer and I shook with laughter. The saffron yellow rock and the native women and Harriet all seemed comical to me.

Harriet turned from me with a frown and I followed her out of the courtyard. I feared she might be angry, but she said nothing. We rode the whole way in silence, perhaps wearied by the ladies of the Poetry Society and their talk of Byron. When we arrived at Government House, I saw that I had soiled my skirts again—perhaps when I was laughing. The servants gave no sign, and I pretended that the blood was not there.

As a farewell celebration before our departure for the Punjab, Henry invited forty people to an evening of tableaux, at the risk of giving offense choosing those he thought would be best at the game. Henry delights in tableaux. At our last Entertainment at which we did twenty-four characters of Shakespeare, Mrs. Langley was quite weeping with laughter at his Hermione (can she ever have read it?).

We went into the drawing room after dinner and the room quickly grew warm with the heat of persons pressed together, although not as torpid and airless as a London assembly room. Our guests sat on chairs and sofas arranged in a circle, the better for everyone to see. A wooden frame draped in canvas with a black deal floor set on four wheels, designed by Henry expressly for tableaux, was positioned behind a screen.

The civil service ladies quite unnecessarily took it upon themselves to open the evening with an artful little scene of their own: "The Genie of India Pouring the Treasures of the East into the Lap of Britannia." Mrs. Langley, dressed as an houri in layers of gauze veils, not surprisingly took the part of the Genie. Mrs. Osborne, the wife of the richest merchant in Calcutta (he is very rich), was in a bedsheet, holding a studded leather shield and a brass hanging-scale. She sat stiffly in a chair held aloft by four of her husband's clerks, her lap brimming with mangoes and bananas. *The exhaustless East pour'd in her lap all gems in sparkling showers.*

Lafayette, not usually the first to decipher a mystery, had it at once. (He has been in a particularly foul temper, having chanced upon his manservant Abdullah straining his morning punch through a sock. Abdullah has a lisp not unlike Harriet's, but he ascribes it to a genie who leapt into his mouth one afternoon during a heavy rainstorm. He has a cleft lip—his mother must have been surprised by a sweep when she was with child.)

Our subject, at Henry's request, was "The Animals of Asia in Consort with the Animals of Albion." At a signal, the screen was drawn aside. There was a ram and an elephant, and a black and white badger astride a peacock. Mr. Calvert turns out to be a good amateur actor; he made a very convincing peacock. The badger, played perfectly by Dean Frazier, was a trifle heavy for the peacock, and Mr. Calvert had the greatest difficulty keeping his legs, sheathed in white scallop-shell gaiters. Fortunately, none of the players succumbed to excitement, as happened during Monsoon when we enacted "The Heroines of Sir Walter Scott" and Lucia had to be carried senseless from the room.

As I watched (I no longer wish to play at tableaux; my own life is enough of a puzzle), I discerned an uneasy movement among the servants. Indeed, several of the Hindus had dropped to the ground. Two of the men serving tea had placed their trays on the carpet, the better to fix their hands in prayer. One of the kitmutgars dropped a full tray with an inspiring clatter of cups and saucers. Even Khalid, watching from the doorway, stood with mouth agape. To my dismay, I realized that the servants had mistaken the animals in the tableaux for gods. I caught Mr. MacGregor's eye and saw that he had come to the same realization. He jumped to his feet, hastily drawing the screen around the platform, and coolly herded the servants to the verandah. Our guests seemed not to realize what had happened, busy as they were deciphering the tableaux.

At last Mr. MacGregor returned to his seat. I could not tell if he'd had any success; his implacable face gives away nothing. The servants crept into the room to stand gravely along the walls, trying to make sense of the discovery that we, too, had gods and goddesses and that our means of worshiping them differed but slightly from their own. No more trays were spilled, however, and no one threw himself to the ground. MacGregor had done his work—more with threats than theology, I suspect.

In the last tableau (a black ewe leading an alligator), the parts had been given after much competition to Lady Steadman (the ewe) and to the lovely Rose Sheridan (the alligator—she was the only one who could slither properly). Miss Sheridan looked like an idol carried home from the South Pacific by Capt. Cook. Across her back she wore an officer's cuirass painted to resemble the scales of an alligator and around her face, poor child, was a greenish ruff with long ivory spindles meant to be teeth. I must say that despite my earlier condescension to Miss Sheridan, I had to amend my view when I saw the good nature with which she undertook her role, if not her position—that is, stretched on her stomach across the floor of Henry's contraption with the leather leash around her neck attached to Lady Steadman's black-gloved hand. Lady Steadman, an old cat with a gigantic ear trumpet whose ancestors had clearly married in India, was splendid as the ewe in a rustling black dress tufted with black balls of yarn, a black astrakhan toque, and a superb gold Portuguese chain around her neck.

As Lady Steadman was stepping down from the moving stage—she is a capacious woman—one of the servants, distracted for a moment by the sight of Miss Sheridan struggling to her feet like a goddess ascending, lost his hold momentarily on the front wheels, allowing the stage to roll forward a foot or two. The sudden motion caused Lady Steadman to lose her hold. She stumbled from the platform, but by some good fortune, Henry, who had just stepped from behind the curtain, his cow's head under one arm, reached to steady Her Ladyship before she could harm herself.

As I struggled through a conversation with Mrs. Langley and

her niece—Mrs. Langley was looking to introduce, if not marry, Miss Sheridan to Lafayette, but the boy had disappeared from the room—Henry passed behind me with Lady Steadman leaning heavily on his arm. She tapped me on the shoulder with her fan to chide me for not visiting her more often. I introduced her to the ladies with me and saw her make an instantaneous assessment of them, all in the blink of an eye, and judge them of some interest, particularly her tableau partner Miss Sheridan, although not worth a great deal of effort. It would not be the ambition she would mind, but the dullness. They made their adieux as Henry passed behind me and whispered, "I am a most steady man." I pretended not to hear him. He guided Lady Steadman to a sofa, where they sat themselves down to watch complacently as the young officers and commercial men and their eager wives moved amidst the chairs, eyes flashing with envy and desire.

In my desperation to escape Mrs. Langley and her niece, I searched the room once more for Lafayette. I'd seen him only a moment earlier talking with Harriet. This is a new habit of his, drifting away from the card games (always obliged to make an unenthusiastic fourth) and the stultifying diplomatic banquets. I once asked him where it was that he betook himself so hastily and inquired if I might accompany him the next time, but he only smiled. Mrs. MacGregor, the shrew, told Harriet that her ayah told her maid that Lafayette is enamoured of the nautch and hurries to the dancing every night as soon as he can escape his duties, that he has a particular favourite among the dancers, that she is said to visit him in the park, that she is bibi to a rich nawab who is known for his temper, that Lafayette has gambled away his estates (what estates?) to buy four villages for her. I still wish he would take me with him.

"Alas, I don't see my cousin, Miss Sheridan," I said. I

saw in the girl's face a look of relief, although her aunt was disappointed—as an aunt has every right to be. Miss Sheridan is not here for the stimulating company and the vivifying climate. I suddenly felt a disturbing sympathy. What is a Mrs. Langley to do but look out for herself? A benefit of which, should she succeed, is to look out in turn for her niece. The very skills that we have so cleverly cultivated as women—our intuition (which is nothing more than paying mind), our contrivance, our mistrust of other women, our extravagance of feeling, our frivolity, vanity, coquetry—are the very things used as evidence of our inferiority. Like the Indian. Our proof of *their* debasement is the fact that they (like women) allow themselves to be ruled.

The two women stared at me in silence, perhaps because I clutched the girl tightly by the hand. Her little fingers squeezed in my own, she was trying not to grimace in pain. I released her. "You must come again soon," I heard myself say. The women said not a word as I summoned Zahid from the doorway where he stood watching me.

I only wished to be alone—there was an unexpected delay when one of Mrs. Beecham's military ladies who'd had too much cherry brandy stepped off the end of the verandah into a thicket of bougainvillea and was retrieved feet first by a man not her husband. Henry, having seen Lady Steadman to her carriage, had slipped away to his despatch boxes. At last the house was silent and Zahid escorted me up the stairs to my room.

I am sitting at the little ivory desk that Harriet had made for my birthday. I can hear the woodcutters talking softly on their way to the forest and I can smell the dust they raise with each silent step.

I think in hours now, not months or years, certainly not a lifetime: Zahid will awaken me at four o'clock tomorrow morning. Brandt and Rosina will rush about in the dark like frightened cats and send the maidservants on useless errands. The Indian servants will be desperate at leaving their families. Henry will jest that leaving two or three wives is surely better than leaving one and Lafayette will disagree. Zahid will remain serene as always, dispatching the bearers with the last of the hatboxes and carpetbags. He will carry my painting box himself.

There will be hundreds of people at the Chandpal ghat, even European women, waving handkerchiefs in the torchlight, weeping as if we were going to our doom. (Brandt could not wait to tell me that, once we are away, there will be many more dances and much gayer parties, with conversation late into the night, some of it even witty.) The gentlemen will wave their hats. Guns will be fired in the air. The sight of Mrs. Beccham in jetted cape and scarlet bonnet will raise my spirits. Harriet, not ashamed of sentiment, will whisper that she had no idea we were so well-liked, but I won't think it the time to disabuse her. The servants who remain behind will put their hands together and say, Ram, Ram, and I will put my hands together and say, Ram, Ram, to them. Radha will invoke the blessings of the elephant god Ganesha at the start of our long journey. She will pray that the fragrance of lotus streaming from the goddess Lakshmi's body will not leave us—it is said to float for a thousand miles.

We—who take but a meagre part of our belongings (my twenty-one volumes of Saint-Simon)—will fill four barges; the natives will carry their things in a shawl. We will travel the first stage of our journey on a flatboat fitted with a little house, towed by a steamer. Another two steamers and flatboats will carry Mr. and Mrs. MacGregor and the Calverts and the many secretaries and aides. Our servants and animals will travel on a third boat and yet another is fitted up as kitchen and larder. Capt. Hutchinson, who will feed us, thoughtfully will carry two dozen jars of Gentleman's Relish. Gen. Stewart, an astutish old man who despises children, will ride in the steamer with Mr. and Mrs. Calvert and their child, Tim, who already disputes him over the hammock. The remaining thousands, most of them soldiers, will go by land, meeting us in sixty days' time in Benares.

At night, the boats will anchor together and I will be kept awake by the natives spitting and coughing. My fever will return and in the morning I will be so shaken with ague that Zahid will have to carry me to my bath. Radha will pour river water over me.

But I will take Babur's *Memoirs* and Frolic and Squirrel, resplendent in his new black travelling cloak, and all my books to read again. (Melbourne's *Milton* is in no state to travel, having been ripped to shreds. I use the onionskin leaves to mend my mildewed drawings.) At the last moment, I will succumb to Harriet's entreaties to bring my deer.

I am not happy to leave this provoking place. How surprising. If I had more strength, it would astonish me.

We are, thank God, come to the end of the Sundarbans, a melancholy, menacing maze of saltwater creeks and low mangrove that lies between Calcutta and the sea—it is a part of the world deliberately left unfinished. The sky is flat and milky. Now and then there is a brackish lake and now and then, without warning, a narrow winding channel—the jalousies were ripped away our second day as we scraped noisily through a tunnel of mangrove. The movement of the flatboat (it is called a budgerow) was not unlike our childhood game of Crack the Whip: the steamer disappeared around a bend and we careened after it. The boat was thrown against one bank, then the other, knocking us to the deck.

I grew desperate to see life of any kind—there was no sign of a living creature other than the two familial tigers I chanced upon one evening swimming noiselessly across the bow. As no one else saw them, Henry thought I'd imagined them and perhaps I had (because of my fever, I imagine all kinds of things that fill me up, then leave me empty). Twice we saw rags hanging limply from stalks of bamboo, like banners on a deserted battleground, to mark where a tiger had seized a man.

Our servants were near to starving. It is an impurity for a Hindu to eat with us, of course, but they will not eat on water, either. They could not go into the mangrove lest a tiger carry them away (it is not just the Bishop's white flock who live in fear of beasts). Our Mohammedan servants cannot take the chance of eating meat that has not been killed by one of them. (I am in great hope that someone will eat Mrs. MacGregor's parrot. Although it has turned out to be much cleverer than any of the children in our party, it never stops screaming, *Stella this day is thirty-four, We shan't dispute a year or more.* Stella is Mrs. MacGregor's Christian name.)

This is what they call dropping down the river.

On the River, 15 October 1837

I was mistaken, as I expect to be about many things now, to think that the servants would be content to roll out their mats on the deck each night; they sleep under our cots, under our chairs, under our very feet. (I used to think of them as animals—not that they were bestial, but because they reminded me of certain creatures: Radha the gazelle, Jimmund the cat, Krishna the antelope. But they no longer appear that way to me.)

The moment the men who serve at table have completed their duties, they pull off their new white livery, splash each other thoroughly with buckets of water and stretch out like crucified thieves to dry. (It seems to me that we often glisten with moisture: rain in Monsoon, perspiration in the Hot Weather.) They remain there until it is time to serve the next meal. At first I was afraid of treading on them, but I've learned to step between them.

We live in a tiny straw house set in the middle of the budgerow. There are no rooms, only blinds of vétiver root, called khus-khus, which the servants keep wet day and night. I lie on my cot, fanning myself, and watch Harriet make yet another entry in her commonplace book (as Bhiraj fans her); beyond, Henry drinks a glass of champagne; beyond Henry, Lafayette sits in a hip-bath of river water smoking his hookah. Beyond all of us, the convention of watchmen who guard our little convoy prepare their pan.

There was a most unpleasant occurrence two nights ago when Lafayette, driven to madness by the bleating of a kid, shouted to have it killed. The servants (they'd been asleep) didn't know what to do, constrained by a number of reasons from carrying out Lafayette's command. When he furiously shouted again, one of the Mohammedan servants simply lifted the animal from its pen and dropped it over the side of the boat. I could hear it bleating as it was pulled downriver by the current.

Now the budgerow carrying the animals has pulled alongside us. My black mare looks at me from the window of her stall, which is not unlike my own stall, and neighs loudly. There are two funeral fires on the near bank tonight; from one pyre they took a half-burned body and rolled it into the river. The other fire is blazing and a man with a long pole stirs it up. He pushes the corpse deeper into the flames and the fire glows brighter. I am only relieved that I cannot smell burning flesh. The feet of the corpse appear to twitch in pain. Harriet confesses that she, too, dreads the smell, but only because she fears that it will make her hungry.

The current runs with such violence tonight that the captain will remain at the helm, his hand on the wheel.

On the River, 16 October 1837

It is our eighth day and already so much has been revealed. It does not hurt that Henry's aides like to gather on the deck of the steamer at night to smoke; we hear every word that they say. Clearly, all the excitement will be had on their boat. Gen. Stewart, who is known for his excellent anecdotes, has wasted no time in falling head-over-gouty-heels in love with Mrs. Hutchinson. Wicked Lafayette noticed at once, during a little musicale Mrs. Calvert gave to us today. Her harp, sad to say, is breaking apart; it hasn't long to go—I reckon only another hymn or two. Although only half the strings remain, she played like an angel, Mr. Calvert singing along girlishly.

Gen. Stewart, whose wife remains in London spending his money as fast as she can, sang "O Ye Bonny Lass" for Mrs. Hutchinson. She is the very same person whom the newspaper in Calcutta daily describes as "the beauteous Mrs. H in an appropriate costume." In addition to loathing children, as I'd already discerned, the General is as happy to kick a cat as to look at one. Mrs. MacGregor caused a tremendous stir when she came upon him dangling her beloved Persian cat, Xerxes, over the rail by its tail. He said later that he was saving the cat from choking to death on a bone—this from the man who commands the four thousand native soldiers required to keep us from harm.

On the River, 20 October 1837

As insects do not trouble us so much during the day (at night they burn themselves in the candle flames, emitting a terrible odour), we sat on deck under an awning this morning, suffused with contentment even if the Ganges is a dull-looking stream with no reflection. The intimacy of the open sky and the white light compelled us to stillness; even Lafayette was forced to a moment's contemplation.

I am reading *Mansfield Park* for the third time. I'd finished the

Pickwick, stitched together in a linen binding of my and Zahid's design, by the third day. I laughed so hard that Zahid, thinking I was crying again, rushed to my side with a supply of handkerchiefs. My laughter was excessive, but then I am excessive all around now.

Lafayette sat alongside Harriet, an uncut copy of Surtees in his lap. It does not take much of a novel to tire him, however; he believes Macaulay's description of the battle of Killiecrankie the finest thing ever written. He taps his moustaches, in very good looks although a trifle sulky. I cannot think why he mopes unless it is the tedium of composing the occasional quayside speech Henry requires him to write or the endless thank-you letters to rajas. Henry is so restless that both Harriet and I would prefer he remain inside our little straw house. He has already put aside *Peregrine Pickle*, bored out of his wits. Without his official correspondence and his petitions, as well as the invigorating though sporadic despatches from Afghanistan, he is deprived of his reason for being. Although I am surprised to see how gravely he has taken his responsibilities, he manages to fuss at his papers, trifling with his correspondence just long enough to miss the last steamer, thus gaining himself a few more *months* to make up his mind! I've suggested that this is a dangerous luxury, but he insists he is simply clarifying his plans and intentions for London. "Melbourne would expect no less of me," he says. I'd have thought Melbourne expected a little more of him. In truth, Henry thinks only of his cool bedroom at Government House. Although Crick has rigged every kind of bed conceivable—a camp bed said to have belonged to Wellington, a cane charpoi, quilted mats—he can find no place comfortable enough to lay his head.

"Mrs. MacGregor has sent another of her ayahs back to Calcutta, this one for drinking a bottle and a half of French brandy," said Harriet.

Lafayette, who is trusted in the servants' quarters, said, "It is a lie. A rumour spread by the other ayahs."

"They were envious of Mrs. MacGregor's gift to the girl of a rather frayed but still plausible Pamela hat," I said.

"I wonder, did Mrs. MacGregor ask the girl to give back the hat once she'd ruined her life?" Harriet was drawing a sailor she'd convinced to pose for her upon a coil of rope.

"Shall I read a little?" Henry asked, disapproving of gossip.

"Do," said Lafayette, tapping his moustaches.

Henry retrieved Sleeman's *Vocabulary of the Peculiar Language of Thugs* from under his chair: " 'India is a strange land; and live in it as long as we may, we shall to the last be constantly liable to stumble upon new moral phenomena.' " He looked up. "I'm not at all sure that I agree."

Harriet caught my eye and smiled. She is a perfect companion. I fear that I have not appreciated her as she deserves. I believe she is finding herself fonder of me, too. If she is pleased by another's conversation, she looks at me in the hope that I am listening. Nothing of interest is said without her repeating it to me. She possesses a rapturous humour.

Henry was about to continue when a khansama brought a tray of sweetmeats and sherry. Abdullah brought Lafayette his hookah. Unfortunately, he'd forgotten the rosewater that Lafayette prefers and my cousin sent him scurrying after it.

"Why are Indian servants so inefficient?" Lafayette bestirred himself to ask.

"The things that distract them are more important," said Harriet.

"More important than what?" asked Henry. He put down the book and went to the rail. "Look at the chaps, Eleanor," he said, peering through his race-glasses. He pointed to some men making their way to a shrine on a wooded point. "They go to worship Vishnu." He was wrong; it was a temple of Shiva with his trident on top, but one is always going to be wrong here.

"They really shouldn't like us as much as they do," said Lafayette.

"Why would you think that they like us?" asked Harriet.

I think much of my servants these days—I don't mean that I think highly of them, although I do; rather that they occupy my thoughts. They are the strictest of judges. Zahid is less forgiving than my own mother at her worst. The moment I do not meet his rather lofty expectations, I instantly perceive the disillusionment in his face—surely it is an unexpected provocation to be amongst people who bear their lives so gracefully. They believe in the unknown world, like women.

"It drives me to distraction," Lafayette said with a smile, "that the bribes I am obliged to give never get me as much as I expected or, in fact, as much as I contracted."

"There is nothing more vexing than a servant who will not put himself in the way of obligation," said Henry with a flicker of a frown. "I find them instinctively honest, but if they are ignorant on any subject, they pretend to know all about it, yet they are unusually gifted at hiding any knowledge they do possess."

"I am only thankful," said my cousin, "that they haven't enough scruples to be tedious."

I turned away to look at Harriet's drawing—unlike myself, she doesn't mind if someone looks over her shoulder. Although we both were taught by Mr. Crabbe (called Windmill Crabbe because of his prodigious skill in rendering windmills), we no longer paint alike. Her drawings have become smaller and more precise, like a detail of a larger picture, whereas mine have grown vaguer and vaguer. My drawing is not particularly good. I don't say this in disappointment; it is simply the sign of an amateur who can tell the difference. I am only relieved that I have not yet succumbed to the Picturesque. But who can say what I'll do now? I might give up my charming human subjects for trees. I must remember to ask Zahid about sketching camels—they have such pretty eyes and yet seldom have I heard someone say, She has the eyes of a camel. The sketch Harriet was making of the sailor was not, as I'd expected, of his figure but of his feet—two feet as carefully rendered as a botanical drawing.

On the River, 28 October 1837

This morning at breakfast, Brandt, who had complained of headache this last week, asked my leave to remain in her cot on the steamer. I sent for Dr. Drummond (I noticed that he wore a ring over one gloved finger), but it was too late. Harriet and I sat with her to the end. As we could not conceive that she wished us to burn her, she was sewn into a canvas shroud weighted with stones and slipped into the river. It is unwise to keep a body more than a few hours here. Mr. Yarmouth read the service. (I believe she was an adherent of Luther, but it cannot signify now.) Rosina wailed in grief, to my surprise. I cannot say that I loved Brandt, but she was an honest woman and, as Henry says, always had a way with a bonnet. (Have I ever had a heart?)

On the River, 1 November 1837

Tonight I celebrate the Durga Festival. The lamps will be lit in honour of the Fair-Complexioned One for nine days. She will take a new form each night, armed with a different weapon to do fierce battle with a Demon who once threatened the gods. Radha has put lamps around my cot and prepared tiny balls of sweet dough called kul-kuls.

I just lighted a candle for Brandt and placed it before my image of Durga. Brandt would have been horrified.

Surder, 15 November 1837

We have moored at Surder to take on coal and sheep (Henry said it seemed Absurder rather than Surder). The settlement consists of a row of shabby bungalows. A little girl on a white pony, a servant holding an umbrella over her head, watched us gravely as the sailors threw the ropes. Three ladies endimanchées stood at the greasy little ghat, one of them with a brown silk sofa cushion tied atop her head—a shawl would have done just as well, but that would have been too Indian. (She'd been gravely ill and had shaved her head in hope of recovery. She's asked Dr. Drummond to send her a suitable wig as soon as we reach Delhi.) One of the ladies, little more than a child herself, clasped a young boy to her side, her eyes shielded from the blinding light by a hat at least a yard across. It seems that when she was obliged to send her children to school in England, she hid the youngest, the boy she held so tightly, in a basket and spirited him from the ship. She, at least, will have a companion while her husband loses his sleep over the endless troubles of the villagers. She confided to me at dinner, before the airlessness of the room and the blackberry wine made her fall asleep, that her husband berates her for playing marbles in the yard with the boy while he waits for his supper. She has gone mad twice this year and expects to do so again soon. My first thought was to hope she'd postpone it 'til our departure, but later when I tried to sleep I could think of nothing but her desperation. It appears there is another woman in the station, young and pretty, the mother of the little girl on the white pony, but so drunk that she is kept hidden. There is nothing to be done, Dr. Drummond says, when brandy is the sickness. Her baby is dying of malnutrition. He says that half the European children will die before they are grown.

We took tea yesterday with the young Mrs. Morrison-and-son and the bald Mrs. Dunlop in a little stucco house surrounded by dull flowers grown in rusty cans so that the plants may be taken along should the women ever leave this place. The conversation careened from death to fashion and back to death again. I am grateful all the time now for my interest in dress. (Once it was the only thing that Harriet and I talked about, but no longer.) Dress has proved to be more than a giddy topic around the dressing table; it is useful in evoking an immediate intimacy, an animated exchange of the comic ("Did you see Mrs. Kelly's lavender boots?") and the tragic (the sergeant's half-caste bibi suffered a stillbirth while crossing the river tied to a horse because she refused to remove her new corset). Harriet and I gave the women two gowns and six pairs of gloves each, as well as Brandt's trunks, and left them to try on their new things—Mrs. Dunlop already screaming for her tailors. She wants her gown for the dinner Henry is giving to the resident. In my old life, the women I encountered were of my own kind. My life—once a fastidious nibble—has turned into an endless disorderly feast.

There are two young clerks here we'd met once in Calcutta. Mr. Lushington, who presented himself with a rush of desperation, carries three novels of Victor Hugo with him (*Les Orientales, Les Feuilles d'Automne, Les Chants du Crépuscule*) and to my knowledge never lets go of them; he was brought up in Paris and Naples. Mr. Francis Graham, his companion, seems near to lunacy. Of an unusual pallor, he told me that he is incapable of listening to one more quarrel over two rupees. The two of them are frantic with loneliness and I begin to see why. (Lafayette says Wynton de Bretaille in Agra is so dispirited that he has taught his cook to play cribbage.)

This morning when Mr. Lushington came on board the budgerow, Victor Hugo under his arm (the severest Mohammedan torture could not induce him to part with the books), Harriet and I fell on him as if he were a brother returned from the war. This has happened to me before. Once, in Berlin, where our tutor Herr Schmidt had taken us to improve our German, we chanced upon a friend of Maman's in our hotel. To the old lady's astonishment, I threw myself into her arms, sobbing with happiness. It cannot have been Berlin alone or Henry's insidious teaming with Herr Schmidt against me that moved me to such a display, but a phenomenon of travel itself. Surely it is a matter of ambient conditions—we fall upon the neck of a bore we'd once met at dinner in London if we meet him on the Corso, but should the poor fellow, misinterpreting our continental ardour, turn up two months later in Hill Street, we are embarrassed by his mundanity, his fatuousness, his preposterous presumption of friendship. Our only thought is to remove him from sight as quickly as possible in the hope of never seeing him again—that is, until we chance upon him next year in the rue Vivienne. Poor Mr. Lushington was eager after his desolate months here for a good chat: Lady Illiers has bolted, the snowfall on Christmas Day was the heaviest in living memory, the Queen netted a purse while the King slept, fifty thousand hands out of work in Manchester. Although distracted by his own concerns, a flux that has persisted for weeks, he cannot keep away. He boasts that he cares for naught but Society. Clearly agitated by the onset of his flux, he excused himself manfully to take himself to one of the small wooden cages bound with hemp to the stern of the budgerow, the only sanitation allowed us. (Harriet and I do not use the little cages; we remain deeply devoted, despite the King's warning, to our pots.) I wanted to be discreet, but I couldn't help stealing a look. Mr. Lushington's lower half was nicely concealed behind a small canvas sail cleverly arranged around the cage like a curtain, but the rest of him was exposed to view. He perched there, the books under his arm, grimacing with discomfort as the river streamed beneath him.

Surder, 16 November 1837

As we were about to cast off this evening, Mr. Lushington, smelling of ghee, rushed on board eager for one last chat. He set right in (Radha was rubbing my feet with tulka to ease my headache), displacing Squirrel to make himself comfortable in my one good chair as he complained bitterly of Mr. Graham. It seems that Mr. Graham drives Lushington to fantasies of murder. "I found him this morning in the bath wearing a lace mobcap. But that is not the worst of it, Lady Eleanor."

As Lushington began to describe Mr. Graham's latest indiscretion (something about a goose), I was distracted by the sound of the men on deck as they prepared to throw off the lines. I cut Mr. Lushington short, alarmed that he'd be left on board. I'd begun to feel sympathy for Mr. Graham. Mr. Lushington's tale-telling only served to make me less disposed to him than his subject—as often happens with gossips. Besides, I'd received a note from Mrs. Morrison (written on letter-paper bearing the inscription *Mind Your Ps and Qs*—could it be from Brandt's trunks?) thanking me for the gloves and gown and I wanted to write a quick note to her. If she does not die of cholera, she will die of despair. Radha, reading my mind, hurried Mr. Lushington from the boat.

Harriet has bought a flock of wild ducks for her zoo. They wasted away for three days, refusing to eat, but then wisely resigned themselves to captivity and now do nothing but sleep contentedly all day and devour barley all night.

The Ganges, 18 November 1837

Because of my headache tonight, Henry insisted on reading to me from *Maid Marian*. " 'Well, Father, added Mathilda, I must go to the woods. Must you? said the baron; I say you must not. But I am going, said Mathilda. But I will have up the drawbridge, said the baron. But I will swim the moat, said Mathilda. But I will secure the gates, said the baron. But I will leap from the battlement, said Mathilda. But I will lock you in an upper chamber, said the baron. But I will shred the tapestry, said Mathilda, and let myself down. But I will lock you in a turret, said the baron, where you shall only see light through a loophole. But through that loophole, said Mathilda, will I take my flight and, Father, while I go freely I will return willingly, but if once I slip out through the loophole—' "

He broke off. "Must I read this nonsense?"

I was watching the women on the bank in their scarlet and purple sarees. Not in all the world have I seen such grace; it is impossible for them to make an awkward gesture. It is the sixth day of the waxing moon, who is no longer Artemis but a dashing young man on an antelope, and the women will walk through the fields tonight to eat certain herbs in the hope of conceiving a child. (Pliny writes of the Druid women of ancient Britain who collected mistletoe on the sixth day of the new moon in hope of a child.) If I tilt my new shutters a certain way, I remain hidden in my place of observation. I felt, dare I say it, exotic.

"I thought you liked Scott. It was not my choice, my dear." I dislike being read to—Maman died while being read a sermon by Bossuet on immortality.

"I could have sworn you asked for it," he said.

The boatmen were making liquor from the flowers of the mahua tree—it has the unmistakable odour of mice. There was a sound like thunder, but it was only hundreds of teal as they lighted on the river, beating the water with their wings. On the bank were the ragged tents of the Leech Gatherers and a gang of thin naked children and emaciated dogs. A cure in doggerel comes free of charge with each jar of leeches—I will buy a dozen jars and, blessed with the spell, I will keep my health (and they will have their dinner).

"Shall I read something other?" he asked, lighting a candle to rummage through my books.

I turned to look at him. "I would rather you find me a melon."

He sighed loudly. "Oh, do ask for something feasible—an emerald, say."

"You have only yourself to blame for giving me the Emperor Babur's memoirs. He writes endlessly of melons and he has awakened an overwhelming craving in me. He taught his malis to grow Persian melons. Delicate pale melons." *Yellow skin mottled like shagreen.*

He narrowed his pale eyes and stared at me. "I know that you dreaded coming to the East, my dear, and hid your fears once you saw what it meant to me, but I would never have taken this appointment at the expense of your health." He said it as if he meant my mind.

"There is something you could do that would please me even more," I said. "There is a book you must lend to me. In truth, I'm somewhat injured— given our reading in the past."

"You want the Rowlandson." He smiled shyly.

"I want the book of Indian miniatures. The men and women. You've kept it for yourself."

He looked embarrassed, but only for a moment. "I meant to show it to you, but we have been so seldom together. There is no privacy here."

"I feel quite neglected. It puts Father's books to shame."

"You've looked at it."

"Twice. Both times interrupted by Crick. I sometimes wonder what he knows."

"Father?"

"Father is dead."

"Yes, I know."

"I was speaking of Crick."

"He knows nothing. He's too busy making money. Like us, he means to make his fortune here. I surprised him last night trading two of my hats for a sack of rock crystal. A rather large sack at that."

"Have you the book on board then?"

"In my trunk. You may have to delay your feasting a day or two."

I dislike it when he is vulgar. "There is no rush at all."

There was the sound of the men preparing their dinner on the bank alongside. I am like my sister now; just the smell of food makes my mouth water. Even with this constant headache, I can eat. Most partial I am to a crab curry that St. Cléry has perfected. I could hear Harriet and Bhiraj coaxing Gazelle and my deer ashore for their evening romp.

"Isn't it extraordinary how Harriet has taken to this place?" I asked. "As we grow nearer the hills, she becomes downright gay. Her very face has changed. Her movements. Even her speech."

"She no longer lisps, you mean. Yes, I've noticed that." He yawned. "She spends an inordinate amount of time with that jemadar of hers." He rose and stretched, his palms pressed flat again the low rush roof. "What do they talk about?" He yawned again. "Dearest?"

"Yes, Henry?"

"Is it not exhausting here in the land of Akbar and Prester John? And now we go to the cunning Sikhs. They are not unlike us, you know." He tested his weight on a slender bamboo post. "Which may make it less tedious. Protestant Hindus, if you see what I mean. Only one god. It makes it so much easier." He considered whether to swing from the post.

"I see what you mean." He always has my attention when he is witty. "The Bishop says it is yet another ingenious Hindu solution to the challenge of Mohammedanism."

"How ingenious of the Bishop." He dropped his arms to his sides and yawned again.

Raj Mahal, 19 November 1837

We have been travelling for forty-two days, two hundred miles from Calcutta, and we are in the hill country at last. We went to pay our respects to Harriet's place of encampment—she swears that not a blade of grass has moved since she was here with Lafayette last year. The country is just as she described; even the jungle of white roses is not an exaggeration. (Nothing is an exaggeration in India.) It is the last scenery we will have for thousands of miles. Lafayette warns that there will be nothing to look at between here and the hills; only the burning plains with rivers wandering through them and, somewhere far behind, the mountains. Once we leave Raj Mahal, nothing but dry gasping plain until we reach Simla.

Zahid and Bhiraj were preparing our easels on a rise a mile distant from the river when Lafayette rode into our little circle with a swirl of excitement, a sack of mail thrown over his saddle. Smiling mysteriously, he doled out the letters as if he were giving sweets at a children's party—we stretched out our hands greedily for one, then another.

We sat on the rocks and ripped open our letters. I had ten of my own: four from my sister, three from friends, three from Melbourne. All full of news of our new Queen! The King is dead! Lafayette knew, but wished us to have the surprise. Melbourne writes that she who had her entire life (eighteen years) shared a bedroom with her mother insisted as her First Royal Decree that from that day forth she would have her own sleeping chamber. My Old Opportunist sounds as if he has plans of the young girl. *She laughs opening her mouth as wide as it will go, showing not very pretty gums, but her lips and eyes are expressive. I aim to be delicate at first.* My sister writes that the girl already has very clear notions as to how the court should proceed. Some of the courtiers are most dismayed. She so disapproves of smoking that the Bishop of Leicester was obliged to lie full length on the floor of his room at Windsor, his head in the grate, to blow his cigar smoke up the chimney. My friend Catherine sent me a miniature of the Queen and ten newspapers (they are not kind about our late King).

We were too elated to sketch after our news and galloped back to the budgerow to read our letters once more. (On our ride home, I saw a little hut with an image of Hanuman made of mud decorated with fresh green saplings wedged into the sand around it. As the moon is full, I will ride back to sketch it tonight. *Love for that moon grips the whole world like the light of the sun.*)

Lafayette fell into a deck chair as soon as we reached the flatboat. He was as exhausted as if he'd just ridden from Calcutta. He looked feverish. "Cousin, will you not allow Dr. Drummond to attend you?" I asked.

"There is nothing he can do for me," he said, pulling off his yellow gloves. I'm sure he did not intend it in any sinister way, but for an instant I wondered. He buried his head in his letters to escape me, I know. In Calcutta, my charming cousin spends his time at the nautch or the racecourse, but here on the budgerow there is little to amuse him. I rely on him to amuse me and when he is out of sorts I grow melancholy, too.

Henry paced back and forth, reading the black-edged announcements of the King's death, while Mr. Calvert, hands fluttering, opened Henry's mail with a silver knife, unfolded the sheets and laid a page in Henry's open hand each time that he passed. Harriet had a letter from Lord Morlington. He is at Allahabad, where there are good coins to be found, in particular the square rupees minted by Akbar that are so prized. Harriet would have told me much more than I need to know about old coins had I not begged her silence in order to read my own letters. My deer lay across my feet and I read every letter twice more.

The letters from my sister made me cry with envy. Mary claims that the French have taken her up because they like nothing better than a brilliant mind in a hideous body. "Otherwise there is a risk of being too much of a good thing. That is why they are so fond of Hume." She has been twice to the new museum at Versailles. She writes that Lady Holland has a native boy in her service who was posted to her from Madras. He is known as the "little imp famous for dressing salad" and she wonders if I am so fortunate as to be possessed of an imp or two of my own.

Henry sent for champagne to honour our new Queen.

Dinapore, 26 November 1837

We arrived two nights ago just in time for a Coronation Ball given by the Queen's 31st Regiment, pulling up to the ghat in a moonlight instantly ruined by a burst of torchlight from the awaiting soldiers. We were passed down a long carpet that stretched from the river to the collector's house while the military band took up "God Save the Queen," sending us into shudders of loyalty about her and ourselves. The great commotion was a shock after our peaceful days on the river; it was the first time any of us had been able to honour formally our new Queen. I wore a gown of cream dotted-Swiss voile with an underskirt of snuff-coloured soie grège (a colour Maman was inclined to call Dust of Ruins) with the new and ever tighter sleeve, thanks to my sister's packet of patterns; Harriet wore honey-coloured shot silk (Melbourne used to say that shot silk, like chameleons, looked faithless) with vines of pale green faille leaves at the waist and a Juliet cap of amaranth tulle sewn with petals of pearl. She looked like an illustration from *The Floral Telegraph:* "Hope," perhaps. As no black could be had for a hundred miles, we were emblems of restraint in our reverence for the dead King. Harriet and I trimmed our hems with bits of black crêpe to give a hint of our grief. We looked lovely.

Henry had asked that the local rajas be invited (Mr. MacGregor had instructed his aides to make sure that they knew to wear shoes so I longed for them to come without trousers). Some of the guests travelled two days to get here. We had the usual assortment of judges, collectors, factors, and magistrates—each desirous that Henry inspect his jail, courtroom, school, dispensary in the morning. The opium agent is particularly keen for Henry to see the godown where each evening the little boy workers are scrubbed within an inch of their lives to prevent their selling any thimbleful of opium dust that might have settled on them. The chief medical officer of the province was too late for dinner, unfortunately. He'd fired all six rounds of his revolver at his carriage when its axle broke on the road, wounding his wife in the foot. One maharaja, emerging from his fortress deep in the jungle, was accompanied by a long train of elvish followers in breastplates of rusty armour with tiger-skin capes and belts of leaves round their fine waists, not unlike Harriet.

The rajas' chowry burdars and Henry's chowry burdars stood in attendance with their silver sticks and peacock feathers while a hive of flushed, overexcited aides-de-camp buzzed around ineffectually. Henry, who is easily bored, looked as if he were about to fall over. He sat at a table with Mr. MacGregor as his interpreter. The wives waited in a long line, nearly fainting with the strain, in the hope of exchanging a memorable pleasantry with us; I wanted to tell them that they are too good to want our paltry conversation. I have nothing to say to them that could convey my sympathy without diminishing the effort of their turnout. As we are less constrained by precedence here, I had hoped to sit next to Sir Rufus, said to be The Most Interesting Man in Allahabad, but we discovered, just in time, that he will not sit with a woman. Harriet was next to an old general who refused to say one word to her, although he did ask Henry, "Pray can you tell me, my Lord, are we in the year 1837 or 1838?" and Henry, hoping the general had important papers to sign in the morning, said, "1838."

Midway through a schottische, a stray, arriving late, wandered into the room in a tattered white muslin Regency gown, a faded sash tied beneath her bosom. She wore an evening hat of white crêpe trimmed with a dusty ostrich feather. She seemed unwell. I sent for her at once and took her onto the verandah. She explained that she'd ridden forty miles on horseback. "I do apologize for arriving after dinner, ma'am, but my pony went lame and I had to walk the last four miles to town—I slapped him, I twitched him, I lit a straw under his nose: still he would not go." She carried a much-mended tapestry bag over her arm. I took the girl to sit with me, sending Zahid for a tray of supper for her in the hope that her hands would stop shaking. "I am devoted to the pursuit of fossils, ma'am," she said. "I have a collection of bones."

Promptly at one o'clock, Gen. Stewart, with many sidelong blushing glances at Mrs. Hutchinson, made a ceremonious and rather high-stepping—given the grief in his foot—tour of the room with a painting of the new Queen on a red and gold cushion. All the English rose and saluted, the dogs barked as loud as they could and guns were fired in the yard. As some of the Indian gentlemen had never attended a ball before, they had rather a delightful time seeing so much vice in the form of leaping white ladies. I thought that my young friend would expire with happiness when kind Lafayette asked her to dance.

Lord Gower's nephew, Col. Tyrfitt, whirled past, and whirling with him was a handsome woman of some age wearing a heavily flowered purple gown of many seasons past. She looked charming, if démodé, until I realized that something was not right. I feared that she, too, had had the same idea, for her pale face began to take on a look of grinning panic. And then I saw that she was heavily covered in powder, white powder on her chest and face and arms, and that the heat of the room had caused the powder to gather in thick streaks on her damp skin and that the movement of the dance had caused her low bodice to reveal the tops of two full and very brown breasts where she had not thought to apply her maquillage. There was nothing she could do, her partner as yet unaware of her deception, their arms entwined in an allemande. I felt an excruciating sympathy for her and a need to come to her aid, to help her wash away the incriminating veneer even if she could not wash away the incriminating colour of her skin. The women watching from the chairs along the wall—they looked like dusty lions—began to whisper behind their fans, their faces bright with derision. To my surprise, tears came to my eyes. I could not bear the thought that women are disgusted by women, and frightened of them, and dangerous to them. There was something so shackling, so imprisoning in the room that I found myself gasping for breath.

"Do you wish to take some air, my dear?" Harriet asked, appearing at my side. She took me by the elbow and led me to the verandah. "I fear this wearies you," she said, wiping the tears from my face with her handkerchief. "Unless it is your corset again."

With her customary grace, she did not press me to answer and I was grateful. After a few moments gazing at the black river, we returned to the ball. I looked for the lady in the purple gown, but both she and her partner had left the room.

I arranged for my young friend to spend the night at the station, sleeping at the judge's bungalow so she would not have to travel alone at night. She was perfectly prepared to make her way home—she rides all over the country looking for fossils. I wish that I could have kept her with me, but she has two young brothers at home. Her father is an engineer at Patna. Her mother is confined in Delhi, suffering from an itch so incessant she has scratched herself raw.

On the River, 28 November 1837

The weather is grown cool; it is crisp and fresh. This evening, a delegation of merchants descended on the boat with the most extraordinary jewels I've ever seen—a diamond peacock holding in his ruby beak a rope of immense pearls from which dangled an emerald the size of a duck's egg. I could not afford to *look* at it.

As I made my way along the deck, I was punished for my greed by falling through an open hatch. I had mistaken the hold for a pile of canvas in the uncertain light. I took a graceful spring and went straight to the bottom. My breath was taken from me—such a strange little moment of death, but one familiar to me from the hunting field. I was not injured, but I am so sore that I cannot walk without a stick.

Near Benares, 30 November 1837

Gen. Stewart says that it is desperate in Calcutta—yellow fever and cholera. Three hundred dead every day. Mrs. Langley's niece, Rose Sheridan, is dead, her beautiful hair shorn. A lock will be fashioned into a silhouette of a willow tree to be worn in a brooch by her aunt.

Near Benares, 6 December 1837

Mr. MacGregor, who seems none the worse for the two bottles of claret that Lafayette says he drinks each day, asked to speak to Harriet and me so as to prepare us for Benares. It appears that our wish to visit a zenana has at last been granted. The Raja of Benares invites Harriet and me to call on his mother at his house across the river called Ranugger—how it is spelt, I don't know.

Mr. MacGregor, clearly fearing that Harriet and I might

unwittingly (wittingly) say or do something that would injure our position here—the purpose of this journey to Ranjit Singh, after all, is to make a clinquant figure of my brother—pulled a piece of paper from his waistcoat pocket which he glanced at quickly. Harriet caught a glimpse of it. He had neatly listed certain points he wished to make concerning our behavior; Mr. MacGregor is said to have considerable understanding of men and their habits, whether European or native.

Number One was his concern that we not mention the practice of suttee during our visit to the zenana. Needless to say, it is not the sort of thing I'd have pressed the women to discuss, although I cannot vouch for Harriet. Sitting on deck this morning wearing a striped silk turban of her own design, a gazelle under her chair, her bare arms brown from the sun, four naked men laid to dry either side, she looked up at me and said, "I've had a stultifying and timorous life."

"Although we have banned for seven years the practice of suttee, some of their shastras—" Mr. MacGregor paused to ascertain the extent of our maidenly ignorance.

Good girls that we are, we both nodded gravely to show that we understood him.

"—promise that a wife who burns herself alive on her husband's funeral pyre shall enjoy his company forever in Paradise."

Harriet looked skeptical.

"What they overlook, however, is that even the shastras say this sacrifice must be voluntary. In our very own Bengal, widows are bound with rope to the putrid corpse and men with poles push them back into the flames should they venture to escape! We know that at least eighty-four wives and slaves perished last month with Raja Budh Singh in Bundi. So you can see why we would prefer you not bring it up."

Harriet had that expression I remember from childhood that usually preceded the deliberate upsetting of the tea tray. "We will do our very best," she said coolly. I was disappointed that she did not point out to him, as she has to me, the exceedingly slight similarity between Indian suttee and the English custom whereby a wife is made to leave her home immediately upon her husband's death to make room for the eldest son.

"Secondly, as you do not yet speak the language, you will be accompanied to the palace by myself and Mr. Calvert. You have been told, I understand, the etiquette of arrival and departure. As the Indians say, 'Good manners keep the heavens up and the sounds of the earth sweet.' You must take nuzzas for the Queen. On entering the palace, you must put your right foot first. You must ask permission to leave; that is very important."

I could not look at him. Ahead of us on the steamer, the Goan maids lighted the lamps. The sound of one of Mrs. Calvert's last harp strings (A major) quivered in the air. St. Cléry, dressed in tangerine silk, sauntered along the deck.

"At one time, not so very long ago," Mr. MacGregor said, "our ambassador was obliged to trot forward, pause, pray to the king, run forward again and pray until he reached an inner courtyard where he was presented with a Dress of Honour by one of the king's ministers, who would then shout Begone! at the top of his lungs until our man, running as fast as he could, had cleared the palace."

"We can do that," Harriet said.

"I should warn you," he said, "that the women of the zenana will find you utterly preposterous, no matter how polite and intrigued they may seem. Rather the way you feel about them. They will say, 'Who are these ugly things? Their clothes are poor, their jewelry fit only for horses. Look at those white arms! They haven't been cooked!' "

"Harriet's been cooked," I said, turning to my sister. She was gazing into the distance, her expression one of rapture—Benares, pink and gray, was rising from the mist. She ran to the bow.

I limped after her, staring in astonishment. Temples, their foundations worn away, hung precariously over the water. Hundreds of people stood on the white stone steps of the ghats and in the river, bathing and praying. Straw umbrellas provided shelter where women sat and talked—the women were small, their skin a most beautiful colour of brown. Merchants sat cross-legged on spindly platforms selling sweetmeats and tiny terracotta pots and candles. Two fat Brahmin priests shaded by an umbrella held a board painted with an image of Ganesh as women poured river water and oil and rice over the god's sweet face. On a large stone in the shallows sat two more priests shaded by a pink silk umbrella. One of them held a tall bamboo to which was tied a green-leaved branch. A cloud of smoke lay over the burning ghats. A man sat weeping near a meagre pile of wood within which a corpse had been laid; men lighted the pyre and the man covered his face with his shawl. Between two slender boats in the shape of golden fish, a man dipped a piece of cloth embroidered in purple and gold into the water. And behind him the gilt and ivory palaces and temples—all reflected in the sacred Ganges.

I felt a sudden pain in my chest, but it was not fear—for an instant I felt the great antiquity of the world and the very thought that I might claim some part of it held an unbearable poignancy—until I caught the dark eye of one of the bearers. He squatted near the rail, chewing pan, spitting, staring at me with malevolence. He did not bother to look away, caring not that I saw his hatred. There was nothing I could do. I could not protect my joy, nor explain myself, nor beg his pardon. I could not convince him that did he but know the disposition of my heart, he would love me in return.

As I hurried away, Mr. MacGregor's voice sounded behind me as he called his aides to his side. (He is under no beguilement of place; he has no interest in the gods.) I thought of the Emperor Babur's words: *I beheld a new world—the grass was different, the trees different, the birds of a different plumage, the manners and customs of the wandering tribes of a different kind, I was struck with astonishment, and indeed there was Room for Wonder.*

Above the coconut palms, yellow planets flew across the sky—only later did I see that they were oil lanterns on swaying bamboo sticks. As we climbed the steps of the ghat, Frolic was nearly carried off by a vulture.

Near Benares, 28 December 1837

It is our last night on the Ganges. Now that I must leave the river, I do not want to go. (All the tricks of mind I once used to conceal my melancholy have had an unexpected effect—my artifice is become real. I am such a susceptible woman that I have made myself happy.) The deer was on my lap, her hind legs hanging over the side of my deck chair. Henry sat beside me in the darkness. I begin to see that his boredom and impatience are the only means he has, given his position, given his race, given his sex, of expressing his desperation and it makes me unhappy that I have been impatient with him.

"I suspect we may have come to India at a disadvantageous time," he said, handing me a glass of champagne. "Far too late."

"I'd have thought too early."

He shook his head. "I have been meaning to speak to you about Mr. MacGregor, my dear. You would do me a service could you find it in yourself to be more attentive to that gentleman."

"How Whiggish of you."

"I know you do not think so, but in his heart he likes Indians. He has confided to me many times that he by far prefers talking to an Indian gentleman than to a European."

"Mr. MacGregor is fond of rajas," I said, "not Indians."

"You misjudge him. He is a man of the new type, fully aware of his place yet fully aware of his duties. He even claims to admire Carlyle," he said, with a hint of a smile.

"Sadly for Mr. MacGregor, Napoleon is at last dead and buried. Or so they say. Mr. MacGregor needs must seek his fame in the mysterious East."

It came to me then that it is Mr. MacGregor who should be king-making, not Henry. Like myself, Henry is interested in a vague but generous justice and a nice bed, but Mr. MacGregor delights in the burden and exhilaration of Empire.

Henry gave to me for Christmas a small rosewood table inlaid in a most delicate manner with English wildflowers. He gave Harriet an Italian sewing box. Lafayette gave us each an engraving of the new Queen. We read *Twelfth Night* Christmas Eve, although not without a sign of rebellion from Lafayette, who asked if it were not at last his right to be Duke. His request went unheeded. I encouraged Harriet, however, to relieve me of the part of Viola. I read Olivia instead.

Camp life is worse than anything I could have imagined! I cannot describe it for sinking into tearful laughter (as I no longer permit myself to sulk). Never have I been so uncomfortable. I had no idea it would be so terrible. *Where is my golden palace? Where my ivory bed?* Of course, I pine for the budgerow now it is gone. I do begin by hating a thing only to fall under its charm. By my calculations, I shall be happy again in three days.

They have covered us in every direction as if we were Indian women; we live inside an enormous red serpent. Harriet, Lafayette, Henry and I are in four red tents, each surrounded by a wall of red cloth eight feet high. The tents themselves are prettily made, embroidered with trumpeting elephants, each tent divided into bedroom, dressing room and sitting room. There are covered passages leading from one tent to the other and around our four tents is yet another wall of heavy canvas cloth. Once inside our enclosure, we cannot see a living soul; person or animal. We would have no notion at all of our ten thousand travelling companions but for the constant noise: children coughing; syces beating animals; dogs ceaselessly barking; the din of horns, drums, trumpets; the chopping of wood; the butchering of animals. And, of course, the Governor-General's party's own particular sounds. I was awakened last night by the hair-raising screams of Capt. Jackson's wife, who writhes with prickly heat.

I never saw Henry hate anything so much. He has already named his tent Foully Palace; he's christened mine Misery Hall. He declared at dinner that he would like to make a big pyramid of canvas and set fire to the whole. Harriet declared it the only life she wants—never to be two days in the same place, always sleeping in tents. "Is there anything more exhilarating than each night sleeping in a fluttering red cave? I will never be able to sleep in a house again."

"As if we were ever in a *place*," said Henry.

Benares, 2 January 1838

Another bag of letters came today. Harriet and I do not pounce on it as we once did, tearing the packets apart as if our lives depended on it. Bishop Maxwell-Lewis writes that there are many deaths in Calcutta, including the famous dancing girl called the Lotus. He sent me four volumes of Pepys. Melbourne writes that the Queen will not live in Buckingham Palace until work is done to prevent the sewers from overflowing into the kitchens when it rains. (How Indian.) As she did not look at a novel until she was nineteen (*The Bride of Lammermoor*), she has asked Melbourne to guide her in her reading (*The Dancing Girl and the Duke?*). The Queen's tiresome mother wishes her to read things of a spiritual nature in order to be a Shining Example, but Her Majesty will rely on Melbourne instead. He says the Queen is best content with a simple life—her favourite pastime is giving her collie a daily bath. He has never been so happy.

I asked Harriet when religion became so fashionable—has it happened while we've been away?—but she did not know.

I have been so intent on looking, so determined to see, that I fear I have clouded my mind. Our prejudices and our ignorance in combination with their strangeness make it difficult to think clearly. I see now that although I have expected—yearned—for an enactment of a fantasy, every exquisite moment only serves to reveal the absurd, the comical, the ludicrous. And every ludicrous moment reveals the exquisite. Things that once would have seemed incredible to me now seem quite commonplace. The promptings of my imagination turn out to be less fantastical than those of reality.

We made our visit to a zenana yesterday, leaving camp on the back of a rather shabbily dressed elephant, Khalid and Salim sitting behind us to hold two velvet umbrellas over our heads. I wore the cendre de rose taffeta, a bonnet festooned with gray heron feathers, and the nutmeg velvet mantle with passementerie so that the women could not see my uncooked arms. I did not wear the coral jewelry that goes so well with the taffeta for fear they would think I borrowed it of my horse. On my thumb was a large emerald ring full of flaws that Mr. MacGregor had given me as a present for the Rajmata, and Harriet, in a red silk plaid trimmed with jet, wore a gold chain, shockingly light, around her neck. It is etiquette to give something that you are wearing—that is the nuzza.

I'd convinced Henry to convince Mr. MacGregor that we could dispense with his assistance, so we were burdened only with Mr. Calvert, who rode a little black horse wearing a tricorn hat (Mr. Calvert wore the hat). I anticipated that Mr. Calvert, who is a bit miss-ish, would find delight in the silks and sequins of the zenana and given the jauntiness of his mien he seemed to anticipate it, too. We were accompanied by quantities of servants. The Raja sent a troupe of Maratha horsewomen blazing with jewels to lead the way. Webb cracked his long whip with great cries of Holla! Holla! and wild-looking horsemen in red dresses galloped backwards and forwards. The Raja's soldiers stood watching from a rise, their camels and horses and elephants stamping and snorting in the grove behind them. The dust was great, but the revelry was even greater. Harriet and I could not hear each other over the cries of men and beasts.

The dust swirled up in clouds. Harriet coughed until she began to gag and we were grateful to have a drink of tea from Zahid's caddy. Bhiraj, something of a dandy, I discover, wore a silk kerchief drawn under his chin and tied atop his blue turban so that the beauty of his beard would not be compromised. He wetted our handkerchiefs for us and passed them under our layers of veils so that we might moisten our lips.

The Raja's gilded boat was waiting to take us across the river. Salim and Khalid slid down the elephant's tail to help us board, pushing aside the mob of servants in a show of their own distinction. There were two silver armchairs and two footstools in the prow, but Harriet and I, our eyes streaming despite our swaddling, were shunted into a red-sheeted enclosure. The Raja, a small, portly, charming man dressed very simply with one strand of not very good pink pearls around his throat (he was not what Mrs. MacGregor calls a show-Indian), sat in one of the silver chairs, donning a helmet consisting of three black Homburgs piled one atop the other.

We were met across the river by more of His Majesty's servants, who lifted us onto two large elephants for our journey of a stone's throw to one of those towering porte cochères built to accommodate an elephant-with-howdah. We were lowered over the side and Salim gave me a quick brushing with his whisk; plumes of dust rose into the air as he cleaned me. Harriet's cape was streaked with dirt. Bhiraj had brought sponges to wipe her down, but with his customary awkwardness he succeeded in making her dirtier than ever.

The Raja, who is a descendant of the sun, led us across a moat into what was once a large formal garden, now choking with roses and blue creeper, and down a weedy path and through a lovely carved gateway with doors hanging from rusty hinges, into a courtyard, at the end of which was a large marble table, not unlike the altar at St. Luke's, on which stood four rows of children beautifully wrapped in silks and brocades. "All these are mine," he said, in passable French. "I do apologize, those three belong to the Treasurer and those—un, deux, trois, quatre, cinq—are the Prime Minister's." There were thirty of them by Harriet's count.

We continued in excruciating slowness, step by step, as the Raja's servants, crawling on their hands and knees, unrolled a narrow red and gold carpet for us to walk on; it led into a courtyard enclosed by a wall high enough that a man standing on an elephant could not see over it—the standard of measurement for a zenana wall. Under the solemn gaze of a line of guards dressed in gold and armed with shining swords and pikes, all women guarding the entrance to the zenana, we followed the Raja through a maze of rooms, one prettier than the next. We climbed some filthy stairs and went down a wet and narrow couloir to a marble archway draped with a heavily wadded striped curtain called a purdah. On a stucco tablet alongside, I noticed two rows of little suttee hands imprinted in red. I had a sense of moral discomfort, but it lasted only a moment.

Mr. Calvert was taken in hand by six veiled attendants. We put aside our shoes and stepped right foot first into the zenana. At once there was a smell of attar of roses, disagreeably strong, and my stomach turned over. Bamboo blinds woven with coloured rib-

bon were fitted between the marble columns of a long verandah—
not unlike Government House. The walls were patterned with tiny
pieces of mirror to make a design of flowers; we were reflected a
thousand—a million—times in the red and green glass. Light fell
through a carved lattice set into the roof, casting a pattern of lace
on the black marble floor. There were silk mattresses with cushions of brocade to lean upon and large cushions of embroidered
velvet strewn against the wall. Niches cut in different shapes held
white marble urns. I could see a shrine at the far end of the verandah, lighted by candles. Inside were a multitude of black stone
linga, flowers draped round them, and a scattering of godlings.
Some of the stones wore pink skirts.

The women of the zenana, every size, age and colour, spoke
gaily together. Some played Snakes and Ladders while others were
busy decorating boiled eggs, painting them with brushes or staining
them in intricate designs. Harriet and I would have been drawing
winsome chickens and bluebells, but their eggs were painted in
striking lines and triangles. No two designs were the same.

Five little ranees sat in low silver chairs against the wall, their
slaves squatting at their feet. Their heads looked too large because
of the quantity of pearls that covered them. Nose crescents of diamonds with flounces of pearls and emeralds concealed the lower
half of their faces. Their immense eyes glittered above the veils of
pearls. They wore tinselly tunics and tight trousers and laughed
violently when they had the courage to look at us. (I think they
laughed at our bonnets and I know we stared at their nose rings.)

The Raja went directly to a handsome, not very old woman
sitting on a mattress, putting his two hands to his forehead and
then to his chest as he bent low to touch her feet. It was his mother,
a clever-looking queen with tiny hands and feet, though scant
remains of her famous beauty (as dark beauties always look best

by candlelight, she'd asked us to come at a late hour). She was dressed in widow fashion with no jewels but for a pair of fine gold bracelets.

The Rajmata indicated that Harriet and I were to sit on a mattress at her side, smiling as we awkwardly made our salaams. Harriet said to me in a low voice, "We flatter ourselves that we are well-dressed, but we ruin the beauty." There was a high-pitched cough from Mr. Calvert, sitting in silhouette behind a screen—two black slave women with swords, borrowed from *Les Mille et Une Nuits*, stood on either side of the screen to behead him should he dare to peek. I recited the few words of greeting I'd asked Calvert to teach me. Harriet, far more at ease, provoked another smile from the Rajmata with her eloquent little speech. The Raja then introduced us to a crumpled lady who clearly had just been dragged from her bed and bound firmly to a swing—she appeared to have no spine. She was His Highness's great-aunt, I believe.

Some of the women would not look at us, whether in diffidence or disdain I cannot say. They did not seem the slightest in awe of anyone, although they attended His Highness whenever he moved, watching him intently. I was most intrigued to see that in the zenana it is women who look at men. Some of the women were remarkably plain, causing me to think how unjust it is to imprison an ugly woman in a zenana. A few of the serving women were distinctly not native—one or two had the fair skin and light eyes of Byron's Circassians.

The Rajmata signed to us to remove our bonnets. We did as we were told and instantly we were harnessed with a dozen flower necklaces. Now the women grew animated. I could not be sure they weren't teasing us; it did not matter, we were all so gay. The Raja, perhaps thinking of other things, shook his head dreamily. He sat in a yellow satin bergère, smoking a Turkish cigarette. We presented Her Majesty with the sorry emerald ring and gold chain that Mr. MacGregor had given us for her. Although she was too polite to dash them to the floor, our bonnets were dumped back upon our heads, a dozen flashing hands knotting the satin ribbons tightly under our chins. "The ladies do me too much honour," she said, although Calvert's translation left out the humour in her voice.

As the astute old queen was fully aware that her gifts to us were all destined for the Toshakhana, she leaned towards us and to our surprise said quietly in French that other jewels had been specially prepared for us, finer than the inferior articles which would be on the list given to Maj. Quinn. Harriet's eyes glittered with pleasure, but there was another cough from Calvert; the man has very good ears. "Best not," he shouted. With an angry gesture, the Rajmata sent away the trays of nuzzas meant for us to steal. Harriet watched them disappear with tears in her eyes. Mademoiselle used to tell us of grocers' boys who the first week of their apprenticeship were allowed to eat barley sugar and raisins to such an amount that they never wished to touch them again. We thought that a cautionary myth, but I am nearing my surfeit of emeralds and pearls and, unlike Harriet, I do not mind so much anymore when they are snatched from me.

The Rajmata gestured to her servants—dressed as exquisitely as the young ranees—to give us each a silver cup with a ruby handle into which coffee was poured. The Raja had disappeared. I began to feel more at ease. Some of the women eschewed the drinking of coffee to eat roasted coffee beans instead, certainly a more direct approach, although rather noisy. Trays were passed round holding a single gilded lime or a tiny sugar pagoda, and bowls of pistachio nuts the colour of green pigeons. Kashmiri peaches, white apricots, dried fruits and nuts, confectionery and cakes were set on low silver tables, the plates decorated with cut-outs of coloured paper. The Rajmata was handed a large gold spoon of almond paste which was passed amongst the ladies after she'd taken a nibble. The ladies took the almond paste without touching the spoon with their lips. I was much relieved that it did not come our way. Their delicacy was daunting.

The Rajmata stared intently at Harriet. She began to speak in her own language, not pausing to allow Calvert to translate. She went on so quickly that he was compelled to speak at the same time. "Her Highness admires very much the colouring of Lady Harriet, her blue eyes and yellow hair, and she wishes to know what it is that she wears at her waist and would she be so kind as to show it to Her Majesty, in return for which Her Majesty would be well-pleased. She would like to present Lady Harriet with a dupatta." Calvert sounded as if he were frowning (my father claimed to have once heard a smile).

As the dupatta was extraordinarily beautiful—one of those pleated and twisted lengths of silk dipped in powdered mica to make it sparkle—Harriet was clearly getting the better of the exchange. My sister, no fool, removed her French watch with its dangling charms and handed it to a maidservant, who presented it to the Queen on a silver tray. The Rajmata held the watch to a candle to examine it closely. "Her Majesty wishes to know if you abide by your watch," said Calvert. The Rajmata passed Harriet's watch back to her, this time putting it into her hand. "My own women sleep all day, dine at midnight and smoke their hookahs 'til dawn. There is no need of a timepiece in the zenana," she said to us in French. She did not give Harriet the dupatta.

"They are like your ducks: asleep all day, feeding all night," I said to Harriet, as the women adorned our wrists and necks with skipping ropes of silver braid and pressed little embroidered bags of spices and betel into our hands. Attar of roses was splashed over us, ruining my gown. The smell of the attar combined with the heavy incense gave me a most piercing headache. Her Highness, perhaps noticing that I frowned with pain, reached into a gold casket at her side to withdraw a small black ball which she held out to me, gesturing to me to eat it as she touched her forehead in sympathy. When I hesitated, she broke the lump in two, giving me half of it, which I obediently put into my mouth. She put the other half under her tongue. My pain vanished as it melted in my mouth. She smiled.

The Raja appeared as if by magic. He wished us to see his collection of paintings, all painted by himself. We asked permission of the Rajmata to leave and she granted it with an elegant wave of her hand. It had begun to rain and there was a rhythmic drumming of raindrops upon our parasols as we crossed the numerous courtyards, mercifully without the red and gold carpet. I longed to be impressed, but the paintings, rumoured to be indecent, were near incomprehensible—all arms and noses and storks' bills. His Majesty gently explained that his themes were taken from the Koka-Shastra. Before a large painting in which a dancing girl in a crimson skirt could be vaguely discerned after much searching, Harriet whispered, "I believe cousin Lafayette is acquainted with that lady."

It was a disappointment to leave the Raja to cross the river in the falling light. I'd been utterly spoiled in one afternoon. The wind had risen and the crossing was rough, but Mr. MacGregor had thoughtfully sent Webb with the carriage and it was waiting for us across the river, accompanied, however, by sixty Indian soldiers on camels, as well as a troop of thirty mounted sepoys with torches. Although filthy and starving, I was, thanks to the Rajmata's medicine, very content in myself, laughing at everything that was done or said. I felt no tiredness for the first time since leaving Calcutta. As I watched the bearers running alongside, their lips stained red from pan, I wondered how it must feel to run barefoot through the cool dust.

The torches illuminated the camels trotting past and the horses prancing, as the trumpets sounded and the men ran after us down the lanes. Rats as big as spaniels bounded along the bank. Numerous madmen were roving the streets. They drown themselves in the belief that death in the holy Ganges will bring eternal bliss. Relays of bearers arranged themselves every fifty feet, wild-looking men who shouted as they lunged towards the carriage, causing Harriet to jump each time in startlement. I was thinking that the camel is a jolie laide with her velvet-brown eyes blinking slowly and her long black lashes; less enchanting when seen from above with her sloping shoulders after Ingres and her piquant ears, when Harriet said, "I shall never again say we live like purdah ladies."

I had no spasms in the night, thanks to the Rajmata's little black ball.

In Camp, 8 January 1838

I went to Harriet this evening to accompany her to the dining tent, only to find her crouched in a corner, wearing a fur coat and astrakhan, the wind whipping through a large hole in the side of her tent—what Maman was apt to call a "thorough" air. She looked a mess.

"Do forgive my asking, sister, but one might imagine there was a stain down the front of your ermine."

"Oh, yes," she said. "It was so cold I wore my coat for tea."

She saw that I was staring at the rip in the side of the tent as she rose stiffly to her feet. "Nothing will induce me to let them make a prison of this!"

I wrapped myself tightly in my shawl. "Our people have behaved badly," I said. "Most shamefully, I'm afraid, although not our very own servants."

She waited for me to continue as Myra rubbed her cold hands.

"How they managed it, I cannot fathom, but it appears that they have stolen the red and gold carpet that the Raja laid for us at the palace."

Harriet moaned in dismay, pulling her hands free.

"They've offered to return it now they're found out, but it is too late," I said. "Mr. MacGregor says, If we forgive them, people will gup-gup that the Governor-General lets his servants show great disrespect to their princes. And all for a piece of carpet! They are to be sent to Calcutta immediately. There is nothing to be done."

After supper, I was obliged, despite a great desire to be alone, to attend a nautch given by the collector. We were deprived of Henry's presence by his teeth. It was a disappointment to him, as he has grown fond of these drinking bouts. Lafayette lounged languidly on the bolsters, chewing anise. The singers and dancers, the best in Benares, acted scenes from the lives of Vishnu and Brahma and sang Persian songs that were astonishingly discordant. Young men (Lafayette said that they were men, and he would know) were dressed to represent a troupe of gods and goddesses. "Is not blue-armed Krishna beautiful?" Harriet asked.

Mr. MacGregor talked at me the whole time, never moving a muscle of his very unmovable countenance: "This is delightful! This is really delightful!"

"Do translate for me, sir," I said at last.

He was pleased to be asked. " 'I am the body, you are the soul; we may be parted here, but let no one say we shall be separated tonight'—I beg your pardon, Lady Eleanor—'separated hereafter.' "

I looked to Harriet to see if she had heard the translation, but she was staring intently at a cross-eyed nautch girl who had cast at least one eye on Lafayette, singing to him passionately with little meaning smiles. Lafayette smiled back at her. Harriet was so embarrassed by the resplendence of Lafayette's countenance that she had to look away.

"Pray, Mr. MacGregor, how does the lady address my cousin?" Harriet leaned across me to ask.

" 'My grave is open, and I gaze into it, but do you care for me?' " said Mr. MacGregor.

"The Captain is much attracted," she said. "I fear it would be too much for him if I forwarded your translation."

"He hardly requires it," said Mr. MacGregor.

As we left the tent, an equerry arrived carrying a bundle wrapped in Benares silk. It was the Rajmata's dupatta. Harriet concealed it under her cloak so that Quinn could not take it from her.

Near Benares, 9 January 1838

Lafayette was waiting at the edge of camp when Harriet and I returned from our walk today. (Surely, there is nothing so lovely as an evening in a village in India—what the people call cow-dust time. The mist rises in a blue haze from the fields of mustard. The sky is a pale lilac colour. The smell of wood smoke drifts from the lanes. *It is only the evening cowbells. Come let us climb that jasmine-mantled rock and look*. The dogs rush out, whining and yipping, and Harriet shakes her stick at them and they sidle back to the huts. The villagers are returning from the fields; the women, the hems of their sarees tucked at the waist, offer us a cup of goat's milk. There are small shrines by the side of the road, holding linga and other stones painted scarlet and white, and as we pass we make our little nod of respect.) Lafayette wished to warn us that the servants who'd been dismissed for stealing the Raja's carpet were in search of us. Three times they have contrived to get into my tent with their relations and three times Zahid has sent them away unhappy.

Lafayette disappeared (for someone so famously courageous in the field, he is craven when it comes to domestic battles) as the tearful leader of the deputation caught sight of us and threw himself on the ground, laying hold of my feet. It is very bad not to forgive anyone who wishes it even less humbly than he does. Harriet and I gave him money to take all of them back to Bengal and he seemed satisfied. We cannot feel so pleased.

As it has turned colder, Harriet acquiesced to stitching up the rent in her red cave. Bhiraj insisted on sewing it himself, refusing to call the darzi. As he is as clumsy with a needle as he is with everything else, Harriet nearly froze to death in the night. She will have it repaired properly tomorrow.

Tamarhabad, 11 January 1838

We have made our first march. My sense of time is already altered, my ordinary means of seeing distorted. All is provisional, all is just within reach—fours hours distant at most. I live only to reach the next camp.

A hundred bugles sounded at five o'clock this morning. The fakirs beat their drums just the other side of our canvas wall to make sure we were sufficiently roused, although the camels had awakened us at midnight as they were loaded with pots and pans, and an advance of tent pitchers and bhistis, making a most fearful racket, departed with them in order to prepare our next camp.

At five-thirty, our beds and chairs were snatched from under us and loaded onto the twenty elephants needed for the two dozen people who make up our own party. Harriet and I made our cloaked and sombre way through the chilly darkness as the heavy fluttering tents were pulled down, rolled up and tied atop the swaying beasts. Henry, resplendent in his very goldest coat, star-and-ribbon and cocked hat, was in a frenzy of indignation because Maj. Quinn, watching him like a hawk with hiccoughs, had snatched away his dressing room before he'd completed his toilette.

We at last set off on our elephants. The syces ran ahead with torches, shouting, as the postilions, blinded by the dust, could not see the way. We had to wait for an hour by the side of the road until the dust had settled so we could ride on, stirring it up for the legions who follow—there are ten miles of beasts and men trailing after us. It was all the syces could do to control the animals, unhappy with the heavy and unwieldy loads hanging hazardously from their sides (not the half-dozen camels loaded with cigars for the officers). Behind the camels and elephants came a train of covered hackeries with camp beds and pianos (alas for the drowned piano tuner); Mrs. MacGregor very grand in a carriage as she read her Bible, Mr. MacGregor ambling ahead on a pony; women en plein déshabille with babies; my deer in her own cart; Gen. Stewart curvetting beside Mrs. Hutchinson, who reclined in a blue satin-lined palankeen; pet cats in swings; servants bearing parrots in silver cages; Jimmund stalking along in his livery, a stick in one hand and Frolic in the other, the dog's nose peeping from a brown woolen shawl. Harriet's menagerie grows so large—Gazelle, three tiny lorikeets who sleep hanging from her coiled braid, a rescued pariah dog named Jack, the ducks and her lemur, Rolla—that Maj. Quinn, his red face twitching worse than ever from far too much responsibility, threatens a closed hackerie for her animals alone. She will never consent to that—the creatures enjoy the change of scene exceedingly.

Our enormous train will be kept to a rate of little more than six miles in the hour, travelling from five to eight o'clock in the morning. The sun is so searing, the effort so exhausting that the whole cavalcade must camp for the rest of the day and night. The troops, whistling and singing, complain if we do not end our march before the sun grows too hot. As the sick and the dying must push on with the others, there are beds on poles for the many dozens of ailing servants, and palankeens for us should we require them. Fourteen of my own people are in fevers and I have only a turnscrew to bleed them.

Our food is in the miraculous hands of St. Cléry, who travels one day ahead of us. Suffering from a liver ailment, he complains bitterly that the moment he tries to rest, les bêtes fling themselves to the ground and are instantly asleep, leaving the dinner to cook itself. If but one hair is found in a dish of food, he matches it carefully to the head of each kitchen servant. When the culprit is discovered, his head is shaved. St. Cléry has always verged on instability, but surely this is excessive. He is somewhat appeased by a slender (and hairless) Singhalese boy who does not leave his side; he sharpens St. Cléry's knives when he is not rubbing St. Cléry's feet. This afternoon St. Cléry left for us a sultana and almond pullao, brinjal pickle, curried lady's fingers, mulligatawny soup, chicken cutlets and a roly-poly pudding.

Harriet and Lafayette sat with me in my tent this evening. She sat in silence, smoking her hookah, a dish of spring water at her side so that she may rinse the mouthpiece each time that she uses it—a safeguard against scorpions devised by Bhiraj.

"Do we think St. Cléry's Singhalese is more for ornament than use?" Lafayette asked, bored with his newspapers (six months old).

"St. Cléry is a trifle rattled of late," I said. "He is in ecstasies over the arrival in camp of the young Prince of Orange."

"I thought St. Cléry fancied me," said Lafayette.

"It is you, Ellie, who have a weakness for handsome young princes, not St. Cléry," said Harriet, taking her pipe from her mouth to speak and putting it back again.

"I do not have high hopes of M. le Prince, despite my alleged weakness," I said. "He is affianced to that same Duchess Olga we knew in Petersburg." My deer made three little circles and lay at my feet.

"Is she not also his aunt?" asked Harriet.

"Ah," said Lafayette. "An aunt who does not scruple to wed a relation."

"Is this a proposal of marriage, cousin?" asked Harriet.

"The nephew happens to be her husband's heir. Would that I had something to give you, my Harriet."

"Fortunate prince," said Harriet. "But then, princes often are."

"She does take the precaution," I said, in defense of the Duchess, "of sending him to India to make him a man." I stole a look at Lafayette. He'd finished half a bottle of port and was gesturing to Abdullah to pour him another glass. His hands shake and I fear that an attack of fever may be upon him.

"That is the thing about India," he said. "No heiresses. None one could marry, that is."

"Mrs. Calvert woke this morning to discover a man on his hands and knees creeping through her tent," said Harriet. "I do hope it wasn't the prince. She called out, awakening Mr. Calvert, and the man ran away."

"I hope it wasn't Lafayette," I said.

"Mrs. Calvert is having great difficulty in managing her people," he said. "Yet another ayah has been packed off to Calcutta. This one was caught selling balls of cotton Mrs. Calvert had used to clean her ears. The mahouts use the wax to rouse their elephants to fight."

"Hardly a reason for dismissal," said Harriet.

"Mrs. Calvert feels that our innate goodness is not sufficiently appreciated by our servants. They really do prefer—even relish—a cuff or a kick to an angry word, she says, but in this instance she was quite sure that the ayah deserved exile." He put his hand over his eyes.

"As long as one can believe in the virtue of one's servants, they do not frighten. Mrs. Calvert finds her servants less threatening if she can believe in their vice," said Harriet.

"Does not Mr. Calvert strike you as a muffin-fight-in-chapel kind of person?" Lafayette asked.

He made me smile (he made Harriet laugh). I have feared of late that my cousin's love of vice had robbed him of his humour—which is curious, as vice tends to do the opposite in our family.

"Sometimes," he said, "Calvert can be persuaded, if the company is small and the wine ample, to do a tarantella on the table, complete with flounced skirt."

"I've not seen it. Poor luck for me," I said.

"He does not perform for women."

"Rather like the European ladies who will not dance before Indians."

"We are none the worse for that."

"No," said Harriet.

I looked at the clock, waiting as I always do for the muezzin's call to prayer. I have grown used to it—more than that, I long for it. Henry has seen that a special tent is erected at each campsite as a makeshift mosque. I sat back in my chair as the imam's prayer floated over the camp.

"So much nicer than church bells," said Lafayette, reaching to run his hand along the deer's spine.

"Is it not disconcerting," Harriet asked, "to think that a handful of somewhat well-intentioned Christians should be worshiping God in this desert which is not their home and that thousands of infidels who understandably detest our faith should be standing around patiently under our command?"

"Our whimsical command," my cousin said, attempting to remove himself from his chair. Abdullah reached to help him, but Lafayette waved him away and fell back into the chair.

"Shall I read awhile, cousin?" I asked. I do not like to see him in that state.

"Do," he said. "Verse. Anything but Tennyson."

As I rose to fetch a book, Harriet put aside her pipe and went to him. She offered her hand and he took it. She helped him from his chair and, still holding his hand, escorted him from the tent. Abdullah, bearing his master's gloves and hat, followed in their wake.

Harriet returned a few minutes later and resumed her place by the firestones. Bhiraj brought fresh charcoal for her chillum. "He cannot find his tent when he is in that way of condition," she said, "and he is too proud to ask his servants."

I'm feeling particularly Indian low and tired, perhaps because I've been reading Blake again. There was a durbar this evening for the neighbourhood raja, and I remained in Henry's tent, awaiting his return. Unfortunately, he brought Calvert, Mr. MacGregor, Lafayette and Gen. Stewart with him.

"The Persians advance to Herat with the intention of taking Kandahar!" Henry said excitedly, as he came into the tent. He poured himself and Lafayette a glass of champagne. The khansamas poured glasses for the other men. "Afghanistan, through one of those sly tricks of geography, lies too close to Persia and Russia for its own good. If we do not take Afghanistan, Russia will help herself to it."

"And then our very own India will be next in line," said Gen. Stewart, working himself into a fit.

Mr. MacGregor coughed loudly. He turned his back, but not before I saw him purse his lips in disapproval. This was not talk for women. Or Indians. He gestured to the others to wait until the servants had left.

"I saw a most beautiful bunch of grapes today," I said, to hide my vexation. Henry glanced quickly at the other men, embarrassed. "A most beautiful bunch of twenty-seven emerald grapes on a green enamel stalk. A jeweler brought them to me." (I must remind myself from time to time that as a young man Henry was called the Comical Dog, although I don't see much comical dogness of late—even his puns are few and far between; the last I recall was, "I'd Ranjit Singh for my supper.") "Not for me, Henry, but to give to Ranjit Singh as a present."

Henry again looked round at the men, this time relieved.

"Ranjit Singh only recently demanded His Lordship send

him guns," said Mr. MacGregor with a sad smile. He has the curved Persian beak of a hawk, and like a hawk he does not care to be regarded.

"But Henry sent him a dentist instead," I said.

"His Lordship has always been preoccupied with teeth," said Lafayette.

I looked at him. His tone was light, but I could not tell if he were teasing.

"Raja Ranjit Singh has two impeccable qualities," said Henry. "His obstinate refusal to quarrel with the English and a willingness to incorporate Mohammedans into his army. He deserves a present for that alone. There is no one so clever."

"Perhaps the emerald grapes should go to Shah Shuja. He lives, poor chap, in sad seclusion at Ludhiana with six hundred wives," said Mr. Calvert.

"No," said Henry. "We are giving him Afghanistan."

As I listened to them, I suddenly thought that Henry's way with me—and Papa's and Mr. MacGregor's and even Lord Melbourne's—is not dissimilar to my way with the people. Wary, indulgent, amused, protective, terrified.

Mr. Calvert pulled me aside. "Did you hear?" he asked in a low voice. "The Raja of Jambar outsmarted us today by going before His Lordship without his shoes."

"Yes," said Lafayette loudly. "We'd taken every precaution to safeguard just such an affront, but the Raja was wearing unusually long pantaloons that concealed his feet." At last I caught his eye and he smiled. He was making trouble. My cousin, who came out to India one of the prettiest, wildest boys I'd ever seen, is become a handsome man (Oliphants as a race are ugly) with great moustaches and fine teeth shining through them and that sort of sportive sourness that belongs to seven-and-twenty when it is unhappy.

"You don't quite understand, Capt. Oliphant," said Mr. MacGregor, with a sigh.

"Yes," said Calvert. "It is just as if I were to sit before Her Majesty the Queen with my hat on my head."

"Good God!" said Gen. Stewart.

I noticed that Henry said nothing. He didn't seem to be listening.

"Are you suggesting, sir, that the gentleman insulted His Lordship on purpose?" asked Lafayette, holding out his glass for more champagne.

"It was quite apparent," said Calvert, "that the Raja didn't know what he was doing, poor ignorant creature. It is sad to think him ignorant, but then they all are."

"I discovered yesterday," I said, seizing my chance, "that the jemadars have been forcing the villagers to sell food to us at very low prices—that is, when we do not steal the food outright."

"Stealing food?" Henry asked sternly, looking up from one of his red leather despatch boxes.

"We will make an inquiry, Lady Eleanor," said Mr. MacGregor, with a little bow. He did not seem insincere, and as there was nothing more I cared to say, I left them to men's business. As I departed the tent, I heard my cousin say, "So, gentlemen, we rid ourselves of Dost Mohammed in Kabul in the interest of protecting our four million pounds of profit per annum and put the wise and well-beloved Shah Shuja in his place?" His voice was brittle with sarcasm.

Radha and Zahid were waiting in my tent. Zahid set up the chessboard—I am ahead three games to two—and Radha made tea on the spirit lamp. Burton recommends chess as a cure for melancholy. *Fit for idle gentlewomen, soldiers, and courtiers that have naught but love-matters to busy them.*

In Camp, 5 February 1838

Despite the cold, we set off by starlight this morning; I saw a star fall into a clump of trees. Sometimes, in the dark, a sudden inexplicable happiness seizes us, and the horses (Henry alone has sixty mounts) and then the baggage animals are teased into a semblance of a canter and there is such a tumult of blows and screams and rattling boxes and chests that it sounds like a hurricane. We do not get very far, wheeling like a flock of confused starlings, but it is thrilling.

Camp near Allahabad, 20 February 1838

We sit before our tents tonight; the band will play from eight to ten. Harriet has her hookah and Henry reads his back issues of *Blackwoods;* nobody takes the slightest notice of anyone else. I have been thinking, and not simply out of greed, that we Europeans have misunderstood the meaning of nuzza. We see it as a straightforward commercial exchange that entitles us to certain privileges and goods and we do not hesitate to use these privileges to obtain wealth and power, but it does not mean the same thing to the Indian. For them, a nuzza—whether it is a gift to us of a sword or a horse or a monopoly on jute—is a ritual, not a system of trade. Dresses of Honour are kept for generations, passed from father to son and brought out for display on special occasions; they aren't for ordinary wear and they are certainly not sent to the auction rooms. We take the nuzza for a bribe, which then entitles us to whatever we want—their country, for example.

In his restlessness, Lafayette organized a game of night polo. The balls are coated in sulfur from the sea, which makes them luminous. I can just make out the soothing sound of pounding hooves and the English officers shouting, "Shabash! Shabash!" As the nights are cold, we will not sit out long. The people wrap themselves from head to toe in their blankets, and so do we.

In Camp, 25 February 1838

Our camp stretches for miles across a plain wholly without interest or charm. It is a desolate place; yellow clouds shut out the sky. Although I can see a long way, I cannot distinguish anything at all: a great dun land. Now and then the sun shines long enough to catch the side of a blade or a tin pot or one of the officers' shaving mirrors and through the smoke of a thousand fires there are startling flashes of light. It is the only moment of beauty.

Last night, Harriet was obliged to dance with the young Prince of Orange; he was very excited and leapt all over the place in the German style, plunging horribly. She was wet through with perspiration, her face bright red, when he at last relinquished her to Lafayette, who had been trying for an hour to retrieve her. The prince, who does not scruple to question me day and night ("Are you sure, Madam, given the state of these monstrous roads, my carriage will not overturn?"), sat beside me. Mrs. Hutchinson, wearing a white velvet bonnet, sang "Fields of Hyacinth and Tulips," and the prince burst into tears. To be fair, the travelling has been difficult. We change horses every few miles, the sand halfway to the doors of the carriages.

Harriet's friend Lord Morlington is spending a few weeks in camp on his way to Lucknow. He is a handsome Englishman—young, big, strong, without a hair on his head, which misfortune pains him; even his long black beard does not compensate. He takes a tone with Harriet of bantering affection. She treats him as one of her menagerie—although she scratches his ears, I don't believe he sleeps in her bed. We went this morning to look at temples with him. He hasn't the usual English prejudice against a veer from the classical; he does not recoil before a Hindu temple, although he admits to preferring a mosque-in-the-moonlight kind of place. (I have seen Mrs. MacGregor wince before a frieze of posturing apsaras as if their degradation would compromise her: "It is certainly not the Parthenon!")

An unusually large assemblage of people belonging to the King of Oudh accompanied us. Because we travel through his country, the King has taken upon himself responsibility for our comfort. He graciously sends attendants with enormous gilded breakfasts and enormous silvered lunches and enormous gilded and silvered dinners. As St. Cléry, in competition with the King's kitchens, furiously refuses to alter his own menus, I have never seen so much food; what is left of the King's food is sent to the villages, even if Mrs. MacGregor says it will upset their stomachs. Harriet chose a dusty spot beneath a crumbling arch and our men spread our rugs and pitched our tables and chairs and easels and the King of Oudh's men set out our picnic. Morlington spent an hour turning over every brick and stone he could find.

"Did you find what you were looking for, my Lord?" I asked.

"No, I'm happy to say."

"What a pity."

"Not at all. I was looking for scorpions." He picked up one of Harriet's sketchbooks and glanced through it, pausing for some time at the drawings of her servants' feet. "Give me one good reason why a Mohammedan should give up one god for three of ours! for a hundred Hindu gods!" he said, looking fiercely from Harriet to me and back again. With his long arms and legs, he lowered himself to the tartan not unlike a camel would do. "I understand perfectly. Like them, I find the essential mysteries of Christianity utterly disgusting. Really, in the end, isn't it always a question of taste?"

One of the King of Oudh's kitmutgars held out to me a tray of fritters pasted with sugared rose petals. I shook my head; I was still too full from breakfast. He offered them to Morlington, who, his beard separated in two and each half tucked behind an ear, had room for a rose.

Cawnpore, 24 March 1838

This morning Harriet sent Bhiraj to me with a note to ask if I would take her place at breakfast next to Lord Morlington, adding mysteriously that she wished to ascertain if it were she who were lunatic. Bhiraj smiled mysteriously as I read the note. Of course, my curiosity knew no bounds.

Morlington did not seem pleased when I sat myself next to him; he has a marked fondness for my sister. He leaves us next week to return to Europe with an important discovery he has made. I asked him about his find with real interest.

"I have proof at last—the proof I've been searching for."

"What proof is that, my Lord?"

"Proof that the North Pole lies but thirty miles from here, near Gwalior."

"I would be much interested to see it," I heard myself say.

"I will be more than happy to show it to you. I have found Magnetic Stones that have the exact representation of Solomon's Temple upon them."

I glanced across the table at Henry and the others, but they seemed quite convinced. Besides, they were talking about horses in that tone of voice I know so well, how such a horse would have suited them only it would not and how they would have bought it only they did not. Harriet, at the end of the table, looked down at her hands.

"When my discovery reaches Europe, which it will, there will be an end to all their science. They will have to begin again."

I was relieved when Zahid placed my watercress before me. I did not know what to say. I knew the man was eccentric, eccentricity being considered, at least by my father's generation, a mark of refinement, a privilege not yet afforded the middle class, and Harriet had told me that His Lordship refuses to ride a train, having once been locked into his compartment in the first days of the cars by guards fearful of panic among the passengers, but this was altogether different. I caught Harriet's eye and she nodded. Poor Morlington has lost his mind. It has been jungled out of him.

Tonight he sent me a piece of the North Pole in a box and a cactus flower in a blue glass. Henry encourages him to leave for England sooner than he'd intended. "Really, the Indian climate has much to answer for," Henry said, rather unsympathetically. Harriet does not seem sorry to see him go.

Powrah, 11 May 1838

The horror here is inconceivable. We have come into the starving districts. There has been no rain for a year. The sun sears the land from first light. The ground is cracked and split; the stone and rock have crumbled into sand. The livestock are dead. The people chew leather, roots, weeds. They club the dying dogs and devour the rotting flesh of hyenas. The bark on the leafless trees is eaten to the height of ten feet—as high as a person can reach standing upon a man's shoulders. There are corpses everywhere. Vultures and crows tear the flesh from the dying. Harriet fires at them, driving them off for a moment, but even the carrion are starving. The living no longer resemble human beings. The women look as if they have been buried. Their skulls terrify me. I cannot write tonight.

Powrah, 18 May 1838

Three hundred people came today—many of them sicken at the first food they take. We began giving food away two days ago. We are near a large village and the suffering is greater. Yesterday there were seven hundred people. There was fighting over the food. (In a moment of frustration, I did say to Harriet, "Surely this is not our fault.") I remained until two in the morning, but Henry and Harriet were with them all night.

Harriet came to my tent near morning. Her eyes were swollen from the dust, her fingers blistered, the trim torn from her gown so that her stays jutted from her sides like broken ribs. She'd been caught in a crowd at the edge of camp who were picking through the dung of our horses for any undigested grain and there was a panic at the sight of her—they feared she would chase them away. Harriet would never chase them away, but how were they to know? She possesses that rare thing, a tenderness utterly untroubled by condescension. (It makes her a little terrifying.)

I wished to send Zahid for tea, but my sister wanted nothing, certainly not food, only to sit with me. The sun had burned the skin from her shoulders through her gown the first day and I could see that it still gave her pain. She pulled off her ruined bonnet, dropping it to the carpet, and sat on a hassock, her skirt hiked to her knees—she wore hunting boots under her gown. "I used not to have a point of view about things," she said. "Not that a point of view implies sympathy." Rolla, smelling her through the walls of the tent, slid beneath the canvas to take the chair next to her.

"It is more often the reverse," I said.

"We're told that the happiness of subject peoples is more important than their freedom, but these people have neither happiness nor freedom. Mr. Bentham's theory assumes that given the opportunity to pursue happiness, we will all pursue the same happiness." One of her plaits had come loose and strands of golden hair glimmered in the candlelight. As I watched her, I realized that my weariness has made me delicate—I felt as if I would cry. I jumped to my feet and walked round the walls of the tent. A slender pink line was just visible beneath the hem of the canvas—I signed to Zahid to put out the lamps. The terrible sun would soon be setting the plain afire. I lifted one of the tent flaps.

To my surprise, Bhiraj's wife, Sunitra, was standing in the passage between the tents, a bundle in her arms. Lafayette was behind her, holding a child by the hand. He looked haggard and dirty, but I reminded myself that we all look that way now. The child appeared to be about six years old. Her head had been shaved, but she was finely dressed in silk leggings and tunic, with bangles around her wrists and ankles. She did not appear to be starved. Lafayette urged the ayah forward and they stepped inside the tent.

Sunitra went straight to Harriet, dropped the bundle in her lap and left the tent. Harriet calmly pulled back the swaddling to take a look. Inside was a miserable elf; it looked like an old monkey with green eyes. The creature was clearly of mixed race. Sunitra returned in a moment with Radha and a small jug of milk. As Sunitra went to feed the baby, the little girl snatched the milk from her hand to feed the baby herself, spilling the precious milk on the carpet. Harriet sat with her legs apart, the baby in the hammock of her skirt, letting the girl do her work, neither helping nor hindering.

Lafayette removed his gloves and poured himself a glass of wine, drinking it down. I noticed that his hands were shaking, perhaps from hunger. There is no food for miles around—we've given it all away—and Capt. Hutchinson has had to send for more. The baby sucked the end of a piece of muslin that the girl dipped into the milk.

Harriet turned to Lafayette. "Who are they?" She spoke in a low voice, as if she feared offending the children by her question. "They are not village children."

"Their mother is dead," he said. "I've brought them to you because there is no one else."

Sunitra lifted the funny-looking baby from Harriet's lap. Rolla watched venomously from his chair, his eyes red in the candlelight. The child did not yet possess the beauty of the half-caste. I looked at Harriet. Something in my face—not sentiment, certainly not a susceptibility to babies—told her that we were in accord. I felt none of those womanly emotions, only that here was a gift; a thing that we could do without too much trouble to ourselves (the thousand servants).

There was the sound of drumming in the lane outside, and singing. The music flared for a moment and then faded away, as did the melodious voices. The baby began to cry and then the girl began to cry, with tiredness more than fear, and at a sign from me, Sunitra, already cooing, took the children from the tent.

"It is the men returning with Capt. Jackson's monkey," Harriet said. She took her bonnet from the floor.

"That is a relief. I was afraid they would keep it."

"I was afraid they would eat it," she said.

A deputation of village men had come two days ago to request of Capt. Jackson permission to carry his black monkey with the white face to their temple. The monkey was a new species of idol to them and had gone off in state with his own bearers to carry him. The captain did not like it, but he could hardly refuse.

"It has turned his head, I'm sure," I said.

"The Captain's head?"

"No."

We fell silent again. Lafayette, lower than I have ever known him, took his gloves from the table where he'd dropped them. His eyes were heavy with fatigue.

"What have you done with the Dutch Prince?" I asked.

"I left him at the hunting camp," he said. He passed his hand through his hair.

"Are you altogether well, cousin?"

"It is only the young Prince. He wearies me exceedingly. I suspect he is terrified, but nonetheless it tires. All the beaters and sirkars remain with him, but he will think himself abandoned. One would imagine I'd left him with cannibals." He allowed himself a smile.

"I was that way once," Harriet said.

"Do you reckon," I asked, "if two thousand years hence when nobody can make out the meaning of the old English word 'oak tree,' some black Governor-General of England and his black sisters will be marching through Dorset to look at the ruins, doubting whether Salisbury ever was a large town, and will find some skeletons and say what distress they must have been in, and the Governor-General's sisters, longing to go home, will make a passing good sketch of the abandoned farms?"

"I don't long to go home," Harriet said.

Radha came to tell us that Capt. Jackson's monkey returns extremely agitated and more snappish than ever. Lafayette seized the moment to bid us good-night.

In Camp, 20 June 1838

It is unbearably hot, the wind very high. The sand fills our mouths and eyes. I have been too low to write. (What does a traveller write, what one knows or what one doesn't know? What I don't know is endless. Sterne would have us do what all travellers do: feel superior to other travellers.)

We have been here for weeks, longer than we'd planned to stay. We work in an agony of restraint. It takes all my will to keep from sitting in the road and crying. Four hundred thousand dead of starvation. It isn't our superior knowledge that we dispense now (*Aesop's Fables* rotting in Bombay), but our food. We feed everyone and give them blankets, six hundred people a day. Even Crick and Webb pass out bread and pots of curds. Four times Henry has sent couriers for help. He's given money of our own and convinces the Board of Control in Calcutta to release more supplies, but it is near impossible to bring the necessary food and medicine over these roads. He has already raised forty lakhs for relief—he is unfaltering, never reluctant or hesitant—and has ordered a Government Inquiry to discover how to prevent this ever happening again. I am filled with admiration for him.

Despite their ceaseless suffering, the people demonstrate their usual gentle courtesy. I am ashamed to admit that I think of them without condescension for the first time. The last month has been the most sorrowful of my life.

Umreetpore, 2 July 1838

We broke camp ten days ago, stopping to give food to the people, taking seven hours to cover one mile. They are not as stricken here, thank God. As we proceeded into the town, the horses went mad. It is because they, like us, are so very dispirited. Webb stopped the carriage and I jumped down in my dusty bonnet, a long black cloak worn over my dressing gown, with Squirrel on my shoulder, followed by the untiring Zahid, Harriet's pariah dog frisking and whining, and the khansamas with bedsheets twisted around their turbans and under their chins—the excitable Bengalis have a dread of demons establishing residence in their heads by way of their ears—to walk through the crowds of people waiting for us. Radha led my deer and Harriet's Gazelle by a long rope lest the animal kick her. Behind us came the carriages with all the horses rearing and screaming, the syces clinging to them, and Rosina and Jones leaning from the windows in terror. Henry gave away all the food that we had.

(Harriet and I find it difficult to eat, but that won't last.)

In Camp, 2 August 1838

Henry, with the consent of a dubious Mr. MacGregor, has admitted the necessity of sending Lafayette as his private emissary to the Amir Dost Mohammed in Kabul in the hope of preventing him from making an alliance with Russia. Lafayette will carry Henry's portrait set in a diamond star on a string of pearls, gold-mounted pistols and a sword in a golden scabbard as presents for Dost Mohammed. I think it a wise course and I am relieved that Henry at last deigns to consider Lafayette's advice—it will do my cousin good to be in the field. He has been very low in spirits.

Our own little girls flourish. They are trundled dutifully into my tent once a day to be dandled on my lady knees. I grow fond of them, and Harriet—who preaches a life of blessed singleness, or is it single blessedness?—is devoted to them. Radha fitted a little pannier to the deer and the baby is trotted from my tent to Harriet's tent and back again. Brown babies are so much prettier than white babies. Harriet named the older girl Tara. The baby is named Vimala. Rosina was wont to call her chee-chee, which means half-caste. The word also means filth. I forbade the word and now she calls the child by her right name, albeit with a hint of derision—directed at me, not the baby. I am teaching Tara to draw. She comes on very well. Like an English child would do, she makes a round sun, a tree and a square box of a house (although its roof is flat). I fear that she is fonder of Frolic than she is of me.

Moradabad, 8 September 1838

I never thought that I would see mountains again. So lovely! A hard dark blue on the horizon and a line of black peaks. There is even a smell of mountains. Looking at them makes me feel less sad.

Lafayette's mission to Kabul does not go well—perhaps because Henry does not offer Dost Muhammad anything worth having (not the pearls or the pistols). Lafayette writes that the Afghans are the most treacherous, clever, cynical and ferocious men he has ever met.

I am reading Lady Mary Wortley Montagu's letters written from Turkey. Her correspondence with Pope is most friendly, given the cruelty with which he depicted her in *Imitations of Horace*. My mother told me that their quarrel was due to a pair of bedsheets borrowed by Lady Mary of Mrs. Pope, his mother, and returned a fortnight later unwashed.

In Camp, 24 September 1838

Lafayette arrived last night from Kabul, looking like a long-wandering knight, his gray cloak the colour of armour thrown over his uniform, attended only by his squire Abdullah and two barefoot grooms with torches. He dismounted in a swirl of manly importance and went straight to Henry's tent, Mr. MacGregor and the secretaries scrambling behind like eager innkeepers. They did not emerge until morning, with the result that Mr. MacGregor and thirty aides depart tomorrow to call on Raja Ranjit Singh in Lahore in the hope of persuading him to make war on the Afghan Amir Dost Mohammed! Lafayette failed to convince Henry of the good sense of Dost Mohammed's demands. Henry scorns Dost Mohammed. He is resolved to put the pretender Shah Shuja on the throne—Shah Shuja with his ragtail troupe of emaciated mendicants and idle knife-sharpeners. *And sixty-four thousand Genii guard the Eastern Gate.* Henry has it in his head that Shah Shuja has a legitimate right to the Afghan throne—in truth, Dost Mohammed is too independent for them. He will not do as they wish. (Lafayette says that Shah Shuja is an insipid despot, not unlike a medieval Scottish baron, his questionable influence extending to one small mud fort and two wretched villages with a handful of terrified peasants. He is said to delight in lascivious torture.)

Henry has drafted a declaration called the Simla Manifesto which sets out the justifications for overthrowing Dost Mohammed in Kabul. He says that the Afghans have lost the right to govern through their own weakness and folly; the only question now is whether incompetence is inherent in their character or whether we can scour enough of it out of them so that we can all go home and leave them to ruin their country themselves. We will put Shah

Shuja on the throne, a vicious tyrant who has three times been thrown out by his own people.

In Camp, 10 October 1838

Henry is almost happy with unhappiness. The Board of Control in Calcutta was appalled by his Simla Manifesto. He's chosen to ignore their astonished letters, sitting of an evening before his tent to listen to a group of army musicians play martial airs atop an elephant, set back-to-back like travellers in a jaunting car.

Dost Mohammed has sent an ambassador to Henry to ask for a little encouragement and power: *The conduct of reckless and misguided Sikhs, and their breach of treaty, are well-known to your Lordship. Communicate to me whatever may suggest itself to your wisdom for the settlement of the affairs of Afghanistan, that it may serve as a rule for my guidance.* Once a drunkard and rapist, he studies the Koran devoutly and redresses all his earlier cruelties—if injured, however, he makes his enemy bite the finger of repentance.

Henry consults neither Palmerston in London nor the Board of Control in Calcutta and disregards Lafayette's counsel, making all decisions with Mr. MacGregor alone, who writes from the Punjab that although he is received with much honour, Ranjit Singh limits his conversation to the Ten Commandments, salt, women and shrapnel. (Interesting, I'd have thought.) Shah Shuja reads edifying poetry; between poems he commands the odd torture. In between maiming and reading, he writes his memoirs. I know this because I read Henry's correspondence in secret. (Lafayette, frustrated by Henry, eschews an interest in statecraft. He spends his time shooting birds. When there are no birds, Abdullah puts a pea on the point of a spear and Lafayette shoots at it from a considerable distance, hitting it every time. When he is in camp, he is too distracted to stop awhile; he is always on his way somewhere. Harriet says that most nights he attends a nautch that Maj. Quinn arranges for a few chosen gentlemen.)

Near Meerat, 2 November 1838

Eleven thousand of us (we have picked up another thousand souls along the way) crossed the Ganges four days ago on a bridge of boats, screaming and yelling as the soldiers whipped the servants and the servants whipped the animals. The elephants were made to go first; many men were lost in the night trying to cross. A hundred camels were carried away, but found again. Once on the other side, Dr. Drummond prepared my tincture of laudanum and I was able to sleep awhile (oh, for my black balls of opium). There are funeral pyres in camp tonight for the few men whose bodies were found along the river.

We continue by land. The roads are so bad that we cannot sit our horses. Pitted with deep sand holes, the track is cut into ditches by the hackeries that go before us. The bullocks bear it well, but it has broken the hearts of the horses. Frolic has been ill and I bled him twice.

Meerat, 27 November 1838

Meerat, a large station with a quantity of white bungalows and barracks, is spread over four miles of muddy plain; there is not a tree or blade of grass in sight. Our two little girls are sick with fever. In a fortnight we will be in Delhi, which place is surely more salubrious. It is difficult to sleep, as jackals scream around the bungalow and the sentries fire at them all night, making the children cry. There was a dance tonight, but I begged fatigue.

Lafayette came this morning to tell me that our troops, grandly called the Army of the Indus (shades of Bonaparte?), composed of our Bengal and Bombay armies, one troop of Ranjit Singh's Sikhs and Shah Shuja's jugglers and minstrels, have mustered at Ferozepore. Henry will invade Afghanistan and depose the Afghan Amir, Dost Mohammed.

I dream of the women's skulls.

Near the Sutlej, 13 December 1838

We are camped on an endless plain east of the Sutlej River; the Raja Ranjit Singh sets up his tents on the west side. It is a wilderness of cactus, prickly scrub, sandy hillocks and the bleached bones of camels. A dilapidated mud-and-brick fort sits on a hill overlooking the river. The town is a wandering collection of wooden hovels, a few dingy shops, and alleyways crammed with maimed dogs, human waste and widows.

Henry met this afternoon with a delegation of Ranjit Singh's chieftains. The beautiful Sikhs sat on the ground while Henry listened to their compliments with a grave look as he waited for Mr. MacGregor to translate for them and then to translate back his own flatteries; it took half an hour to determine that Ranjit Singh was in good health, and to ascertain that indeed roses had bloomed in the garden of friendship and nightingales in bowers of affection sang sweeter than ever, now that the two great empires have at last joined hands. Uzeez ud-Din, Ranjit Singh's chief adviser, led the delegation. He was dressed as a fakir ought to be dressed in coarse brown cloth, but I could see an exquisite gold tunic thickly embroidered with emeralds and pearls when his robes parted. Despite the gold dress, he did not look over-clean. I know all this thanks to my hiding place in the passage.

Gen. Stewart told me that Ranjit Singh is a great man, even if he sometimes comports himself indecently atop an elephant.

Near the Sutlej, 20 December 1838

At last I have seen Ranjit Singh, the One-Eyed Lion of the Punjab! We went to him suitably accompanied by the 16th Hussars, a body of Indian cavalry, the 13th Foot, two regiments of native light cavalry, the 2nd Royals, a company of Highlanders playing their pipes, the Queen's Buffs, a long train of artillery drawn by camels, Col. Skinner's wild horsemen wearing steel caps and orange dresses, and a phalanx of elephants dressed for battle.

Henry arrived on his elephant, swarmed by a great crowd of handsome Sikhs and less handsome British officers, all pushing and shoving. (Ranjit Singh's troops are better dressed than ours, with very good horses, and nobody knows what to say about it, so they simply say that the Sikhs are sure to run away in a real fight.) The procession of their chieftains was four miles long. They wore collars of rubies and emeralds with lengths of silver tissue draped over their heads. Ranjit Singh's bodyguard was dressed in yellow satin with gold kincob shawls, their shields and lances studded with gold. As we neared the end of the review, one of the horses lunged at Harriet's mare. Bhiraj spurred his pony between them, showing a degree of self-possession for which I can never sufficiently respect him. He suffered a sprained wrist, but he saved Harriet.

We were taken into a large canvas tent enclosed on three sides. I was placed next to Ranjit Singh; on my right was Kurruck Singh, his son and heir. The moment Ranjit Singh sat down, four jeweled attendants, each with only one eye, came and knelt before him. Uzeez ud-Din placed a bottle of spirits and glasses at Ranjit Singh's side.

Ranjit Singh looks like an old mouse with gray whiskers and one eye—small, wizened, ugly, pockmarked. He wore a simple red cotton dress with an edging of the commonest gray squirrel's fur and a red cotton turban. He can neither read nor write. He possesses eighteen wives. He is mad for guns, horses, boys, women and drink. He physics himself with powdered pearls, corn brandy, opium, musk and meat juice. Although he has been known to step down from his chair to wipe the dust from the feet of a Mohammedan beggar, he is utterly indifferent to the well-being of his people. He has created no law courts, no hospitals, no schools, no prisons; made no roads, bridges or canals. His vaults are stuffed with treasure, but he will not pay his soldiers. Although he murdered his mother, those who cross him are not killed, merely relieved of their noses and ears. He is excessively beloved by his people.

He sat with one leg curled beneath him, his left foot in his right hand, one dusty shoe placed beneath his gilded chair. He insisted that I taste his drink; even without Mr. MacGregor's winks and nods, I knew that I must do it. I could not swallow it for it burned my lips. So he would not be offended, I turned aside to let it run out the side of my mouth, ruining my gown—fortunately, I was on his blind side.

I tried hard to converse with his son Kurruck Singh, but he appeared to be an idiot —he made bewildering hand signals which Uzeez ud-Din then turned into long, incomprehensible speeches. Behind me, Ranjit Singh's handsome favourite, Heera Singh, who has some English, whispered to me his own translation of Kurruck Singh's questions ("Do you eat pig? dogs? Will you eat that little black dog soon?"). Lafayette told me later that Kurruck Singh affects to be insane so that his father will not be jealous of him. Oh, that I could know what they are thinking, without the veil of politeness and Mr. MacGregor's false words and our strangeness!

Our audience at last came to a close when it was apparent that Ranjit Singh was too drunk to remain in his chair. Uzeez ud-Din waved his arm and a man dressed in a finely pleated pink dress trotted into the tent with a saddle on his back. He knelt before Ranjit Singh's chair and His Highness was lifted onto the man's back and his feet fitted in the stirrups. The man crawled out of the tent on his hands and knees, Ranjit Singh hanging from his back.

Lahore, 2 January 1839

It has been raining for ten days. We are encamped in the old bed of a river and the trenches dug around our tents overflow with water. It is a quagmire of mud. Everyone is ill. I shake with ague. Zahid must carry me to the dining tent.

Our Christmas was most quiet. I gave to Harriet a lotus-shaped mouthpiece for her hookah in gray jade with diamonds and rubies that I bought from the Toshakhana and to Lafayette a silver dagger hilt from the Deccan. I gave to Henry a pair of seventeenth-century red sandstone brackets of elephants which undoubtedly he will make into bookends. Henry surprised Harriet and me by producing two pairs of French evening boots: mandarin-orange satin for Harriet, yellow for me. Harriet gave me (away from the others) an ivory opium pipe with a woman sitting on a pot de chambre holding a dog. She was most pleased with a shotgun that Lafayette had ordered for her from London.

Henry was too distracted to read *Twelfth Night*. It is the first Christmas that we have not read it.

The Residency, Delhi, 5 January 1839

Delhi is surrounded by a high gated wall of red sandstone. Indian gentlemen of rank attended by trains of followers swarm the dirty streets on horses, elephants and camels, all beautifully dressed (noblemen, followers and animals), but the magnificence is deceptive—for miles around, there is nothing but ruins of mosques and palaces. The Emperor lives in the centre in a ragged palace with crumbling walls. Harriet and I went there with our sketchbooks our first afternoon. (Henry could not attend because of some obscure point of etiquette which I could not, would not bother to understand.) It is a melancholy place. I looked through a splintered ivory lattice the colour of old teeth into an overgrown garden leading down to the Jamuna River and thought of the hundreds of royal women who never walked outside the walls. The marble screens in the women's rooms are pocked with black holes where the jewels have been prised loose—nothing will ever be put in their place. There were charpois in some of the rooms piled with guards, asleep, and a dry marble bath where twenty cheerful servants squatted to chew pan. I made two sketches of them.

In the garden, an old man was reading on a stone bench. A chowry burdar stood behind him, keeping the flies from the pages of his book. Our people fell to the ground when they saw him, their foreheads pressed to the dirt. The old man is their Emperor. They hold him in the greatest reverence. *Found the King in the Parke. There walked. Gallantry great.*

Harriet and I made a deep curtsy, and he lifted his watery eyes to gaze on us. Did he sit in the same arbor as his Mughal ancestor who delighted to watch his ladies slide down the sloping bank into a tank of lotus? With a forlorn grunt, the Emperor went back to his poetry and we tiptoed away, the servants bowing until he was out of view. We English delight in tormenting him, taking away more and more of his privileges; soon he will have to ask permission to recite his ghazals. I find I am no longer very fond of Englishmen (Out of their own country, that is, Lafayette always adds loyally). Delhi is a very suggestive, moralizing place. Such stupendous remains of power and wealth passed and passing away and somehow I feel that we rapacious English have just gone and done it—merchandized it, revenued it and sold it all.

Such beautiful capes of real Russian sable lined with shawl I saw tonight (merchandizing and revenue-ing at its best), brought by the Mughals to tempt me to ruin. I was desirous of them but, as the fur is Russian, I cannot have a cape for reasons of state. Nothing frightens us so much as Russia. I bought instead some quartos of Andalusian Arab verse and two books of devotional poems. Lafayette bought an ivory and gold toothpick case decorated with diamond sprays and a tiny portrait of Warren Hastings. The Mughals beguile us of our rupees.

The Residency, Delhi, 18 January 1839

Of all the things I ever saw, the Qutub Minar is the finest. Did we know about it in England? Why did they not tell us? Did Henry know? Built of red granite, 240 feet high, 50 feet in diameter, it rises in five graduated tiers with galleries, carved with verses from the Koran, each letter a yard high. Standing in a wilderness of ruins, each tomb is more beautiful than the next. It is perfect. We stayed for hours, staring in awe.

The Residency, Delhi, 2 February 1839

Harriet and I went this afternoon to see a large stone step well into which men are so kind as to dive. They fly through the air, joining their hands as if to enter the water with a prayer, the black water closing silently over their heels. Harriet said it gave her the greatest thrill she's ever felt in her life and she paid the men to do it over and over again until I began to fear they would harm themselves. One after the other they threw themselves into the pool, sixty feet down, then ran up the steps and stood dripping on the edge, ready to dive again for Harriet. We stayed until it was too black to see.

Harriet said tonight that she wishes to die at the Qutub.

The Residency, Delhi, 8 February 1839

Harriet came to my tent this evening, the baby Vimala in her arms, accompanied by Bhiraj and Rolla, still sulky even though he has a new crimson frock which particularly suits his black hands (Rolla). She eased herself onto a sofa, careful not to wake the baby, who was wrapped in a shawl.

"I think this Delhi a very unwholesome place," she said. "These sudden hot days after the cold."

I lifted my deer from a chair and sat down. "I dragged Henry out in the rain today to see the European burial ground. We could not discover one soul who lived to be more than thirty-six years old. It will give Lady Morris pleasure, however, to know that her husband's first wife is certainly dead and buried—at least she is buried—under a remarkably shabby stone. I made a drawing of it for her."

"The Europeans here are not very distinguished," Harriet said. "Have you noticed?"

"I must admit that I am not sorry to see the Dutch Prince leave us. In truth, I am filled with relief. Overflowing."

The Prince of Orange, inordinately fond of music, spent much of his visit tormenting my sister. As he travels with his own spinet, she was summoned to perform duets with him, fearfully difficult pieces of Bach and Gluck, while he turned the pages of the music, brushing her cheek with his scant whiskers every time he leaned forward, at the same time whispering "Ma fleur!" violently in her ear. The Prince has a piercing voice, squeaky at the best of times, perhaps because of his youth.

"His Highness confided to me that he admired your 'vital spark,' " I said.

"I have," she said, reaching to pick a flea from the baby's head, "as much vital spark as a maid lighting a tinder box." She has grown as deft as an ape at finding fleas. Bhiraj stepped forward to take the flea from her fingers, and dropped it to the carpet.

"It was burning most brightly at the step well, if I remember." She looked at me.

"The diving boys."

She smiled. "I've been there twice again." She shifted the baby in her arms. "I'm returning it now. Like a lending library. You can have it in the morning." She looked down at the brownish face. "Sometimes a sad and sickening feeling comes over me, sister. Sometimes when I hear the muezzin calling the people to prayer, I'm filled with terror that I am in this strange country with its grinning idols and human sacrifice—and then, just as quickly, I remember what joy I have felt here and I am filled with remorse and shame that I should feel such revulsion."

At which moment came a great shout of Pambu! Pambu! The baby awoke and began to scream. A serpent was moving gracefully across the blue Herat carpet. As it was not a cobra, which they will not kill, Bhiraj cut off its head with his knife. It was a polonga snake, whose bite is fatal. *Now the sneaking serpent walks in mild humility.*

"Well done," Harriet said, and left to return the baby.

The Residency, Delhi, 12 February 1839

A disaster has occurred. Gen. Stewart's sepoy regiments were assembled at the parade ground to receive medals awarded by the Prince of Orange upon his departure. The English officer who was handing out the gilt medallions to the Indian troopers chose to make his speech in dialect. He mistook suwars (Urdu for pigs) for sowars (troopers) and billi (cats) for billa (medallion), shouting to the men, "Here, Pigs, a Cat to wear around your necks!" He has been sent to the North-West Frontier.

The Residency, Delhi, 15 February 1839

Maj. Quinn has written for two thousand bearers to take our goods to Simla.

We must leave Gazelle and the deer here in Delhi with Capt. Crawfurd, as they would not survive in the mountains. When I told Harriet that the Captain claims to love animals, she said, "All Englishmen say that."

I am teaching Tara to speak English. (Jones taught her to say

"I want doesn't get," the favourite sentence of all nurses, but I have convinced the child otherwise.)

Simla, 20 April 1839

We are seven thousand feet above sea level! It really is worth all the trouble. Now I come back to the air, I remember what it is to breathe. It is a cool sort of air, sweet and pleasant to the taste. It goes to my head. *Riding the blue sapphire mountains wearing moonstone for slippers, blowing long horns, O Shiva!*

But if we are elated, the Bengalis are miserable, suffering from the cold and so afraid of the precipices that they will not go to the bazaar to buy food, with the result that they are starving as well as freezing. They creep along, their shoulders to their ears, convinced that their long poles will save them should they stumble into a ravine. They are miserable out of our own hot oven of Calcutta; they cough and sneeze day and night. Yesterday, Harriet came upon a group of them who were looking so unhappy that she sent Maj. Quinn round to all the houses to make a list of those who were settled. She found that sixty-seven people had no place to live. She was very angry. They feel the cold most keenly, and their helplessness, but they never complain. She has arranged to put them under tents for the present; the houses must be ready before the Rains come. I wonder they are all so patient.

There is a fine half hour before sunset when I seize the moment to go for a gallop. It is cool and crisp. A sea of pinkish-white clouds rolls through the hills. There is the melancholy call of doves and barbets and the rush of streams tumbling through the valleys, and the sudden and unexpected trills from the penny pipe whistles of the men.

Our house wants only the furniture and carpets and chandeliers we have carried from Calcutta. The rooms, though small, are very fine. There are fires in every room. We have no need of punkahs; hanging from the ceiling are Oriental lamps fed with oil of geranium and lavender. From the drawing room I see deep valleys of blue and from my bedroom I see the mountains. The malis and I have already planted dahlias of that rhubarb-and-magnesia colour that makes you hear the spoon grit against your teeth. They will be the only double dahlias in India, although nothing could be so lovely as the blue Himalayan poppy. There are small owls in the garden—the rare *Phodilus badius*—which is described in my Indian field guide as "spotted with black and buff above and chestnut-coloured underpants." It gives a whistle of three notes that sounds like a man calling a dog. Frolic nearly lost his mind the first week, but he ignores them now.

I convinced Henry to ride with me this afternoon to the valley of Annandale—the banks of thick white fog and the English cuckoo make him long for England. *Cuckoo, noisy among the shenbaka flowers, honey on your beak, the god who holds a white conch shell is not yet revealed to me.*

"This place has that particular suburban whimsy that I detest!" he said, as we rode through the town. Simla, tacked all hodgepodge onto the side of a hill, fairly bustles with rows of shops with mock-Tudor facades and little painted signs bearing the names of the villas: My Captain's Delight, The Wee Priory, Britannia. The customary means of transport is a wicker tonjon on high fragile wheels harried by four shouting and shoving men, who push it as fast as they can down one hill to get it up the next. "I thought Simla was supposed to be our kind of English," he said.

"Your library will soon be ready," I said. "I've found a painter to make borders round the doors and windows. We will have the image of a cheerful middle-sized house in Wiltshire when I am through with it. You will feel as if you never left England—except, of course, for the festoons of white orchids swinging from the eaves."

"And the borders."

We edged our way past trains of slender mules and slender handsome Pathans, all (mules and men) with long black hair. The ground was bright with ferns, the banks covered with wild iris and bright purple lupine. Threads of cloud floated past; the mountains had let their gowns slip from their shoulders. The syces raced ahead to dig up wild tulips for me. They dash about the hills and the instant they spot a promising-looking plant they pull it up, cutting off the bulb, but it does not signify, as I am very happy.

We paused at a waterfall where a string of boys in yellow and red shawls dropped stones into the pool below. As we watched, one of them slipped and fell into the water. "He looks like a goldfish in a bowl," said Henry.

Simla, 30 April 1839

Lafayette came this afternoon while the little girls were with me. I dress them in white cambric, which particularly suits the green-eyed baby, but Lafayette prefers to see them clothed in the style of their country. I was happy to oblige him, but it was startling when they returned looking like tiny nautch girls in their bangles and bells and red petticoats, their eyes smeared with kohl. It is unsettling to think that these dark-eyed houris will someday be transformed into lady's maids. The older girl, Tara, watched solemnly as Zahid cleaned my brushes. Lafayette took the baby on his lap. I was painting.

"Henry has requested I make a likeness of our Queen as a present for Ranjit Singh," I said. "I am creating Her Majesty from descriptions in old newspapers and letters—robes, crown, and all. Everything but the ugly teeth. It's easier than you might imagine."

Lafayette gave the baby to an ayah and took a pile of my old copies of *Petit Courrier des Dames* in his lap instead. It was a strangely domestic view except for the myriad hues of skin colour. Tara leaned against Lafayette's chair, playing with a lock of hair at the back of his head as she looked over his shoulder at the illustrations of Paris frocks. He seemed more at ease than I have seen him in some time. He has faults enough for ten, but his charm and beauty never fail to win me. I made tiny white satin shoes for the Queen and beckoned to Tara to come to see them, but she would not leave Lafayette.

"The child is much attached to you," I said.

"Yes," he said, unwinding his hair from the child's fingers. He put aside the fashion plates.

"I have had to post Rosina down the hill," I said. "I feared at first that she had plague. She had the parched mouth and rapid pulse, but not that little straining under the skin. Of course, it did not help that a lizard fell on her head the night before her departure."

"From the east wall?"

I nodded. "I could do naught but commiserate on her early death."

"It can kill you with the brush of a woman's sleeve," he said.

I looked at him but his eyes were closed, his head resting on the back of his chair.

Simla, 2 May 1839

We have had a most provoking contretemps, just the kind I've come to dread. I used to rather enjoy things of this nature, but no longer. I was reading the latest chapter of *Nicholas Nickleby* and Harriet was sewing when Mrs. Robinson, a wan and limpish woman in a pink satin bonnet, was announced—she is the wife of one of Mr. Calvert's secretaries. She wasted no time. "I've come to tell you, Lady Oliphant, that the ladies have settled that they will not dance at the Queen's Birthday Ball."

As neither of us is Lady Oliphant, I deferred to Harriet.

"I'm afraid that I don't understand, Mrs. Robinson," she said. She did not put aside her tapestry.

"We know you have invited the Indians, as well as the Un-covenanted Service. I, for one, have no choice but to remove my fancywork from the Charity Booth, now I learn they are to be part of it." The lady had donated a dozen shoe-trees hand-painted with English wildflowers and three dozen tea towels done in crewelwork.

"Surely there is a better word than 'Uncovenanted,' " I said, looking to Harriet, "but what in its place?" Uncovenanted Service really is one of our choicest Indianisms. It accompanies our very worst Indian feelings. We say it the way we say, Poor chimney-sweeps. The Uncovenanted Service is made up of dignified, highly paid, well-educated clerks in the public offices, but as some of them are half-castes, we with our pure Norman or Saxon blood cannot really think contemptuously enough of them—I often hear Mr. Calvert and Mr. MacGregor insisting that they *cannot* allow Mr. P or Mr. Z to sit down in their presence!

The English have a greater tolerance, and sometimes even liking, for an Indian they consider to be their equal than for a pure Anglo-Saxon whom they deem inferior. Although they don't say it, and perhaps do not even think it, it is not simply the race of a person that signifies here, but his social rank. This has led to some embarrassing misconceptions. The fact that a Brahmin is of a higher caste than a raja is most difficult for them ("Aren't Brahmins cooks?"), although the precision and orderliness of the caste system tends to put them at ease. They know it from the military and from the nobility and from their own domestic hierarchies. (My brother-in-law Buckingham regards his tenant farmers with the same disdain that Mrs. MacGregor reserves for her maid-servants.) They prefer Mohammedans to Hindus only because they are heirs to the Mughals, a noble warrior class (and without the hundred gods). We educated Europeans consider ourselves children of the Enlightenment, but it seems to me that the Enlightenment did much to encourage the view that dark-skinned people are by their very nature beneath us.

"It is not the dancing *with* that we ladies mind," Mrs. Robinson said, "it is the dancing *before*. We have no intention of dancing before natives."

Harriet turned to me and said, in a perfectly clear voice, "Elle se flatte." She gestured to the servants and waited until they had left the room; only Bhiraj and Zahid remained. "I assure you, ma'am," she said to Mrs. Robinson, "that the black would not have rubbed off on your fancywork."

"Their women do not dance before our men," said Mrs. Robinson. "They're all locked up!"

One of the disservices of purdah, I've come to see, is that it allows us to be officially discourteous. European women in India live to incite their menfolk, enflaming their ignorant assumptions rather than calming them—putting out the fire altogether would be too much to ask. (Henry told me that the magistrate in Ralipore last week fined a man two hundred rupees when he learned from his wife that the man had not allowed her palankeen to pass him in a lane.)

"Well, my sister and I must make do without your company, Mrs. Robinson," said Harriet. She declined a glass of tea from Bhiraj, perhaps because her hands were shaking.

Mrs. Robinson, somewhat surprised, retied her damp bonnet strings—India takes the stiffness out of ribbons, leaving our bows to droop about the face. The tightness of her knot revealed the depth of her indignation. "This is a most distressing place for a lady," she said.

"I assure you," said Harriet, "that I have never been less distressed in my life." She looked particularly lovely, her hair springing in damp curls at her temples.

Mrs. Robinson rose to her feet, knocking her reticule to the floor. Zahid picked it up and handed it to her. "When you have been here a sufficient time you will see that I am right," she said. She made us an angry little bow and followed Zahid to the door.

"I promise you I am dancing every dance to show what I think of their nonsense," Harriet said, as our visitor went down the walk.

"It was so much easier when we didn't know any Mrs. Robinsons," I said.

"Yes. I try with all my being to assume the complacence that accompanies good health and an assured income, but in my heart it is all contempt."

"Lafayette tells me that it was nicer here before the women came."

"He was nicer."

Simla, 9 May 1839

It was the Queen's Birthday Ball tonight. There were illuminated banners with the words *Lady Eleanor* and *Lady Harriet* picked out in white rosebuds and a large *Afghanistan* and *VR* in jonquils. There were bouquets of lily-of-the-valley for those of the ladies who could bring themselves to attend.

The Sikhs had seen English dancing before and were quite aware that the ladies were ladies and not nautch girls. I did espy two of the chieftains give each other a nudge as Gen. Kenton whisked past with his buxom daughter (the military ladies suffer no qualms about dancing before natives), but I could see that they thought it amusing rather than depraved. Harriet and I made our usual effort, more out of habit now than the pleasures of vanity, but the dresses of the chieftains were far more exquisite than our own. Sleeves are so tight now, we ladies can barely raise our arms to dance, but Harriet kept her promise.

As we walked home, escorted by Zahid, Bhiraj and thirty torchbearers, I said to her, "Twenty years ago, no European had ever been here, and here we are, with the band playing 'Masaniello' and eating salmon from Scotland and sardines from France and observing that St. Cléry's potage à la Julienne is perhaps better than his other soups and that some of the ladies' hats are a trifle piquant and all this in the face of these hills, some of which have remained untrodden since the Creation; and we, one hundred and five Europeans surrounded by at least three thousand mountaineers who, wrapped in their hill blankets, look on at what we call our polite amusements and bow to the ground if a European comes near them. I sometimes wonder they do not cut off our heads and say nothing more about it."

In the light of the torches, I saw her nod her head.

Simla, 23 June 1839

A black rash covers my body. Tonight my dear Radha performed the balaiya lena on me, taking all my evil and pain onto herself; she drew her hands over my head and then cracked her fingers at her forehead. My pain is less blinding. She wishes to summon a native doctor, who will feel her pulse so as not to defile me—no, it is not that at all. It is so that he will not be defiled. And if the pulsing should prove ineffective, he will sniff some of my sweat rubbed onto a handkerchief. I have refused, even though his way is as good as any. I am damped instead with one of her concoctions of gram; it clings to my breasts and thighs as I step from the bath. Mademoiselle insisted that the surface of my bathwater be sprinkled with talcum so that I could not see my own body.

I used not to think about my body; in truth, I took it as it was, not minding it, even liking it from time to time—liking it with Henry—but now I detest it. It revolts me. (Surely there is no pollution that does not possess some logic.) My weak gray thighs, the black coarse hair spreading across my lap, the stinking hole, the stench of my arm pits. It is the smell on my fingers that makes me sick.

Simla, 2 July 1889

The Rains have begun in earnest. I thought that like meat we would keep better here, but I was wrong. The beaten-down earth of our roof is wet through, and streams of mud cascade from the ceiling. There is a particularly abundant flow over my bed, pouring onto me. My legs are fouled with it, and my sheets. The stench is unbearable.

Harriet says it is not the rain but the flux, but I know otherwise.

Simla, 12 July 1839

It appears that I have been ill.

Simla, 26 July 1839

My recovery is slow. Twice a day, Zahid carries me to a chair by the window so that I may see into the garden while Radha and the maidservants change my bedsheets.

The Wolf Catchers are here today. As it is known in the hills that Harriet will buy any specimen of fauna or flora that is brought to her, she is offered everything from house flies to the rarest Himalayan butterfly. Two small and sinewy men and a withered crone (Kali come for me? *I close my eyes and she's there, garlanded with human heads*), dressed in sackcloth and ashes, drag four dead wolves behind them to claim the bounty of seven shillings. Two live wolves are bound tightly by the legs and slung from a sagging pole; their heads are not hooded and their orange eyes roll in terror. Even I can see that the wolves have been sold many times over. I trust that Harriet will not be swayed to buy them. She already has two dead wolves. Now Bhiraj chases the men and the old woman from the garden. I can hear their curses above the roar of the rain.

Simla, 18 August 1839

I have just learned that Ranjit Singh died without warning on the twenty-seventh of June. They kept the news from me 'til now. He was fifty-eight years old. He asked that his jewels, his horses, his palaces, his slaves, and the thirty-seven emerald grapes that Henry at last consented to give him be sent to different temples so that the Brahmins would pray for him. His heir, Kurruck Singh, and the sirdars who sat round his bed burst into tears as the treasure was hauled away and asked, What will become of us if you give everything away? Ranjit Singh wept, too, but said it must be so. Then he ordered the Koh-i-noor diamond sent to the temple of Jagannath, but the sirdars wailed that there was not another such diamond in all the world and he consented to let it remain in his treasure house. The distribution went on through the night, sufficient to endow fifty temples. He was joined on his funeral pyre by his favourite one-eyed horse, four of his one-eyed attendants, four of his wives and eight slave girls chosen for the honour (the women had twenty-four eyes between them). The instant he died, his kingdom fell into confusion. His soldiers murdered their French and English officers and marauded wildly over the country. Perhaps this will furnish one of those pretenses for interference that so delights us. Once we begin, I know what becomes of any country we assist—we swallow it whole.

Later, when I could not sleep, I sent Radha with a note to Dr. Drummond for more laudanum. It eases my mind.

Simla, 1 September 1839

Harriet came to my bedroom this afternoon with a sack of letters, eight from our sister and three from Melbourne for me. As she leaned over to neaten the counterpane, the pale and slender line parting her golden hair shone in the light of the candles. (Sometimes I feel that she has left me far behind: Harriet is the light over Benares; I am a dry riverbed—or do I romanticize both of us?) She held a glass of water for me to drink. I cannot describe the pleasure, the ecstasy of cold water—I had not held naturally cold water in my hands or tasted it for three years.

Mary writes that she sent us seven trunks of gowns and bonnets last February (they must be at the bottom of the sea). *Do not be alarmed when you see the oval shape of the hats. The profile has become unfashionable, so rid yourselves of your old bonnets! Only a sunflower of a face is admired now. The embroidered yellow Limerick gloves I have sent are also most desirable.*

"She would smile did she but know we keep our gloves in lidded jars," Harriet said.

"Did I dream it, Harriet, or did the housekeeper at Bowood always wear black kid gloves?"

"You did not dream it, Ellie."

"Was she in mourning?"

"I think not. The red lisle stockings."

She opened one of my letters with her ivory knife and handed it to me, but the pain in my head is ceaseless and I gestured to her to read it. (It is a pity about profiles. I have read that the aborigines of North America will not allow themselves to be painted in profile as it is only half of them.)

"Melanie Erskine is dead in Madras," Harriet said, after a while. "She drank a glass of milk while suffering from a spider bite."

"That is sad news. I am sorry for her husband."

Radha came in with the tea tray—the worst possible moment, but how was she to know? Harriet put aside the letters to pour. I could not take my eyes from her. She is no longer a pastel primrose of a girl, but queen-of-the night.

"Why is it, sister, you never wed?" I asked.

She handed a cup and saucer to Bhiraj, who handed it to Zahid, who handed it to me.

"There was Willoughby. And His Grace the Duke. And Capt. Pendleton," I said.

"Perhaps I was waiting for this." She gestured shyly towards the mountains. "Can you tell me I was wrong to wait?" She put down her cup and opened another envelope. "Lord Morlington writes from Nice to wish me a Happy Birthday. He is being treated in a maison de santé."

"I forgot your birthday, sister," I said. "Forgive me."

"You were very ill, dearest. You forgot everything."

"Did they give you a ball?"

"Yes." She looked up as Bhiraj prepared her hookah. "Will it bother you if I smoke?"

I shook my head, watching Bhiraj fill the chillum with charcoal. "Indians and ladies?" I asked.

Harriet looked at me.

"At the ball."

"Yes. And the Simla Amateur Players made me a little tableau. Mrs. Korning took the part of Thais, the courtesan who persuaded Alexander to burn Persepolis. She stood there as if she'd done nothing else her whole life."

"She was brought up in France." There were footsteps on the roof—the monkeys arrived for tea. They are so brazen they come through the windows to steal fruit from the tray. Harriet sent Bhiraj to shoot at them with a toy bow and arrow. "And the lovely Mrs. Hutchinson?" I asked. "I believe I dreamed that she ran off with a Sikh chieftain. I was so jealous that I wished her dead and buried."

"She is dead."

I looked at her.

"By her own hand," she said. "I was waiting to tell you."

I was dumb with astonishment.

"She ate a fatal amount of thorn apple. Dr. Drummond was called, but it was too late."

My eyes filled with tears. "How terrible her suffering must have been!"

I am sure that I dreamed of Mrs. Hutchinson and the Sikh chieftain. He wore a crown of wild celery, like Theseus. An enormous squid with seven heads and razor teeth slid from beneath Mrs. Hutchinson's skirt. There were yelping dogs. Mrs. Hutchinson danced "O Ruddier Than the Cherry," lifting her skirt and slapping her thighs—*I am possessed by nymphs! I am possessed by nymphs! We are coming from far away!*—as the chieftain clapped his hands in delight.

"It is more commonly used to stimulate the sexual organs to pleasure," I said.

She looked up from her magazine.

"Thorn apple."

"I didn't know." She did not go back to her reading, but sat there smoking, watching me.

If I did not tell my sweet Harriet the whole of my fever dream, it is because my dreams give me a glimpse of what it is to be mad. The sly madwoman must be very protective of her domain. The slightest intrusion may despoil it. Once a sane person catches even a glimpse of this other world, he cannot help but be beguiled, even if he does not know it—which is, after all, the nature of bewitchment. When my imaginings possessed me, when I was in my fever, I began to feel a deep peace in my own absence. I relinquished all pettiness, all envy, all longing and fear. Nothing could stir me. I was afraid of nothing. The rats careening about the room drove Squirrel to his own lunacy, but they were of no concern to me. I had very little self to trouble me. Renunciation is a most seductive thing. I feel its temptation even now. I understand why women refuse to walk or eat or marry, why they climb into bed and never rise again, retreating into a dream. I understand why they eat thorn apple. But my self has returned with my health—how foolish not to know that my transport was only temporary! I am ashamed to say that I snapped at Radha this morning; I nagged Henry about Afghanistan. "You know, I sometimes miss being dead," I said.

"Yes," said my sister. "I imagine one might." She ripped open a large scarlet and gold envelope. "His Highness Maharawul Bansda asks us to the wedding of two of his dogs next month," she said, making me smile. Perhaps I am not ready for renunciation after all. She opened another letter. It was from Mrs. Beecham in Calcutta. "She writes that the city garden you made near the Esplanade is full to bursting every evening. The natives call it the Lady Baghan, after you."

I was feeling weary. Harriet saw that I was failing and gathered the letters and papers. She gestured to Radha to prepare me for sleep (a little wiping, a little laudanum and a fluffing of my pillows). She kissed me good-night (we did not embrace as girls) and left me.

I awoke in the middle of the night and could not sleep again. I was sad thinking of all the people we have met these last years and how many of them are dead. I made my way across the room to a table by the fire, careful not to awaken Radha, asleep on her mat, where I write this. She had placed a carpet over a screen to keep the draught from me—some mornings the coconut oil in the lamps is as hard as a rock. I will write to Capt. Hutchinson. Sometimes it is frightening to be so far from all that I know. I must ask Radha to find me opium tomorrow.

Simla, 4 September 1839

Outriders have come with the news that the pretender Shah Shuja, with the help of thirty thousand of our soldiers, has taken the town of Ghazni in Afghanistan. Gen. Stewart boasts from his bath chair that the only distress suffered by our troops is a lack of wine and cigars. (The 16th sent back their second pack of hounds for want of suitable coverts.)

The defeated Dost Mohammed flees north to the Hindu Kush with his sons and a few loyal chieftains. More than a thousand Afghans were killed in the battle and sixteen hundred taken prisoner. The English officers were shocked by the brutality with which Shah Shuja's men treated their bound prisoners, amusing themselves by hacking them to death with knives.

Simla, 12 September 1839

Kabul is taken. The victorious English officers and their wives are billeted in a settlement outside the gates of the city as Shah Shuja discovers that he does not like foreigners enough to lodge them within the safety of the palace compound. Mr. MacGregor writes that, despite this insult, all remains couleur de rose.

Although the people of Kabul are said to be restrained in their rejoicing, the news that Dost Mohammed is overthrown and Shah Shuja put in his place is greeted with exultation here. Lafayette does not share in the high spirits, despite Henry's relief at the news. I do not know what to think.

Simla, 14 September 1839

A courier arrived from Afghanistan in the middle of the night. Mr MacGregor was riding near Kabul when a horseman raced down from the hills, jumped from his saddle and seized Mr. MacGregor's stirrup. MacGregor was astonished to recognize the Amir Dost Mohammed, who asked for the protection of the English government. Mr. MacGregor embraced him and promised him a large pension (at the expense of the Indian people). The Amir is taken from Kabul under strong guard to the north of India. Lafayette says that Dost Mohammed may have had the fate of his women and family in mind. It seems that we hold them hostage in the Punjab. Really, the English are ruthless in the land of Tamerlane.

Simla, 28 September 1839

The Rains have ended. The Himalayas have returned after three months of fog. The hills are blue. We are on an island in the sky—isolated, inaccessible, encircled. I hear from miles away the call of the cranes as they make their way south from Mongolia and I know that in a short time it will be winter again. The beauty of the mountains eases my mind.

Simla, 30 October 1839

My dear Radha is ill with fever. Mrs. Jackson and her son died suddenly two days ago, stricken with cholera. I pray Radha does not have it—but then if she did she would be dead by now.

The season is over. A great many Europeans go down the mountain this week.

Simla, 28 November 1839

Lafayette thought to lift my spirits today by showing me the Book of Splendid Hierarchies that he's designed—Henry still holds to the belief that the more we give the Indian princes of form, the less they will think of substance. I tried to admire the two winged dragons flanking something that looked awfully like a pullet brandishing an arrow, designed for the Maharaja Rana of Jhalawar, but I fear I was not very convincing.

Radha, thank God, is recovered. The few scars of pox on her face will fade with time, says Dr. Drummond.

Near Ferozepore, 8 December 1839

We have left the beautiful mountains.

Lahore, 4 January 1840

We have had an agonizing week. Rolla died after two days of illness. He caught cold like the rest of the camp in this swamp of Lahore and died of an inflammation of the stomach so virulent that no medicine was of the slightest use. It was the severest torture to hear his screams. As Harriet could not bear it, I nursed him to the end. He was a clever little person. He held out his black hands which are shaped exactly like ours as he was dying, whimpering like a child. We did everything that could be done.

It was a most solemn Christmas.

Lahore, 1 March 1840

Henry left a book on my table tonight entitled *The Ancients' Guide to the Senses*. It seems that there are Eight Ways to Bite, including one with the lovely name of Pearl Bite. Perhaps for eating rice. (I know very well what a Pearl Bite is.) He has recovered his spirits now Kabul is ours. I wish I could feel so sanguine.

In Camp, 12 April 1840

I dreamed last night of the Raja of Benares. *I made him the most radiant inclination of my entire life, every inch of it full of most voluptuous enjoyment*. We sat in a long gallery printed and gilded in curious and lovely patterns. There were no tables or chairs. The only piece of furniture, what we might call furniture, was a hideous English barrel organ. There was a full-grown tiger, tolerably tame, and a large pot of milk for its dinner. The Raja wished to take me into the zenana, but I pleaded weariness. I knew I would be overcome by jealousy. I could not bear to think of the women awaiting him on their silken cushions. *With cloud-blue skin and garment of yellow silk, he boasted to me he rules the hearts of sixteen thousand shepherdesses*.

Soonair, 2 May 1840

Harriet came in just now to tell me that her maid Jones has eloped with an Irish soldier! Harriet called her several times tonight to undress her, until at last Sunitra crept in to tell her that Jones had stolen out earlier, carrying two bandboxes of Harriet's bonnets. One by one, the ayahs slipped into Harriet's room with tales of Jones's lovemaking. Lafayette always claimed she had a cuisse legère. Harriet had no idea of any of this. Henry said, "Better Soonair than later."

My sister writes that Hester Stanhope is dead in the Lebanon. She, who claimed to be a seeress, lived at the end in indescribable misery; impoverished, mean, mad, completely alone but for her servants, who abused her and robbed her of everything—money, books, souvenirs. Her uncle Pitt was Papa's neighbour. Pitt was so in love with her that if she were in the next room and he heard her voice, he would call out, "My darling niece, what are you saying? I must know!"

In Camp, 6 June 1840

A curious thing has happened. I'd put a little gold ring and a small amount of rupees in a work basket to add to my purse for the hungry. The rupees and the ring were gone when I looked for them this morning. I'd have preferred to let it pass unremarked, but Zahid was with me when I discovered the theft. I understood that he was asserting both his honour and our intimacy when he strode through camp muttering, Best put back the rupees! Best do it now!

but the rupees were not forthcoming. I have allowed, even encouraged, those servants who are indispensable to me, like Radha and Zahid, Salim and Khalid, to exercise an attitude of authority with me that, in truth, I forbid my friends and relatives. Even so, the influence of my servants is an illusion—it is I who hold the power no matter how hard my servants and I pretend otherwise. It is our intimacy in complicity with our estrangement that makes it so confusing. (My mother's footmen were not allowed to look at her, or each other, when in her presence.)

The Guards arrived in force, a captain shouting that the Rice Test must be conducted. A priest was hastily summoned. He gravely measured out so much rice powder according to the amount of the missing rupees and ring. It is considered a sacred rite and the people believe in it. The servants to be tried were assembled. They said their prayers, washed themselves and took a share of the rice. They spit it out in a liquid form, thereby proving their innocence. My chobdar, Ali, a remarkably kind creature who has been at Government House since he was twelve years old, could not bring himself to touch the rice. He is by nature very timid and always trembles if anybody speaks quickly to him. He cleans my tent, and I am very fond of him. He protested his innocence and I quickly stepped forward to declare that I believed him; the Rice Test was over.

This evening all the others came round to say that they were certain it was not Ali after all, although this morning they were ready to hang him from a mango tree. I regret being compelled to let the servants go in Benares for stealing the Raja's carpet. Zahid seemed pleased when the trial was over that he'd done the right thing, and perhaps he had.

Ali was the thief. I am quite sure of it.

In Camp, 16 July 1840

Letters have come with news of the Queen's marriage. The wedding almost did not take place, as the Queen suffered an attack of regret only days before the ceremony. Once Melbourne assured her that even though she would be just a wife, she would still be Queen of England, she recovered. He has sent me half a year's worth of *Oliver Twist*, which he cannot bring himself to read— he finds the story too distressing.

In Camp, 4 August 1840

My dear little flying squirrel that Harriet gave me when he was three days old died yesterday. He never ate anything but two or three teaspoons of tea, but he found a meat pie that the servants had taken away from luncheon and it killed him in two hours. When I was fretful at night, he would hold out his paw for my hand and bite it all over. When I was dressing, he sat on Radha's shoulder and watched with great black eyes as she did my hair—if he were impatient of her efforts he would leap onto my back and arrange it to his liking. I can never witness the death of a loved one again.

In Camp, 4 September 1840

The rain has ceased. I find that I miss it. It was very pleasing to lie on my bed listening to its endless fall. It is collected in large casks and sometimes a jar will crack apart loudly and the water rush out with a long sigh of relief. The days have grown clear and bright; sometimes there is a low white fog around the tents. Lafayette claims to have taken a shovel, thrust it into a bank of vapour and pulled it out laden with mist. I've asked him to bring me some the next time. I sleep with a light shawl and only one punkah.

Kurnaul, 19 October 1840

It is the third time that we have been here. The camp is pitched in precisely the same place: the camp followers cook in their old ashes; Frolic roots up the bones he buried last year; we disturb the same ants' nests. Lafayette says, This is our third Kurnaul season, the way people say, Our third London season. I never meant when I started in life to march three times through Kurnaul.

We sat in front of the tents tonight, playing with the two little girls as we sipped gritty tea, filthy to the eyes, sneezing, groaning. I flag more than I used to do. Sometimes I feel a difficulty in carrying on, but it is only because my body is weak. My mind is not weak. I am thirty-eight years old. I feel utterly detached from the past.

I left Lafayette and Harriet with the children and went to my tent. I sent Radha away, wishing to be alone. I took some opium, but when I tried to rest, my head began to spin. The jackals were making a fearful racket tearing up a dog, which caused the other dogs to bark. I gave up and came to my writing table.

In Camp, 2 November 1840

I have had letters from my sister. Despite my advice, she abandons Paris to live again with her husband. She's been appointed lady-in-waiting to Her Majesty, which I suspect is the real reason that she returns. Melbourne writes that the Queen is endlessly perplexed at the discovery (who would have told her?) that some people occasionally do not like the English and their interfering ways. Why do they dislike us? she asks Melbourne. She cannot conceive why it should be so and asks him again and again to explain it to her. Melbourne himself seems to grow less vicious, less susceptible to pleasure, more virtuous and dignified with each year—his timing has always been superb (he used to claim that free trade was a delusion, the ballot rubbish). I cannot imagine that he whips Her Majesty. She has given him a reason to live and he has given her a life.

Henry has discovered that I was sometimes apt to read his government despatches, and instructs his aides to keep them under lock. He found one of his letters from Palmerston on my bed.

In Camp, 20 November 1840

We sent to Delhi for my deer and Gazelle this morning and learned that they are both dead. Gazelle died three weeks ago. Harriet is bereft and blames herself. I can hear her crying in her tent. We are heartsick.

In Camp, 12 December 1840

I have had a letter from Mrs. MacGregor who travels through the Khyber Pass with her ayahs and gowns and parrot and cat and diamonds to join her husband in Kabul. She is unaware that her safe passage has been financed by Government to the cost of eight thousand pounds—paid to the Afghan chieftains to leave European travellers unmolested.

Capt. Jackson loiters behind Henry's chair tonight with an armful of papers. London is well-pleased with the news that Dost Mohammed has been deposed and Shah Shuja put in his place. My brother is made a marquis.

The Residency, Delhi, 4 January 1841

Henry excused himself early from the whist table tonight with a little stretch and a quiver of a yawn. I, too, pleaded weariness soon after, leaving the others to hazard their rupees.

I went down the verandah to his room. I feared that I'd find Crick, grinning like a hobgoblin, but Henry was alone, sitting at a table. The room was in darkness but for the candle on the table, flickering in a light breeze from the river. He slowly turned the pages of a folio, the line of his jaw rose-coloured in the light reflected from the gilded pages. I watched for some time—to my surprise, it made me feel sad.

He didn't look up at the sound of my footstep, nor did he speak. I slipped into the chair next to him and he slid the book across the velvet cloth to me. (In my memory, it is the way he taught me to read, but it cannot be so. He was away at school when I learned to read at the unkind hands of Mademoiselle. Rather, it is the way that he taught me to *look*.)

The book was open to a painting of Monsoon time. "Morning Wind in the Garden of Desire." The sky on the high horizon was black, dotted with birds riding the storm. The trees dipped and swayed in the sudden wind. The man and woman lay in a marble pavilion, the hem of her gauze skirt wound around her waist, the better to see her opening, swollen and pink. Behind them, a golden swing awaited the handmaidens celebrating the coming of the Rains. In a tower at the edge of the painting, two solemn maid-servants watched the lovers. (I noticed that while the prince is without clothes in these paintings, he refrains from removing his hat.)

There is a ritualized form to the paintings, just as there is a ritualized form to our looking. I turn the pages; I take as much time as I like; he watches me. He cannot glance at the book unless I invite him to look. He cannot rush me. The rules are the same when he is in possession of the book and I watch him. The only movement permitted the other is the use of his hands. By the time that we reached "She Bends Her Body like a Snake Untamed by

Spells"—a woman astride a prince, her legs around his neck—
Henry was using his hands and I had stopped turning the pages.

Now I sit outside my dressing room. I write by the light of
the moon. I have an overwhelming desire to bathe. I will wash in
the dark. I don't want Radha to smell my body.

The Residency, Delhi, 8 January 1841

I have been thinking about looking. Looking in the way that
Henry taught me to look. My father had books of that nature in his
library, but it seems to me that those books were concerned with
governance, not sexual congress. The drawings were of priests
and kings and abbesses and duchesses—most of them French, of
course. Clearly, they were meant as insult to the clergy and the
nobility, particularly before the Revolution—used in the service of
revolt, not the interests of the flesh. The images were political, not
sensual: Bonaparte fondling an English mare; a naked but mitred
Bishop (like the rajas in their golden caps) beating a lascivious nun
with his crozier. One of Papa's books was called *Thérèse Philo-
sophe;* another, less philosophical, was *Les Nymphes du Palais-
Royal.* If men and women, kings and bishops and laundresses and
nuns, are equal behind closed doors, then they are equal in other
places as well. Clearly, this is a dangerous idea, but then for women
all books contain dangerous ideas; that is why Maman forbade the
reading of novels before bed. The French pictures did not always
cause me to stir. But the Indian paintings are different, and that is
because they are about pleasure, not vice.

(I am amazed that I write this—I, who fear that I cannot tell the true from the false, am writing words that will be taken for the truth. But why do you assume this is real? The writing of women is always read in the hope of discovering women's secrets. Will my secrets be discovered?)

We leave Delhi tomorrow, making our way to Bengal at last.

The Residency, Agra, 19 January 1841

Henry came to my room tonight in flowered dressing gown and slippers, a cigar in one hand and Alfred de Musset in the other. I was sitting late at my worktable, mending a blister on one of my drawings of Zahid. I laid down my penknife and reached to untie my apron. "Oh, do leave it on," he said. "I always liked you in an apron."

I picked up a sheaf of damp rice paper to fan it dry. "Do I remind you of Mademoiselle?" I asked. I gestured to Zahid to bring Henry a brandy.

He smiled. "Pas du tout. I've come to ask your advice. I'm concerned about Lafayette."

"I wouldn't be."

He waited to speak until Zahid had left the room. "Calvert has discovered that he's joined a private club where they smoke hemp. Each of them is given the name of a bird, and they are expected to sing accordingly."

When I said nothing, Henry said, "They smoke it rolled in pound notes."

"What kind of bird?" I asked.

"What?"

"What kind of bird is Lafayette?" Really, he is so stupid sometimes that it renders him innocent. He knows nothing.

"We are not in a Paris drawing room, sister." He rose in irritation and went to the window. I noticed for the first time that his hair is thinning. There is a white line across the back of his neck where his hat protects him from the sun. "Your apron has to do with home," he said, looking at me over his shoulder. "I mean home in the sense of pretty scullery maids. It doesn't deeply stir my emotions, but it does give me a thrill."

For the first time in my life, I thought he was not quite boring, but nearly so. Verging. I was shocked—not because he was tedious, but because I thought so.

He slid his fingers along a louver. "Six of the Raja of Kanthi's wives have thrown themselves on his funeral pyre. The Board of Control suspects the Raja is challenging us." He pushed open the shutters with two hands and stepped onto the verandah.

"I rather doubt it," I said, but he only smiled.

The Residency, Agra, 29 January 1841

I sat with Harriet at dusk in the latticed chibootra overhanging the river. Beneath us in the aviary, the men prepared the pigeons for an evening battle. (The Emperor Babur inherited his first kingdom when his father was killed in a pigeonnier that tumbled into a ravine.) I took my drawing pad from Zahid and began to sketch.

While Zahid does not hesitate to tell me when the colour of a bonnet does not suit, he will not answer when I ask, Ought not this sky be a little pinker? He stands to the side, not even venturing a glance, which at first I thought an absence of curiosity or even an absence of aesthetic, but now know to be an abundance of sensibility.

I thought it best to say it at once: "I am worried about our little girls, sister. Vimala cannot keep food in her stomach and spits up everything she is given; St. Cléry makes a special porridge for her, but still she grows thin. Tara's fevers bring on convulsions. I think it wisest to send them back to Delhi to the orphanage run by Mrs. Jansen. It will give them a chance to recover their health."

She was silent for a long moment, and then she said, "Lafayette will not let you."

"This adventure in Afghanistan wearies Lafayette—his good sense suffers. The children are too ill to travel with us." There was the drone of insects as darkness came on; it sounded like the opening notes of a raga. "He doesn't sit with them through the night," I said.

"Neither do we."

It was too dark to draw and I put aside my paints and walked to the edge of the tank. "I remember when the mention of an orphanage used not to reduce a lady to tears," I said.

"He is much attached to them," I heard her say. "It delights him to dote on them."

"He cannot dote on them if they are dead." Floating amidst the lotus was the body of a dog. "We will send for them when they are well again." I turned to her, but she was making her way down the pavilion steps, Bhiraj following with her pipe.

Gwalior, 15 February 1841

We marched fifteen miles today over a heavy road and I was grateful that I'd insisted on sending the children to Delhi—I dreamed of them last night. Lafayette is very angry that I sent them away. I promised Harriet that we will send for them before the Rains begin.

Kutolghun, 3 April 1841

It is difficult to write this.

Last night I was reading when I thought I heard a gunshot very near. I could not be sure as the drumming of rain on canvas distorts all sound. I put on my cloak, picking my way across the planks laid in the passage between the tents. My lamp went out. I could see a light flickering in Harriet's tent. I lifted the flap and stepped inside.

Two oil lamps were burning low and the dying light leapt fitfully across the red walls of the tent. Indeed, we lived inside a giant serpent. Harriet's scarlet riding habit lay in an untidy mound on the carpet; it looked like a pool of blood. The familiar stench of mould and rotting mud did not conceal a faint smell of gunpowder. Harriet's new shotgun lay on the carpet, too, its silver fittings flickering in the uneven light. Then I thought, That is a woman on the floor. It is Harriet.

She lay across a man's body, a blue turban cloth in her hand. The man lay on his back. His white dress was black with blood. Her hair had come unbound and strands of it lay across the man's face. She turned her eyes to look at me blankly—she was not dead.

I fell to my knees beside her, putting my fingers to his neck, my mouth to his mouth. There was no heartbeat, no breath. "Get up!" I heard myself shout. "Bhiraj, get up!"

She pushed me aside, taking his head in her hands. I thought how strong her hands were: not gentle, not womanly. "You see!" she said to me. "He is looking forward to the shoot tomorrow, but I forbade him to touch my guns! It is not his place to clean the guns. He forgets who he is—but who am I to remind him?"

There was a noise behind us. Lafayette, carrying an oil lantern, stood in the doorway of the tent, wet with rain. I jumped to my feet and the muddy hem of my gown dragged across Bhiraj's face. "There has been an accident," I said, "a most terrible accident." The sound of my own voice startled me—it was hollow and light. There was a taste of salt on my lips. I wiped my mouth with my hand; there was blood on my mouth.

"Are you mad?" he asked.

Harriet crawled slowly across the carpet on her hands and knees to pick up the shotgun. She sat back on her heels, holding the shotgun loosely in her hands, pointed towards Lafayette, and for a moment I wondered if she meant to kill him.

Perhaps he had the same thought, for he turned and left the tent, only to return a moment later with Crick. Lafayette nodded and Crick stepped forward briskly and began to roll Bhiraj's body neatly in the carpet. He did not like his handiwork and unrolled the carpet to begin again.

"You cannot do this," I said, going to Lafayette. "I beg of you." I took his hand in mine, but he pulled it from me.

"You are all dogma and no system, cousin," he said. "We cannot bear a scandal. Not now."

"A scandal?" I did not comprehend him at first.

"It had to end badly," he said. "Did you not see that?"

Harriet laid down the shotgun and covered her face with her hands.

Crick allowed himself a quick laugh. With a moan of despair, Harriet lunged across the room and threw herself at him. He shook her off easily, knocking her to the ground. He grabbed one end of the rolled carpet and Lafayette took up the other and they dragged it effortlessly out of the tent. It had happened so quickly.

Harriet lay sprawled on the ground. The rain seeped through the canvas to form a shallow pool of water. The top of the tent swelled and billowed like a crimson sea. The sound of the rain was like a thousand drums.

Zahid showed no surprise this morning to find Harriet and me on the floor of her tent, our faces marked with blood. He brought a note from Henry. My brother is gone. Harriet, Lafayette and I, and the few thousand stragglers left in this Great Progress of ours, are to follow him to Calcutta. I sent Zahid to ask the bearers to begin packing.

Kutolghun, 8 April 1841

The camp breaks up so effortlessly it seems never to have existed at all. The grasscutters are sent home to their villages; the camp followers wait patiently outside my tent with hands outstretched for a last gift of rupees; Maj. Quinn sells off the unnecessary animals and furniture; a fleet of boats is loaded. Thirty camels will carry our belongings. What is left of the extraordinary crowd of cavalrymen and thieves and milkmaids and Irish gunners that once moved through this country in a train ten miles long, sleeping and eating in a camp that covered five acres, will soon be gone, seeping across the plain.

Harriet stands apart, strained, watchful, twitching her skirts. She will not speak. Lafayette was right: Bhiraj is not missed in the tumult of departure. If asked, I am to say that he has gone to visit his brother the wolf boy in Lahore. Sunitra has disappeared from camp.

In Camp, 9 April 1841

Henry writes from Allahabad, delighted that he need not rely on his palankeen as all the magistrates and collectors place their buggies at his disposal. He goes very fast and rests all the hot part of the day in a dark bungalow, doing thirty miles at a spell in a carriage drawn by four camels. As Hindustanis believe that the meeting of the Ganges and Jamuna in Allahabad is a sacred place, he had to delay his journey one day so that his people could bathe at the junction of the rivers. Henry does not bathe. Like Lafayette, he remains an English gentleman with an English gentleman's views, and his experience of the world serves only to remind him that those views are the very best indeed.

Ghazeepore, 14 April 1841

I have had news from Mrs. Jansen at the orphanage in Delhi. The baby Vimala is dead of cholera. She apologizes; twelve other children have died. It is a terrible shock to us. The child Tara is too ill to travel. I cannot sleep.

Harriet still does not speak.

Barrackpore, 2 May 1841

At last, thank God, we are home. We arrived late tonight, running down a fisherman's boat in the dark. I was very alarmed by the screams of the men, but they were picked up immediately. The servants wept with happiness to be home at last. I, too, was moved to tears and had to stop myself from running across the lawn with them.

Harriet went directly to her room. Lafayette, who'd ridden ahead, was smoking his hookah on the verandah in his Turkish trousers, surrounded by burning neem leaves to keep away the mosquitoes. He did not rise to greet me. Henry was reading in bed and sent his apology that he is very much overworked by government and overbitten by mosquitoes. We will meet at breakfast.

Now I sit at my desk, looking into the garden. It is the middle of the night; the heat is very great. The house looks so solid after tents and boats. Night-blooming cereus covers the verandah. There is a smell of bruised grass as people come and go with our ivory tables and trunks of silks (we forget shawls and trinkets and go into the furniture and upholstery line now). The insects are dreadful, but I am hardly aware of them—only the welts on my face and hands remind me I am stung.

Barrackpore, 12 May 1841

I have built a little school in the park—virtually overnight, in true native fashion—and engaged a most intelligent native schoolmaster who in a few short weeks has taught the local children to read English, which shows it can be done. As a gesture of peace, Henry had the little boys learn *Who is that this dark night, neath my window playnet?* which they recite—shout, really—every evening on the verandah. The little boys chase after me, calling, "Good morning, dear sir." (Can they suspect that I've always thought myself more man than woman?) One of them slipped into the zoo last week and lost an ear to Harriet's white monkey.

I see Henry and Lafayette only at table. We do not play cards or make tableaux. We pretend that nothing has happened. Harriet no longer appears in the public rooms. One of the sepoys on guard at dinner last night went berserk. He rushed wild-eyed at the table with a drawn bayonet, slashing away at anyone who tried to stop him. Two of the aides were injured. I jumped up, knocking over my chair. Henry said, "Sit down, madam," in a stern and unfriendly voice, and I did. It took four bodyguards to hold the man. His screams were horrible as they dragged him away. It is the heat that makes us do these things.

Government House, 29 May 1841

One of Henry's equerries, the widower Capt. Jackson, very generously got up a prospectus of six plays as a Benefit for the People of India. There was a long list of subscribers, but the actors one by one fell out: one man took a fit of low spirits; another who customarily acted women's parts would not cut off his new moustache; another went off to shoot bears near the Snowy Range and was brought back rolled up in a blanket by six bearers nearly blind. When the gentlemen gave it up, the men of the Uncovenanted Service said they wished to try the parts.

Although the Uncovenanted Service succeeded in taking over the plays, a great many of our Calcutta gentry boast that they will not go to see them.

Government House, 12 June 1841

Despite the furnace of heat in which we live, Mrs. Beecham and I went to Capt. Jackson's Benefit. Lafayette had loaned them the regimental band, and the house was half-full. They acted remarkably well, one Irishman in particular. He looked like an actress dressed in men's clothes; ringlets and a little tunic, and a hat on one side.

Barrackpore, 14 June 1841

It is more fiery than a furnace, more fiery than hell. It *is* hell. Thank God, it is too hot for the dogs to bark. For once, even the crows are speechless. The deer in the park have jumped over the wall and run away. Every surface is black with the discarded wings of insects. The dust of their carapaces is in my hair and under my nails. My rooms are infested with flying beetles whose stench drives my people away. Maggots devour the paint on the walls. My hands are covered in weals of eczema where the white jute moth has lighted. (At least there will be a festival tonight for the snake goddess who lives underground, fortunate girl, in a city made of rubies.)

As I was taking my rest this afternoon a monstrous creature, armed to the teeth, came trumpeting across the floor. A pale spiked thing as big as a land crab, it moved very fast from corner to corner. Radha said it was a butterfly and managed to sweep it from the room. I cannot tell whether she really thought it was a butterfly, not that I have any objection to her classification. It is impossible to know. I ask no questions now. I loathe information.

Barrackpore, 2 July 1841

It is come at last. The beauty of it! Green everywhere.

Government House, 20 July 1841

We live in a net of rain. My rooms awash with toads, mice, lizards, snakes. The mango bird moans for pleasure in the bacilli tree. *Now droops the milk-white peacock like a ghost.*

Harriet has lost weight. Her knees and ankles are swollen. *A water lily gnawed by a beetle.* She has an odour about her. We indulge her because we are afraid of her now.

Barrackpore, 4 August 1841

Harriet refused to bathe except on Friday because it is considered an auspicious day—those who bathe on Friday are forgiven their sins—but now she refuses to bathe at all. She does not dress. Her room is a dank cave, the air thick with the white smoke of incense. Her shutters are never opened; lamps are not lighted. I am the only one whom she will see.

"It is stifling in here," I said this morning, as she allowed me to brush her hair. "It is difficult to breathe." There was the smell of stagnant water beneath the heavy scent of incense. I could barely see her. Nothing could conceal the smell of her naked body. "It is not Friday, I know, but surely any few sins you may bear have long been forgiven, sister. Mayn't I make a bath for you?" Her breath was fetid, her bare shoulders oily with sweat. *Where is she concealed? In what strange forests do you pause, my doe?*

"What did they do with him, sister?"

My eyes filled with tears at the sound of her voice. I had not heard it in weeks.

"They took him to the river."

"Did they burn him?"

"No."

She did not speak again. She allowed me to wash her.

Government House, 13 August 1841

To my surprise, Harriet has agreed to my entreaties to take passage on a ship bound for China. She will be put ashore at Singapore to stay with Lady Merryon for five weeks, in the hope that a change of scene will improve her health. She refuses to take an ayah with her. I gave her the first two chapters of *Barnaby Rudge* for the journey and she thanked me for my selflessness, making me smile.

Government House, 29 August 1841

Harriet has been gone a fortnight. I am sad without her.

Government House, 5 September 1841

Frolic's mouth is so diseased with ulcers that he can no longer eat. He suffers hideously and it is a torture to watch him. The dog-sellers collect at the gate with every kind of dog in bamboo cages, all the dogs barking loudly. Today I found a particularly tactless gentleman on my verandah waving a brown and tan terrier to tempt me. It is odd to see an Asian with a most English dog. It makes both of them appear less than they are.

Zahid has just brought me a letter from Harriet. (My letters arrive opened now, as Henry in his Great Mughal way reads the post before we see it.) *The powder magazine is above my cabin and cannonballs break loose and run about the deck, but it is preferable to the noise of ropes and the creaking of bulkheads. A gale of wind—now it is over I can never be sufficiently obliged—made us put in to Prince of Wales Island. And here I will remain. I have no need to go to Singapore. I am waited upon by convicts, some branded on the face for murder; they say their crimes were merely sins of their youth. The steamer will collect me on its return to Calcutta.*

I'm craving jelabees made with sugar and ghee tonight. Zahid will fetch me some while I wait for the opium pansaree (a finer word than drug seller). *Sugar I love but I haven't the slightest desire to merge with sugar.*

Government House, 25 September 1841

Harriet has returned from her journey plump and brown. I was very happy to see her. She has a strange calm. I can trick her into smiling now and then.

Three days ago at midnight, there was an eclipse of the moon. The land in every direction was completely black. The natives were terrified; they believe it foretells sickness and death.

Government House, 29 September 1841

I dreamed this morning that a troop of vermin dressed in the red and silver uniform of the Chevaliers Gardes marched once around my room, then up and down the gallery for an hour to the raucous shouts of the ladies in the crowd, many of whom wore red gowns. (I remember Papa describing the women of Paris— he watched from the window of the embassy.) I wasn't shocked by their indecorous cries; rather, I yearned to join them, but I could not move. Harriet later explained that it was not, in truth, the Horse Guard but the servants killing rats. It is an act of merit to kill vermin on a Monday.

Harriet said that my dreams come from my deepest part—a place without boundaries where women are kept alive. Does this mean that I am alive? If I am to dream unbidden thoughts, must I then permit myself to think them?

Barrackpore, 2 November 1841

I could not bear Frolic's agony a minute longer tonight and ordered Jimmund to take him to the stables. I knew asking wouldn't do it, but commanding did not do it, either. Zahid had to summon Khalid. He would not do it. Harriet shot poor Frolic in the head. Jimmund cannot stop crying, and neither can I.

Government House, 31 December 1841

We have had horrific news this New Year's Eve.

On Christmas Day, the Afghans seized Mr. MacGregor and his officers while they were riding. Mr. MacGregor struggled valiantly, crying, For God's sake! For God's sake! as Dost Mohammed's son Akbar drew forth the pistols given him by Mr. MacGregor the day before and shot him dead. They swarmed over Mr. MacGregor and cut him to pieces with knives. His head was placed in a chaff bag and hung in the bazaar.

The Afghan rebels confine the English soldiers and their families to the cantonment. The coward Shah Shuja claims to have had no choice but to go over to the rebels once the English were made captive. The women and children suffer; two babies have been born in the freezing huts. The rebels deprive them of firewood and food.

Government House, 19 January 1842

After much delay and confusion, our troops were at last on the way from Peshawar to Kabul when news came that our officers had turned over the Treasury and all their cannon and accepted the terms of Akbar to depart the country. Orders had been made and countermanded so many times by our generals that the outbreak of Afghans loyal to Dost Mohammed was not thwarted when it was still possible for us to send troops. The rebels gained confidence from our inaction and easily seized the strategic positions overlooking the fort and the cantonment.

Henry is paralysed with worry.

We have just learned that on the sixth of January, seven hundred troops, thirty-four Englishwomen and their children, Lady Plumb, and Mrs. MacGregor in her black mourning gown, three thousand sepoys and thousands of camp followers did as Akbar ordered and abandoned the city of Kabul. In three feet of snow, they began the long march through the narrow canyons to Jelalabad, the Afghans trailing them with raised swords. By two o'clock in the morning, the English had moved only five miles from Kabul, the rebels firing on them from the cliffs. Behind them, the Kabul cantonment was afire. The mountain passes were soon choked with terrified camp followers running in panic. Women and children fell in the snow, too exhausted to continue. The soldiers could not hold their rifles in their frostbitten hands. The sepoys deserted.

Dost Mohammed's son, Akbar, suddenly rode into their midst and offered to take the dazed women and married couples and children under his protection; the fact that his father, Dost Mohammed, and his womenfolk are our hostages surely influenced this extraordinary proposal. The surviving women and children were taken by Akbar to his fort while the wounded remnants of our army struggled on, marching through the night, their way strewn with frozen corpses and dying animals. On the twelfth of January, what little was left of the Army of the Indus was massacred by Akbar's men at Gandamak. The only survivor, Dr. Brydon, has crawled into Jelalabad insensible.

Government House, 8 February 1842

Henry has lost his mind. He said last night that the widows of the soldiers killed in Afghanistan best get busy and find themselves new husbands as they receive no widow's pension and no money to return to England. Harriet said, "I will give them money to return if they wish," and left the room. "Our sister is not yet herself," he said to me in concern.

Gen. Stewart has died of fever in Kabul. Mrs. MacGregor, a hostage in Akbar's fort, keeps up her spirits by tending the sick and dying. Her letters are carried to Jelalabad in secret by her ayah's brother (Henry says it is fortunate that she did not dismiss *all* of her maids).

Government House, 26 February 1842

The door of my room does not shut, like all doors in India when there are doors, and as I write I see four hircaras sitting cross-legged in the passage, wrapped in their brown shawls, playing Parcheesi—it is a game like our draughts. The sweepers sit on their heels, palm branches in their laps, watching them. The khansama leans forward to move his piece and I hear the jingle of the keys tied around his waist. Now and then the men look up and smile at me. Zahid told me they sometimes ask if I am mad. It isn't an insult; they have a great regard for madness. It is at times like this that I wish I could speak Hindustani. I am sure that I would say something.

I try to read, or to draw, but the pleasures of a lifetime no longer suffice. Henry gave me a book of Browning to improve my spirits, but I could not read Browning at the best of times. Still, were it not for the shaming loss of Kabul and the suffering of the people, I am not unhappy.

Barrackpore, 6 March 1842

I am alone in the house. Henry has gone to the play; Harriet is mothing in the park; Lafayette is at the club. Zahid takes his dinner at home. Radha has gone to fetch the pansaree.

There is no news from Kabul.

Barrackpore, 12 April 1842

The wind has been blowing since nightfall. The trees moan and the river rises in waves like the sea. Feeling restless for want of air and exercise, I found myself longing for a walk through the green English countryside. (I'd forgotten about England.) I dressed in the moonlight without Radha's help—you see, it can be done—and asked that my black mare be brought round. I rode until five o'clock, then went back to bed 'til I was awakened for breakfast.

(As I rode home, I saw Jimmund and his wife asleep on Frolic's grave. Frolic often slept at their house; he brought them good fortune.)

Government House, 6 May 1842

There has been no word for a month from Akbar's English hostages in Kabul. We grow desperate for news.

Barrackpore, 8 June 1842

There is an odd stillness to the air. I know that dawn is near when I hear the chant of the men urging the oxen up and down the path as they bring water from the river. I hear the stick as it falls heavily on the backs of the animals, and the strain of the ropes, and the creak of the yoke, and the swoosh of the water as it is emptied into the tank. And then the beasts stumble back to the river and it begins all over again. It does not stop 'til nightfall, the time of the amorous bird of night (it is calling to me now).

Monsoon is late this year.

Barrackpore, 10 June 1842

From the verandah I watch the black figures crowding the ghat, carrying candles cradled in leaves to float on the river. On the water is a dark shifting shape with enormous wings silhouetted against the sky—a body with vultures on it. A man flies a paper kite with tiny lanterns tied to its string. There is a fire on the bank where they are burning someone. It isn't a child; they do not burn children. They shroud them in crimson and carry them to the river, where they lay them on tiny bamboo rafts, cover them with flowers and set them adrift in the stream. Eels gorge on the corpses.

As some of my sketches have been passed around the town, I've been asked to touch up the faded portrait of a dead wife or a pastel of a far-distant child. It has been hard to deny these melancholy requests, but I cannot help these people.

Government House, 12 June 1842

The Rains have come at last.

Maman used to complain bitterly, holding her two flaccid breasts in her bejeweled hands, that she'd ruined her bosom on behalf of her children's health. It was years before I took her to mean that she had suckled us herself. She'd been reading *Émile;* she should have blamed Rousseau. Despite Maman's sacrifice, Henry has prickly heat. He likens it to being pierced by hundreds of thorns. The only cure for St. Sebastian is sandalwood dust, but he will not take it. He loathes the smell—too bazaar.

Barrackpore, 31 August 1842

We have had a rather uneventful month. One of Mrs. Calvert's spaniels was killed by marauding leopards. Dr. Drummond's medicines and instruments were stolen and his stomach pump cut to pieces. It is a blessing for our people, as Dr. Drummond forces them to undergo all kinds of medical experiments, including pumping their stomachs. Lafayette has been shooting quail—St. Cléry's boy arranges them artfully around the kitchen on silver mesh chains, singing Calcutta street songs. *Himalaya and his queen are like chakori birds at dawn—starved for moonbeams.*

Barrackpore, 2 September 1842

I am pained by the change in my cousin. It is not his dissipation that I fear, nor the cynicism that he affects, but his disdain. It is troubling to feel him so distant. We have been intimates since childhood. We share the same grandfather, Lord Charleston, he who would have been the first governor of the Carolinas (and a traitor) had he not perished in a shipwreck en route to the Colonies. It is I whom Lafayette enlisted when he came down from university to tell his mother, my dear aunt, that he had doubts about the Blessed Trinity, an admission I thought unnecessary, but one he felt honour required. (It is hard to conjure a picture of myself ten years later explaining to Lady Charleston her son's entanglement with Indian ladies. It would be far more difficult for her to countenance than a loss of confidence in the Holy Ghost.)

Last night I walked through the dusk to his bungalow, tapping the ground with my stick to warn any loitering snakes (and my cousin) of my passage. I had asked Zahid to inquire whether the Captain was expecting guests and he had reported that my cousin dined alone. Through the bacilli trees with their white flowers, there was the light of the torches which day and night St.

Cléry sets round his bungalow in the hope of discouraging jackals. He insists, with no evidence at all, that his proximity to meat gives him a succulent odour most alluring to the sensitive nose of carnivores. I could see him through the trees, sitting on his verandah, the Singhalese boy on his knee. In order not to embarrass him (would it embarrass him?), I turned onto the path that strives to hold back the Bengali jungle with its orchids and tigers from our English border with its zinnias and lady birds, coming upon Lafayette's bungalow from the tamarisk grove.

The house sits in a clearing cut from the trees. The cane panels that he finds more conducive to coolness than window glass were thrown open. The smoke of burning neem leaves drifted through the muslin window hangings, making the bungalow look like a steamboat on a duck pond. As I drew closer, I heard the sound of a woman's laughter. As quick as an adder, I stepped behind a tree, fearful of trodding on a branch; no longer mindful of serpents, I was mindful of twigs.

A woman came onto the verandah. Except for her silver anklets, she was naked. She did not have the voluptuous breasts and rounded buttocks of a Hindu goddess; she was slender, high-breasted. Lafayette lay on a divan. I felt the rising excitement of looking. There before me was one of my Indian miniatures. My hands between my legs, the smell of river and leaves in my throat, the familiar and elusive pleasure swept over me. My heart was beating so loudly, I was afraid that he would hear it.

She went to him. I felt a terrible jealousy—not of their play but of her ease; *she* was not watching. And then, to my confusion, the suffusion I felt began to seep away, draining from my body, replaced by a terrifying emptiness. For the first time, I did not want to look. I gathered up my skirts and crept away.

As I left the grove, I heard singing. The boy was teaching St.

Cléry a song. There was low laughter as St. Cléry tried to follow him. Suddenly I could not bear to return to the house. I wound my shawl around my shoulders. I was wet with perspiration and the breeze had chilled me. I went to the Persian charbag and sat in the swing built for the coming of the Rains.

As it grew dark, the scent falling from the trees lured me into a sleepless dream. Small creatures scratched in the underbrush and the larger creatures who stalked them found them and I felt neither fear nor pity.

The sky had begun to lighten with gray banners of light when I saw Lafayette. He was returning to his bungalow from the stableyard—I hadn't seen him pass by; I must have fallen asleep. My gown was damp with dew. I called out to him.

He did not seem surprised to hear my voice.

"Sit with me while the sun rises, cousin," I said.

He sat next to me on the swing. His weight tilted the balance in his favour and I had to place myself so as not to tumble into his lap. For an instant, I felt myself alarmed at the thought of touching him—beneath his tunic he wore a native skirt passed around his waist and through the thin muslin, I could see his thighs.

"It is painful to feel you such a stranger," I said.

"I might say the same, cousin."

The sky grew pink around the edges. The smell of the earth changed with the coming of day. In the darkness, there was the sound of day before there was light. The banyan grove was raucous with crows—it was not the gradual awakening of an English wood but a spontaneous explosion of shrieks. Mist rose from the black river, as people, first three, then five and six, began to appear along the banks. I felt an immense sacredness—the trees, the river, the sky. In India, it is the land itself that is the god.

"You did not tell me that the child was your own," I said.

"What would it have served had you known? Would you have taken her to London? Put her in service to the Queen?"

"I might ask you the same."

"I would have had time."

"Time? There is no time here."

Together we watched as the park filled with malis and maidservants and officers and syces, all laughing, grumbling, shouting. St. Cléry, in lime green silk, strolled contentedly to the kitchen house.

"You have misjudged Harriet," I said.

"I judged her as the world would judge her."

"That is the very thing she relies on you not to do."

He shrugged. In his world it was permissible, even desirable to keep a bibi, even to sire children with her, but it was not permissible for my sister to have an Indian as a friend. That he was her servant made it more distasteful, but even one of Mrs. MacGregor's show-Indians would have been unseemly.

"Sooner or later," I said, "they will ask us to go."

"I hope nicely."

"They are always nice."

"I suspect we'll be punished for our rudeness as much as for anything."

Radha and the other women were on the lawn, collecting the blossoms that had fallen in the night. I slid from the swing, setting it in motion.

"I will speak to Harriet," he said. He reached for my hand to kiss it.

I made my way to the house, the hem of my gown dragging through the wet grass. As I went along the verandah, I stopped in Henry's room to wish him good morning. To my surprise, he was crouched in a corner, bent over a trunk from which he was pulling papers. He handed the papers to two of his servants, who carried them across the room to thrust into the fire. "I feel this as a great relief," he said, as he saw me. "It distracts my mind." Some of the letters he was burning were from Mr. MacGregor in Afghanistan—I recognized his handwriting. He took more papers from the despatch boxes on his desk and flung them into the fire. He seemed strangely removed, as if he were concealing from himself what he was doing. Crick bustled into the room, carrying a portfolio. "Ah, good," said Henry. He looked at me with bitterness and said, "Af-ghan Away!"

I watched as they burned the documents. Flushed by the heat of the fire, Crick glanced at me now and then with a complicit smile. Henry is wrong about him. It is not that Crick sees nothing—he sees everything, and it is all the same to him.

For the second time I did not want to look, and for the second time I ran away.

Barrackpore, 2 October 1842

I went onto the verandah late last night and to my surprise saw Henry—I could just make out his white breeches—walking quickly across the lawn. I put on a dressing gown and went into the garden. I did not take a candle lest I attract the notice of Crick and the other servants. It was very black: no moon, and the stars invisible above the trees. I heard a large animal in the shrubbery and stopped to listen. I did not hear it again and hastened on. Henry was gone. I called his name softly. There was no answer. He was not in the park, not at the tank. Not at the swing. And then I saw him.

He could not hear my step on the grass. I reached down and touched him on the shoulder. He rolled slowly onto his back. "Tell me, sister, how are we allowed to keep this country one single day?" he whispered. "That is all I want to know." His face, as white as alabaster, was wet, perhaps with tears.

I held out my hand, but he did not want my help. "Lafayette wishes to stay," he said. I waited as he rose to his feet, but he had nothing more to say. I once knew everything about Lafayette.

"Do you mean to say that we are going home?"

He didn't answer. I could see the dark house through the trees: lovely house, lovely place. I could hear Harriet's ducks complaining in the zoo. They are unaccustomed to solitude.

"Do you abandon me?" he asked.

"I don't abandon you, my Henry."

"What do you call it then?"

"India."

To my relief, he laughed. "And what, pray, does that avail me?"

"Everything."

We walked towards the house. It was black under the banyans; the trees, strangely enough, had a smell of ear wax. We stepped onto the path of white seashells, a pale stream in the blackness, but our shadows did not return to us.

"Crick has asked me to advance him quite a sum," he said.

"I'd give it to him."

"Yes, I rather thought I would." He brushed the grass from his shirt as we drew near the house. "I've made many mistakes in my life," he said, "but loving you is not one of them."

I shivered in the breeze from the river and took his hand.

Government House, 6 October 1842

Letters received by overland courier from London contained the news that Peel, our new prime minister, replaces Henry with Lord Ellenborough, who is expected in Calcutta in a month's time. Melbourne kindly writes to say that this appointment was made before Henry's own wise decision to take a much-needed rest—that is, Ellenborough's appointment as Governor-General was decided before the disgrace of Afghanistan, which, if true, adds yet another note of mockery to this pitiful adventure of ours.

We sail on the *Hungerford* in fifty days. I've asked Radha to come with me to England. *If coming had been my choice, I would not have come. If going were my choice, would I ever go?*

Now that we are leaving, I begin to study Hindustani. This evening I sent Radha to lay champa flowers on the ghat; white flowers belong to Shiva, but Vishnu the Protector loves all flowers.

Barrackpore, 16 October 1842

I arranged a pleasure trip on the Hooghly for Harriet on the night of the full moon when the Bathing Festival is celebrated. There were nautch girls on the river in little boats, their movements somewhat circumscribed given the precariousness of their dancing platforms, but the baboos surrounding them seemed not to mind. The women, dressed for the occasion in all their shining finery, danced a little and kissed the men a little and then danced a little more—if there are no kisses, there are no rupees. Or perhaps it is the other way around.

Puppet shows and little scenes were acted in ramshackle stalls built for the night on the banks of the river. We moored to watch them. In one of the stalls, two men, one dressed as a European woman, danced a quadrille that was most convincing. Another actor, wearing black jackboots and other accoutrements of an officer, forced himself between the dancers, shouting in English, "I'm the King of the Palace of Trifles! I've no savings, no land, no happy subjects. I sell women in my ballroom. Let me dance! I'm the King of the Palace of Trifles!" In the next stall, an actor robed as a sadhu, his face smeared with white paste, ogled the women come to watch the procession—at least, I think it was an actor.

I kept stealing nervous looks at Harriet and she at last smiled, if only to keep me from gaping at her. She thought that she saw Lafayette in the crowd, but I did not see him. The ghats, the boats, the housetops and verandahs were jammed with people and painted bullocks and barking dogs. The noise was exhilarating. The ceremony would last through the night. We turned and floated up the river to Barrackpore.

The bank quivered with thousands of lights—fireflies chasing each other through the vines. How come they to act in unison? It is most mysterious. They chased each other along the river, making little arcs of fire. I had an overwhelming desire to walk home, but we could not stop. (Do you see that I call it home?)

I slept soundly despite the happy din, only to be awakened near dawn by Zahid, who wished to tell me that Harriet was standing at the ghat in her nightdress. *I came by the way but didn't go back by the way. I was still on the riverbank with its crazy bridges.*

And so she was. A few figures still danced along the river, the festival at last come to an end. The silence came as a surprise. I must have been listening to the music in my sleep.

"What has happened?" she asked, when she saw me. Gray

light was rising from the ground. "Surely what I think has happened is as real as what did happen."

"You sound like an historian."

She smiled. "Is that what I am?"

We walked along the river. "Do you remember, sister, when we went to look at Sir Jocelyn's souvenirs?" she asked. "I wandered away to steal a look at Napoleon's death mask and as I was finding my way back through that maze of rooms I saw Sir Jocelyn in the drawing room with two of his jemadars. They didn't see me. I watched as Sir Jocelyn took a pair of white gloves from a silver tray held by one of the men and put them on. He then took hold of the other man's ears and pinched them hard. No one said a word. The man whose ears he squeezed did not even grimace. Then Sir Jocelyn let him go and, removing the gloves, put them back on the tray and left the room."

It was not difficult for me to imagine it: Harriet behind the door; Sir Jocelyn in his filigreed salon; the servants dignified, silent.

"That is how I feel," she said, as we reached the ruined temple. The cuckoos were awake—the ones who live on raindrops. "My ears have been pinched, and now I am let go."

Government House, 4 November 1842

We gave a ball last night to our new great friend, the exiled Amir Dost Mohammed, visiting under guard from the north. As an honoured guest of the English, he is generously allowed to tour about as a show of our majesty. (We do not recognize his son, Akbar, as ruler of his country, however.)

He is a dignified Former King with a long sharp nose and a gray beard and moustaches in need of a trim, well-mannered and very intelligent in his ways. He said to Henry, by way of Mr. Calvert, that try as he might he could not understand why the rulers of so great an empire should have crossed the Indus to deprive him of his poor and barren country. He had not seen a European woman in society before, but as he would never betray astonishment, I only know this from Zahid. We played two games of chess before dinner, his sombre attendants hovering over us; we each won one. *My five best chessmen have led me on and now there's my minister trembling, exposed on that pawn's square and my horses hang back and my elephant—why?*

It is the last ball that we will give in India. Even the Maharajadhiraja of Burdwan was in attendance, he who mines all the coal in the country, arriving with his old adviser, Gen. MountSorrel. There is that in MountSorrel's eye that makes me grateful I am not his wife, or the Maharajadhiraja, for that matter. After dinner, Harriet and I sat with Bishop Maxwell-Lewis to watch the dancing. He was wearing a Mandarin skull cap of purple Chinese silk embroidered with gold dragons. The red eyes of the dragons glinted in the candlelight whenever he turned his head. Despite the strong smell of mothballs in the room, I could detect a faint scent of tuberose emanating from him.

Harriet is somewhat restored, but I wonder if it is not the excitement of departure that flushes her cheek—I pray it is not fever. My anxiety for her stretches my imagination. She was lovely in a muslin of orange-yellow, the dye made from the urine of cows fed on mango leaves. I wore a gown trimmed with the iridescent beetle wings I bought in Benares. She excused herself and made her way across the room to an awkward-looking little person who sat stiffly in a chair against the wall. Harriet sat next to her and talked to her quietly, the other ladies watching in astonishment.

The orchestra began to play. For the first time at Government House, there were native musicians in the band. Unfortunately, Maj. Quinn had dressed them in kilts, and pink tights to simulate the color of white flesh—he did all but paint on the freckles. Mrs. Beecham, with very long ringlets hanging to her shoulders and a gold wreath to keep them in place, led the dancing—her sidestep with an occasional Prince of Wales step was executed with such elegance that she made me long to dance. I watched as, across the room, one of the rich indigo planters from upriver made his way towards Harriet. Clearly some of her charm was restored—she contrived to convince the planter in a sentence or two to take the plain young lady as partner in her place. The girl, rather startled, rose to dance with him. Lafayette lounged moodily between the doors leading to the verandah, smoking a cigar. He wore a gold kincob waistcoat with emerald buttons. Behind him, the lovely faces of the ayahs floated like moons as they watched the dancing from their vantage place in the vines.

Henry was at the far end of the room, sitting on a white satin settee with Dost Mohammed. Henry obligingly wore some of Dost Mohammed's gifts: a string of pearls as big as peas; a diamond bracelet on one arm, a large emerald bracelet on the other; a cocked hat embroidered in pearls. Once we would have smiled at the sight of him, but no longer. Dost Mohammed wore a coat of striped green silk with ceremonial sleeves reaching to his knees. He was without expression. Henry had not assumed his customary look of languid distraction so that anyone so foolish as to think of addressing him would be dissuaded simply by looking at him.

Ordinarily, his detachment (for which he has been bred by generations) carries him through such evenings, but the events of the last year have changed him—he looked as if he might run from the room. I felt pity for him. It makes me sad at heart to feel the difference in my regard for my brother. It causes me to wonder if my early and long adoration of him, and dependence on him, made it inevitable that were I ever to find the temerity to leave off my girlhood, his fall from grace would be calamitous. (It is only memory now that provokes a thrill.) I wonder that I am so hard on him—it is as if he has betrayed me, when in truth it is I who leave him behind. I sat there, looking around the glittering room, and tried to take it in, tried to penetrate both the darkness and the brightness for the last time, to pierce beneath the surface of things, but, as is its privilege, it would not yield its secrets to me.

The Bishop was watching me closely, as he had all evening. I pretended to take no notice. "The merit of our kind," I heard him say, "is that wherever we venture, we make trouble." He took two glasses of champagne from a khansama and placed them on the little table before us, nodding a greeting to Mr. Chaudhury, who was serenely dodging the dancers with Dr. Khan. "Freedom of thought and all the many virtues of an enlightened society tend to make a man restless, especially if he does not possess them."

"Do you speak of the Indian or my brother?"

He did not answer.

"You don't approve of him."

"I approve of him as much as I dare."

I did not press him. My craving for moral certitude is diminished now—I, who once flattered myself on my code of conduct and my proud acceptance of its obligations, now pride myself on my paganish equanimity: I, who concerned my Whiggish self with flower shows and guild school prizes.

Across the room, the young lady, her bodice dark with perspiration after her romp with the planter, was returned to her chair next to Harriet, smiling over the top of her paper fan.

"A large packet of Russian letters was intercepted in Delhi last week by our spies," I said to the Bishop. "The letters are thought to be of the greatest importance, but no one can read them. The aides have spent the last few days making copies of them, which are sent to Bombay and Delhi in the hope that some literate Armenian will be found who can translate them. I am praying that they are love letters."

He did not speak for a moment and I wondered if I had gone too far. "You know," he said at last, "one would have kept you at arm's length in the sixteenth century. Fortunately, you have little power in the nineteenth."

In the centre of the room, Mrs. O'Reilly had fainted. Several of the younger officers carried her onto the verandah. Mrs. Calvert swept past to give her assistance, stopping briefly to give me the news. "I fear that she has seen the mermaids again," she said, and took herself off to do good.

"We ladies swoon with clocklike regularity every evening," I said to the Bishop. "You could set your pocket-watch by us."

"The occult is very fashionable here."

"It is not the Indians who have a fancy for it, but we Europeans. St. Cléry often sees tiny men capering in the pantry."

"Like Blake, who saw a procession of creatures the size and colour of grasshoppers bearing a body on a rose leaf."

"They must have been Indian grasshoppers on their way to a burning." A flushed Mrs. O'Reilly, trailed by Mrs. Calvert, hurried inside for a quadrille. "In truth, we faint because of the fleas. We are all stricken—they are everywhere, even in the garden. We scratch ourselves raw in private and swoon in public."

We both nodded to Capt. Catroux. An extremely tall man, he wore a flaxen wig. The Bishop took a sip of champagne. "Capt. Catroux's finest roles, they say, are his Juliet and Desdemona."

I did not answer, distracted by the sight of our prisoner leaving the ballroom with his attendants in a slow procession. The English made way for him, staring at the legendary Dost Mohammed, nodding a cautious greeting, making an occasional half-bob of a curtsy. He carried his humiliation admirably.

Government House, 5 November 1842

Today the father of the plain-looking girl whom Harriet befriended at the ball, recently raised from the ranks for his good conduct, came to say he was most grateful that notice had been taken of his daughter, who was appearing in society for the first time, especially as she did not know how to be a Lady.

I dreamed of water voles along the Isis, their coats, dusted with snow, the colour of the ermine muff Henry gave to me one Christmas in Vienna. The nearer we come to Europe, the whiter become my dreams.

Barrackpore, 8 November 1842

Radha, dragging a wicker trunk, has just come into the room. She's bound her head in a cloth to keep the dust from her hair—

the ends of the cloth rise in two graceful points like the nubs of antlers, reminding me that she was once a gazelle.

Barrackpore, 10 November 1842

I wished to make a last visit to Bishop Maxwell-Lewis before we leave. (I also wished to escape the arrival of Lord Ellenborough.) On my way to the Bishop, I passed a miserable group of shouting European ladies who'd been put out of their palankeens in the middle of the road, their bearers refusing to carry them an inch farther 'til they were paid more money. I was tempted for a moment to offer my assistance as mediator, but I hadn't the heart. I might have ruled in favour of the men and then I might not have.

The Bishop awaited me in his Chinese garden. His pink monkey sat in a bed of crocus, holding a nut in his hands as if to make me a pooja. The Bishop poured tea into two small jade cups without handles. He was wearing a brown velvet skull cap, a silver cross around his neck and shoes made of straw. "I thought I might see Lady Harriet here with you today."

"It is my sister's last day to teach at our school," I said. The monkey plucked at the ribbons on my slippers.

"Ah." He sat on a carved stone bench. "The school."

"They are translating 'The Fox and the Grapes' back into English. A translation of my brother's translation into Hindi." I looked round the Bishop's garden. He has devoted the last twenty years to it. At the edge of the ornamental pond, a flock of ducks with crimson heads shifted mindlessly from one foot to the other. One of them lifted himself fussily into a shrub and I saw that the inside of his wings was crimson, too.

I drank the delicious tea in one gulp and held out my cup for more.

"Do you like it? It is called Monkey Tea. It comes from wild bushes in Yunnan so tall that only trained monkeys can reach the leaves."

I looked at him. Despite his unclerical nature, he is without a trace of affectation, blessed with that natural, modest, cheerful manner of the good society of my youth.

"What a lovely silk you are wearing," he said.

"It is from Benares."

"Of course, the ladies here would never consider wearing Benares silk," he said. "Being in Asia, they must be absolutely sure to be European." He pinched the silk between his thumb and fore-finger. "It has an unusually fine rustle to it."

Surely we have come to a sublime degree of refinement when a silk is valued for its sound and tall monkeys pick tea.

"Have you been happy here?" the Bishop asked idly (there is nothing idle about him).

I did not know what to say, how to describe such a depth of happiness. I watched the monkey and the monkey watched the Bishop. The Bishop watched me; I was desperate under his forgiving gaze. And to think that Henry complains about the Jesuits.

He reached down to pick up a nut. "A concoction of this, by the by, makes a very good ointment for sore lips." The monkey fol-lowed the nut avidly with his eyes. "The roots of the banyan are used to cure thirst. And lovesickness, of course." He smiled. "Your cousin has been twice to see me for a cure."

Despite my curiosity, I disliked asking for an explanation lest the Bishop think it none of my concern, cures tending to the personal.

He blew out the spirit lamp under the teakettle with a little ivory horn. A young boy of indeterminate race—Burmese, perhaps—came from the house to sprinkle water on the path, and I fastened my eyes on his delicate feet. The Bishop brushed the boy's arm with his fingertips as he returned with a dish of pomegranate seeds and when the boy smiled I was startled to see a boundless malice behind his mask of a face.

"They've had enough time now," the Bishop said, "to wonder just how it happened. It's a lovely jest: we've given them the means to use the greatness in themselves." He turned away from the boy to smile at me. "And they will use it against us."

I began to feel a headache—perhaps it was the tea or the licorice plant at my side or the smell of the bodies on the riverbank (it must have been low tide) or the whiff of sandalwood on the nasty boy or the golden pollen staining my slippers or the constant stench of shit or the pandanus tree at the bottom of the garden, emitting that oily bittersweet smell that is said to attract snakes. I am a snake.

"Are you feeling quite yourself?" I heard him ask. He put his hand on my arm for a moment. His hand was spotted black from the sun.

I could only nod my head, fearful that he would hear the serpent in my voice. I began to gather my things: my parasol and the vulgar bouquet of hundred-leaf roses the boy had picked for me. "It is a pity, my Lord," I hissed, casting about for something to say, "that your episcopacy did not take you to China."

"Oh, my dear," he said. "I would have hated it."

I ceased my fussing to look at him. I'd so wanted to talk to him.

"Much too real, you see."

"There is nothing so real as this place," I said, with a sudden loud laugh. "In the way that a dream is real. The strangest and most awful things seem like nothing, providing, of course, that you don't wake up! The whole country and our being here and everything about it is a dream. Everything is improvised, even people. Especially people. My brother, surprisingly, is very good at tableaux given his natural reticence—did you know that? Prince Potemkin, who knew everything, used to erect false villages when the Empress rode into the country. I myself can no longer distinguish between what is real and what is chimera, yet this feeling that I have, this elation of toiling through isolation and wonder, will soon be gone and I will mourn for the rest of my life its going! Of course, I've lived a trifling and timid life 'til now. Without peril or grandeur, bolstered by old, old ideas. I always did suspect, I always knew that there was some other place and I am grateful for that—my longing for that other place is what first led me to books—but now that I am somewhere else, I have lost my terrible repose. I struggle night and day to untangle this wretched puzzle. Of course, I see now that the narrowest crack would have threatened my world, but this is a veritable chasm. A chasm!" I at last stopped, out of breath, and found myself standing. He looked at his feet. "And nothing will ever be the same," I said.

He walked me slowly to my carriage, holding the monkey by the hand.

Yesterday, while the unexpectedly sinister Lord Ellenborough and his aides-de-camp hovered uneasily in the gallery—happily, we do not have to walk a Lady Ellenborough through her paces as she sensibly deserted her husband some time ago for an Arab sheikh— Harriet and I, accompanied by a solemn Zahid and an escort of smiling guards (still saluting with the left hand), were taken into the small drawing room for a farewell party given us by our people. We wore new gowns that the darzis had made especially for our journey—I was in a gold-sprigged muslin cut to an old gown from Paris (I have given away my gowns to Mrs. Beecham); Harriet wore a gray gauze of her own design with a blue-black shawl the colour of a Calcutta crow. I put on my last pair of papery Chinese slippers, crisscrossed at the ankle with ribbons embroidered with white champa flowers. Radha wore one of the sarees she has had made for England. Harriet and I wore all our jewels.

Salim and Khalid gave us ropes of jasmine buds. Harriet wound the jasmine around her neck. I could feel her trembling beside me. With her ruff of pearls and jasmine, she looked like an Elizabethan courtier. On the verandah, the four musicians she had engaged sat on a striped mat playing the ragini Dhanashari. *Charming and with drawing board in hand, painting the beloved, her breast is washed by drops of tears which the girl lets fall.*

St. Cléry, out of his mind with joy now he is going home to his wife in Martinique, nonetheless made a very fine tea. We asked for guavas and cream, jamuns, jellabees, almond cream with silver leaf, pakhoras, mango ices, and that puffed luchi bread that Harriet loves so much. Everyone was there but for the errant Jones and those who were not allowed to attend for reasons of caste. Bhiraj was sorely missed. Khalid could not look at me for fear of weeping. Rosina wept copiously. The Singhalese boy sang two love songs.

I did not let go of Zahid's elbow. Harriet's face was whiter than her collar of jasmine buds.

Government House, 28 November 1842

There has been an auction for five days of the last of the gifts given us during our time here—golden beds and black pearls and turbans of purple and gold, swords encrusted with diamonds, elephants and horses and tinkling caparisons. I hadn't the heart to attend—not because of greed—but I sent one of the aides to buy a gold bracelet given me by Ranjit Singh. *A pearl goes up for auction. No one has enough, so the pearl buys itself.*

Lord Ellenborough begins to make public statements criticizing Henry's Afghan campaign, giving us a taste of what awaits us in London. Crick announced that he is staying in Calcutta to open an English-shop. (Harriet was surprised at the enormous sum he appears to have saved from his wages.) Rosina goes into service with Lady Payne, née Mrs. Langley. I have arranged for Zahid to attend Lord Ellenborough when we are gone. I've bought a house for him by selling to the Parsee merchants some of the jewels I kept hidden in my workbasket; I've learned that he is possessed of three children. I have provided for Salim and Khalid and the others—Imperialism at its best.

Harriet sleeps in a tented enclosure in the garden, open at the top so she may look at the sky. She reads by the light of the stars, despite Bhiraj's belief that stars were made for three things only: to make beautiful the sky, to stone the devil and to guide travellers at sea. She has found a keeper for the zoo. Salim and Khalid have packed up her laboratory; the door and windows are bolted and chained. She leaves behind her cabinet of curiosities and her commonplace books for the Asiatic Society.

Barrackpore, 2 December 1842

A missionary lady from Norfolk came to bid us good-bye today, claiming four hundred souls just last month, many of them young Brahmins. She explained that thanks to people like us, their good English education makes them easy to convert. Harriet flew from the room like lightning. The woman cares nothing for their loss of caste or their estrangement from their people. I see now that a mission is a most practical way of justifying conquest.

Lord Ellenborough announced that henceforth the Lady Baghan will be known as the Eleanor Oliphant Garden in my honour. They've roped off certain paths and lawns where Indians may not go. Perhaps that is to honour me as well—was that not my intention once? I walk every evening by way of the swinging bridges to a flat open plain (this place of music and rivers) from where I can look on Calcutta, its white palaces gleaming in the dusk.

Henry visits the Bengali schools, giving generous prizes and gifts. Ten young Hindu men have qualified as surgeons at the college Harriet and I endowed our first year here. (He paces up and down the verandah at night. I have said and done all that I can to help him.)

Lafayette prepares his kit for the North-West. He's bought

three new horses and is taking my lovely black mare. He no longer shuns Harriet and me, but our intimacy has not returned. He begins to speak again of writing his book on the Punjab. Lady Plumb and Mrs. MacGregor remain Akbar's hostages in Kabul. We send them food and clothes and medicine, but it would be a miracle if anything reached them. Lord Ellenborough is assembling an Army of Retribution to take an appropriate revenge on Afghanistan.

I know what England will be like: cool climate, good roads, white people, food inedible, language not difficult, costume unbecoming. What I don't know is if guavas will keep until we get there. I never dreamed it would come to this—scheming to carry home guavas (high-flown Indian sentiment). What a pious little escapade this has been.

Capetown, 14 February 1843

Our journey has been most uneventful. We carry a great deal of howling livestock so that supplies will be ample for the battery of Irish troopers who accompany us and for some time the ship smelled like a slaughterhouse, the smell of blood and marrow quickly overwhelming the smell of India. Harriet and I stood at the rail, sniffing like dogs for as long as we could catch the faintest trace of it—seven hours—but the scent of smoke and incense and mustard oil and attar of roses suffused our hair and our clothes for many days.

Harriet, a bit feverish, has spent the journey staring out her porthole with her shawls pressed to her chest. I am respectful of her moods, but it is lonely for me. At first, I read the Cantos to her. *Just as a swimmer, still with panting breath, now safe upon the shore, out of the deep, might turn for one last look at the dangerous water.* She pretended to listen in order to please me, but I could see that she was not interested and I soon stopped. She is wasting away. She grows paler, thinner, weaker with each day. Even her hair seems less golden, but perhaps it is just the light at sea. I live in a hammock in her cabin (suspended over two months of dirty linen, eating guavas) so as to be near her; she awakens near dawn wet with perspiration, convinced that she has heard the shriek of some small bush animal as it meets its fate.

Henry shambles along the deck in a tricorn (tied with a shawl when it is gusting), his hands clasped behind his back. He has been in a dudgeon since I told him that Harriet and I were taking a small house by the river in Chelsea and would not live with him. I cannot tell if he grieves to lose an intimate or a housekeeper. He has been steeling himself for his reception at Whitehall. Now he's received his letters during our stop here and learns that he is to be—through loyal Melbourne's efforts—First Lord of the Admiralty, he is less despondent. Harriet's and my house in Chelsea belongs to the Moravian Brethren, but I've decided not to proffer this information lest our old friends think we return Evangelized.

We wonder all the time what Lafayette is doing; the subject is one of the few things that can awaken Harriet's interest. "Do you think, sister, he is in the hills? It is cool at night at Raj Mahal; good for sleeping. Or perhaps Benares. That's it; golden Benares." (Our subject is India, not Lafayette.)

Radha was seasick the first few weeks. Like most Hindustanis, she has a terrible dread of the Black Water, but she recovered quickly, finding her way around the ship like a sailor. I am teaching her particular phrases and she comes on rapidly. "Excuse me, sir, but I do not know London." Henry says that anyone in his right mind will see just by looking at her that she does not know London, but I am determined that she not be humiliated.

Cheyne Walk, 14 April 1843

I was most unprepared for London. It is as if we've been away for a hundred years. The very sounds are foreign to me: no crows, no pariah dogs, no jackals or flutes or drums. There are hawkers, but their cries are parochial—knife grinders and rag-and-bone men dragging through the mud. No pearls, no monkeys, no betel. Worse still, there is no colour. Not even a sun in the sky. The air is black, the people pale. Everyone is dressed in gray. Most disturbingly, but for the fog, but for the river at low tide, there is no smell.

Harriet lies in our sitting room on a couch of Mysore silk, one of the spoils we carried with us to England. She has been there since we arrived; she does not stir. Her skin is yellow, her lips dry and cracked. "For the first time in endless months, I don't fear that I'll go mad," she says, each time that I walk through the room. "Did you know that, Ellie dearest? That I feared I might lose my mind?"

"No, dear, I did not know that."

"Did we forget anything?"

"I think not."

"But can you be certain?"

Radha brings a hookah to calm her.

We have been in our new house almost a month. Harriet will not see anyone, even our sister. I lie to Mary, saying it is best to wait until Harriet is recovered, affected as she is by a mysterious tropical ailment which is most certainly contagious. In the evening, I sit across from her in my mother-of-pearl chair and have my dinner on a tray. Radha makes pots of sweet milky chai for her—it is the only thing she will take.

She asked last week if I would read to her from this journal. It did not seem an inappropriate request as we both know that a journal is always written for another, no matter how much we pretend otherwise. I have been reading it to her each evening. (Is it possible that, in all these pages, an Indian never once speaks?) I do not read every passage to her as there are some things that I do not want her to know. When I see that she flags, I slip away, leaving her with two candles and her Indian bird books. The couch is made up each night with a bolster and shawls by Radha. She wishes only Radha to attend her—she is too weak to care for herself. Radha bathes her and brushes her hair. She sits with her until she is asleep.

I sleep in my bedroom at the top of the house next to Harriet's empty bedroom, listening in my dreams for her call. Radha rests on a mat in the hall so that she can hear should Harriet need her. Our other servants, good Englishmen and -women that they are, are appalled by our arrangement, I can see, but (because they are good Englishmen) say nothing. Radha is a most enterprising companion; she ventures into the high street without a fear to search out the things that we require. She came back this afternoon very pleased with herself. "I have found a pineapple," she said.

I notice that my monthly blood is darker now, and thicker, like silt at the bottom of an emptying well. Could I be coming to the end of all that? I am desiccated. *My body is in eclipse; when is the release, O Lord of the meeting rivers?*

Cheyne Walk, 11 May 1843

We have had a letter from Lafayette. Harriet asked me to read the letter aloud. He stopped in Delhi on his way to the army in Jelalabad to visit the little girl Tara, only to find that she, too, is dead.

"There is something I must tell you," I said. I sat at the end of the sofa near her pale feet. She had a look of pity on her face. I closed my eyes.

"The baby Vimala was Lafayette's child," I heard myself say. For a moment, I grew dizzy. "He believes that is why I sent the children to Mrs. Jansen."

"Yes," she said.

I opened my eyes. I sat there pressed against her feet, my thoughts strange and wild. For a moment, it was difficult to breathe—like the time I fell into the open hatch on the budgerow, a little death. I rose from the sofa and went to the window. The bright river moved past; the tide was running. It is a busy, prosperous, purposeful river. Unlike the Ganges, it reflects light.

"We cannot escape our caste," I heard her say.

I turned away from the shining river to look at her.

"I sneezed twice today," she said.

"Good or bad?"

"A good omen. The strangest thing," she said, "is that I feel there is nothing I cannot do now."

"Yes, yes," I said, going to her.

"I once held the belief that nothing is ever truly understood except in longing," I said. "It is a most convenient philosophy for women as it encourages us to ask for very little. I am so thankful for all that has happened, not least because it has cured me of almost everything I once believed. Losing something is not as fine as possessing it."

"No," she said. "But then I never thought that." She took my hand in her two hands and patted it in reassurance. Her face was wet with tears. I leaned down to kiss the top of her head. "We aren't meant to have it—not any of it," she said. "That is the secret. All we can do is wait."

I sat with her until she fell asleep.

Cheyne Walk, 16 May 1843

Harriet died this morning at seven o'clock. Radha and I were with her. She was not in pain—she has never been in bodily pain from this sickness. I sent for Henry and he came straight from Greenwich. He is sad and gentle. She left no papers, no instructions, no letters. In truth, she died with no desires.

Cheyne Walk, 20 May 1843

I've arranged for the painters to come at the end of the month, the soonest I could engage them. I wish them to paint my room. We haven't had time to unpack all our boxes—there is no rush to do it now. The servants will see that the trunks are stored properly. I need only a table arranged with my most precious things, and candles, books, my journals, paper, ink.

I've received many kind letters. I've at last seen my dear sister, who came from Balmoral three days ago. Melbourne has left his card twice, but I do not wish to see him. Lady Lansdowne sent a note and a book, *Piety Exemplified in the Lives of Eminent Christians*.

I have written to Lafayette. I beseeched his forgiveness. I sent him my last portrait of Harriet.

Henry came every day. They are starting a subscription to erect a monument to him in Calcutta. "For my work on behalf of Agricultural Reform and Famine Relief," he said, at my look of surprise. "Afghanistan is not mentioned, and I am grateful for that." Before I could congratulate him, he said, "Not a day has passed that I don't wonder how I dare to show my face."

"How do you?" I asked.

"It is all I know how to do."

I took his long fingers in my hand and kissed them and I could feel some of the weight, but only a little, fall from him. "Fortunate you," I said.

The last time I saw him he confided that he has asked the widowed Electress of Hanover, now possessed of four castles and a diamond mine in West Africa, to marry him in the New Year. We did not make our fortune in the East, after all. I wished him much happiness. (He invited me to accompany them on their wedding trip to Rome.)

My headaches return, but I have used the last of my opium. As Radha further acquaints herself with the city, she will find some for me. There is nothing she cannot do. I've moved Harriet's bed into my room so that Radha need not sleep on the floor.

Cheyne Walk, 26 May 1843

It was difficult at first to convey to the painters the exact shade of saffron yellow that I desired, but happily Radha has a saree of almost the same shade and she was able to show them. It took some doing, but the walls and floor and ceiling are at last the colour of the saffron yellow rock that Harriet took me to see in Calcutta. (She said it was a goddess.) I cannot help but be happy in this room. I need never leave it. Truly, there is Room for Wonder.

ACKNOWLEDGMENTS

Throughout this book, I have availed myself of the letters and diaries of three women: Emily Eden, Fanny Eden and the sublime Fanny Parks, and, in some instances, I have taken the great liberty of using their very words. I have also relied on Janet Durbar's book, *Golden Interlude; Ladies in the Sun* by J. K. Stanford; Lytton Strachey's *Queen Victoria; The Victorian World Picture* by David Newsome; *Bound to Exile* and *Glorious Sahibs* by Michael Edwardes; *The Days of the Beloved* by Harriet Ronken Lynton and Mohini Rahan; *The Garden of Life* by Naveen Patnaik; *Indian Mansions* by Sarah Tillotson; *A Glimpse of the Burning Plain* and *Plain Tales from the Raj* by Charles Allen; *Shiva's Pigeons* by Jon and Rumer Godden; *Indian Tales of the Raj* by Zareer Masani; *Paris Between Empires, 1814–1852* by Philip Mansel; *Lady Caroline Lamb* by Elizabeth Jenkins; *Baghdad Sketches* and *The Southern Gates of Arabia* by Freya Stark; *A Year with the Gaekwar of Baroda* by Rev. Edward St. Clair Weeden; *Life with Queen Victoria* by Victor Mallett; *The Memsahibs* by Pat Barr; *Letters from India* by Lady Wilson; *As We Were* by E. F. Benson; *Memoirs of a Bengal Civilian* by John Beames; and *British Social Life in India* by Dennis Kincaid.

I am much indebted to Clarissa Avon for allowing me to read the private papers of Emily and Fanny Eden in her possession.